THE PERFECT FOOL

NICK MORRISH

CATISFIELD BOOKS

Published in 2024 by Catisfield Books.
www.chrisblackwaterauthor.co.uk

Text copyright © 2024 Nick Morrish

Cover Design: Nick Morrish

Cover Image: CSA Printstock

The moral right of Nick Morrish to be identified as the author of this work has been asserted in accordance with the Copyright, Designs and Patents Act 1988.

All rights reserved, including the right to reproduce this book, or portions thereof in any form. No part of this text may be reproduced, transmitted, downloaded, decompiled, reverse engineered, stored, or introduced into any information storage and retrieval system by any means, whether electronic or mechanical without the express written permission of the author.

This is a work of fiction. Names, characters, places, incidents and dialogues are products of the author's imagination or are used fictitiously. Any resemblance to actual people, living or dead, events or locales is entirely coincidental.

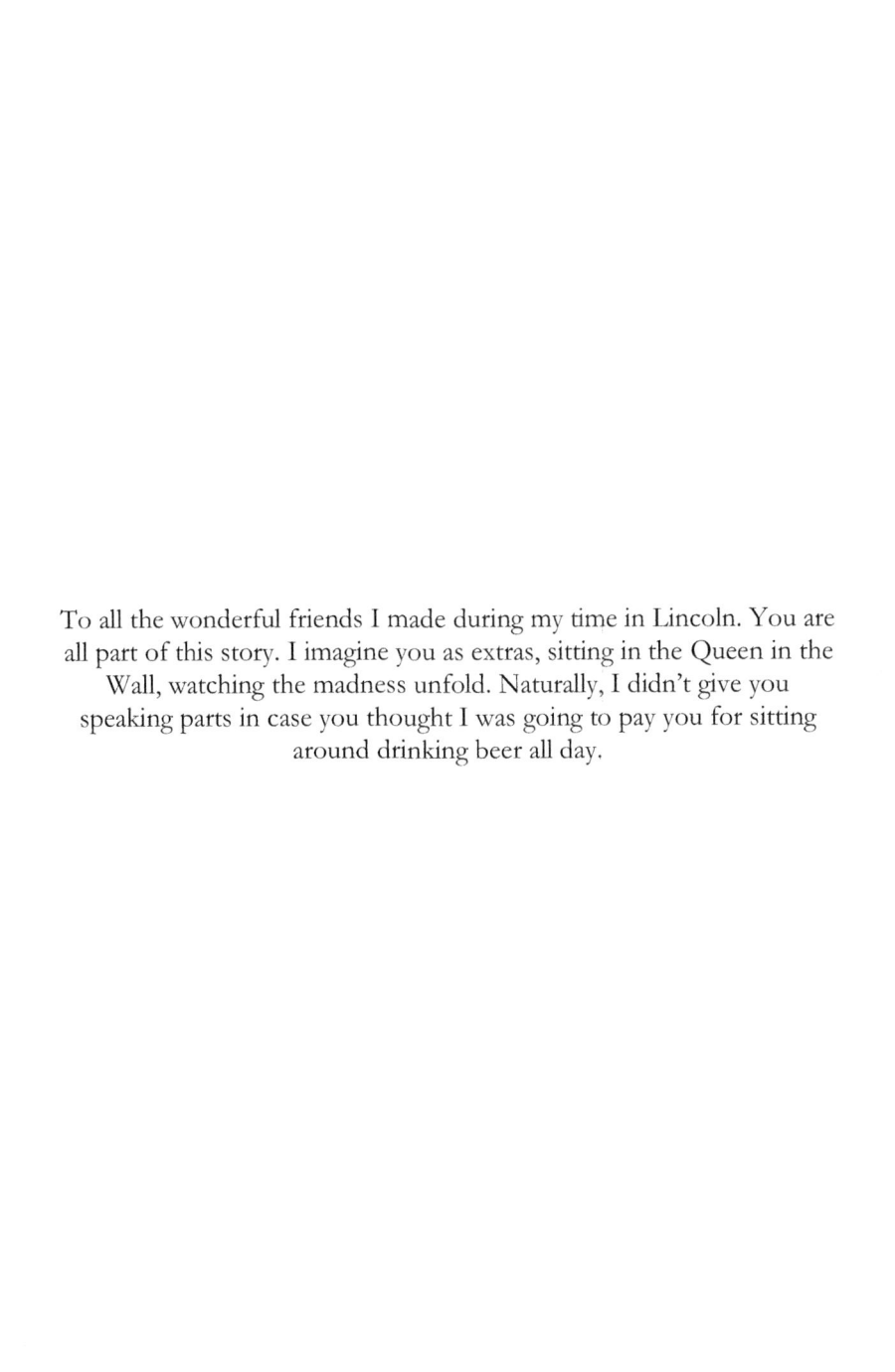

To all the wonderful friends I made during my time in Lincoln. You are all part of this story. I imagine you as extras, sitting in the Queen in the Wall, watching the madness unfold. Naturally, I didn't give you speaking parts in case you thought I was going to pay you for sitting around drinking beer all day.

Contents

1. London Calling 1
2. More News from Nowhere 6
3. The One I Love 12
4. Where Do I Begin? 20
5. The Prophet Speaks 26
6. Different for Girls 33
7. Sisters Are Doing It For Themselves 40
8. Spirits in the Material World 48
9. Avalon 53
10. Eton Rifles 58
11. Lords of the New Church 65
12. Stay With Me 72
13. Mystic Mile 80
14. Another Brick in the Wall 87
15. Watching the Detectives 94
16. Inspection (Check One) 100
17. Firestarter 105
18. Walk on the Wild Side 113
19. Come As You Are 117
20. Just What I Needed 124
21. The Road To Hell 131

22	I Predict a Riot	138
23	It's The End Of The World As We Know It	143
24	Feeling Good	150
25	Blinded by the Light	157
26	The Knife	161
27	Don't Come Around Here No More	167
28	Suspicious Minds	172
29	Dazed and Confused	178
30	Dancing in the Dark	185
31	Save Me	188
32	Losing a Battle, Winning a War	194
33	Messiah Ward	198
34	Hounds of Love	203
35	Blood on the Rooftops	209
36	Celebration Day	216
37	Afterglow	221
38	Supernaturally	228
39	Fool on the Hill	234
ACKNOWLEDGMENTS		240
ABOUT THE AUTHOR		241

1   London Calling

Dillon read the email again. It claimed to be from a national newspaper inviting him to their head office for an interview. It sounded too good to be true. The highlight of his journalistic career so far had been a half-page expose on the alleged failings of the Lincoln Internal Drainage Board. But a quick call to The Sunday Echo confirmed the offer was genuine. They would even pay expenses.

He was certain they'd mistaken him for someone else but, on the appointed day, he pulled on his best and only suit and set off. The early morning London-bound train had been cancelled due to a national shortage of enthusiasm so, at the crack of dawn, he clambered into his ageing Land Rover Defender and drove south. By the time he reached Knebworth, overnight road closures on the Biggleswade bypass meant he was already running late. He was desperate to make up time, but if he pushed the Defender any harder he might never get there at all. The Great North Road plunged downhill and he gradually picked up speed until he reached the entrance to the Hatfield Tunnel.

As he exited the dim, amber glow of the tunnel, a burst of low-level sunlight blinded him. Dillon hunched over the steering wheel like a myopic mantis. Peering through the glare, he realised he was bearing down on a jack-knifed lorry. He swerved right and skidded alongside the mangled central barrier. Ahead was a sea of red lights and crumpled cars and, beyond them, a giant yellow digger was casually clawing up all three lanes of the motorway. Bizarrely, its driver appeared to be wearing medieval armour.

Dillon gaped goldfish-fashion and stomped on the brake pedal. The Land Rover shuddered violently as worn pads cut into warped discs. Realising he was never going to stop in time, he fishtailed towards the digger and struck its massive rear tyre head-on. Dillon was thrown forward and the Defender span uncontrollably before coming to a lurching halt a few metres from the rift.

Dillon sat there stunned, his hands locked in a white-knuckle grip on the steering wheel as the acrid aroma of burning brakes drifted up through the vents. The windscreen was enveloped in dust but appeared intact. Something metallic was tapping urgently at the side window.

With eyes streaming, Dillon felt for the door handle and stumbled out onto the road. As the dust cleared, he found himself facing an outlandish character wearing chainmail armour, complete with helmet, sword and an elegantly embroidered tabard. Behind him, more armoured men stood guarding the trench.

'What the hell are you doing?' said Dillon. 'Are you completely insane? You could have killed me!'

'Have patience,' came the reply from behind the sinister-looking visor. 'As soon as our labours are complete, you may continue on your way. We are presently excavating a site of great spiritual significance.'

'You're doing what?' Dillon's voice went from baritone to screeching falsetto. 'Since when has the A1 been spiritually significant? And why are you digging it up in a suit of armour, for God's sake?'

The object of his ire paused to wipe the spittle from his tabard. He drew his sword and advanced towards Dillon. The knight was a head shorter than him, but his armour was no fancy-dress outfit and his blade looked very real.

'Take not the Lord's name in vain, else his wrath be upon you. We are the Knights of the Wasteland. We have devoted our lives to God and you can be sure we are about his business now.'

'Oh, that's great. Religious maniacs. And here's me, thinking you were just ordinary nutters.'

'It is not madness to follow a just cause,' said the short knight, waving the pointy end of his sword in Dillon's face. 'We are servants of King Arthur. My companions and I have ridden these many months on a sacred quest. You oppose us at great peril to your soul.'

'I wouldn't have to worry about my soul if it wasn't for wazzocks like you trying to separate it from my body,' said Dillon, backing away. He didn't think the knight was going to stab him, but he might accidentally remove an ear.

The knight peered over Dillon's shoulder with a vaguely worried air, as if noticing for the first time the disruption their efforts were causing. A traffic patrol car pulled up and one of the officers got out to inspect the damage. Several trucks, an ice cream van and a dozen expensive-looking cars lay stranded in the ditch. A cacophony of angry horns echoed down the tunnel as more early-morning commuters found themselves faced with an impromptu roadblock.

Dillon tried to pull himself together. He would be seriously late for his interview, but if he arrived with a hot news item, they might be more understanding. According to his CV, he was a young, dynamic, investigative journalist. He should be asking incisive questions, not trading insults with these halfwits. What doesn't kill you makes a good story, he told himself. In truth, he had scarcely applied finger to keyboard for months; not since his job had fallen victim to artificial stupidity. But his reporter's instincts were still sharp, even if no one seemed keen to put them to good use.

'All right then, what is this quest of yours? This is the first time I've heard of anyone making a pilgrimage to the Hatfield Galleria.'

'Our liege lord sends word from the hidden realm of Avalon. Soon he will lead us into battle with the forces of evil. But first, there are certain relics that we must recover if we are to triumph. I fear such things are beyond the ken of narrow-minded churls.'

'Up yours, Lancelot!' said Dillon, quickly abandoning the professional approach. 'What happened to your horse? Did Merlin turn it into a JCB?'

'I am Sir Kevin de Bord-Foss, Knight Errant and Guard-Dolorous,' the knight declared with an amateur-dramatic flourish. 'Many are the times I have ridden into battle astride a noble steed. Yet if I must delve into the earth, I shall use whatever infernal machinery is at my command.'

It was an impressive speech in its way, thought Dillon, as he struggled to hold on to his righteous anger. Meanwhile, irate drivers were emerging from their vehicles and converging on the source of their frustration. On the embankment to the left, an angry mob of workmen waved sharp implements like a fluorescent-jacketed peasants' revolt. Finally, the banshee wail of an approaching police convoy heralded an end to this stage of their quest.

Sir Kevin unhooked an ivory horn from his belt and sounded the retreat. His fellow knights, some carrying muslin-wrapped bundles, clambered over the remains of the central barrier and legged it across the northbound carriageway, seemingly oblivious to the screeching brakes and honking horns of the oncoming traffic.

Through the gloom of the tunnel, Dillon spied a high-speed police pursuit vehicle coming far too fast down the hard shoulder. The traffic officer leapt out from behind his patrol car and yelled a warning to its driver, before abandoning his post and diving over the barrier. The oncoming vehicle locked its wheels and, with an elegant demonstration of Newtonian mechanics, shunted the stationary car into the ditch beyond.

The driver clambered out and scrambled back up to the road with some difficulty, her uniform plastered with mud and tarmac. The newly arrived police interceptors jumped out to help her, but seeing the look on her face, quickly backed away.

There was a tense moment as all four officers squared up to each other. The growing crowd edged forward, hoping to see a fight. Eventually, the patrol car driver decided to direct her ire elsewhere and marched over to the abandoned digger to give the nearest tyre a vicious kick.

'Where did the bastards go?' she snarled.

A dozen hands pointed across the motorway in a dozen different directions. She kicked out again, missed the wheel this time and cracked her shin on the footplate.

'Bollocks!' she bellowed, clutching at her leg while trying to maintain a dignified police presence. It wasn't a great success. Small children were pointing at her whilst their parents videoed the scene and posted it on their socials.

Turning back to the cars, she shouted across to her traumatised colleague. 'Get on the radio, Higgs, and make yourself useful. I want a chopper here and I want it now!'

There was a brief and agitated conversation between PC Higgs and someone with a strong East End accent, who sounded as if he was shouting the wrong way through a megaphone.

'Sorry, ma'am; no chopper. They had a flock of parakeets in the air intake.'

'Right, that just about bloody well does it. Thank you very bloody much. I'm not going to let them get away with it this time. Just you wait …'

Muttering obscenities under her breath, she hurdled the barrier, weaved her way through the rubbernecking traffic on the northbound carriageway and jogged off down the most likely-looking track.

No one seemed keen to follow her. Her colleague examined the wreckage of his patrol car whilst the others climbed back into their pursuit car and set about keeping the hard shoulder clear for the oncoming emergency vehicles, whose sirens were already echoing down the tunnel.

'I take it you've come across these Knights of the Wasteland before?' Dillon asked the disconsolate PC Higgs.

'Yeah, sad to say. We've had a few run-ins with them this year. It's getting beyond a joke.'

'So why were on earth were they digging up the motorway?'

'It's some bloody stupid quest. Monty Python and the Holy Grail. That sort of thing.'

'You mean they really are looking for the Holy Grail?'

'Apparently. They've been digging all along the Great North Road. This is the first time they've had a go at the motorway section, but the old Roman road has more holes in it than a Swiss cheese.'

'How come I've never heard anything about this on the news?'

'Well, it's bad enough with this lot at it. We don't want a load of copycat weirdoes joining in. We usually just stick a few cones round the hole and blame the Highways Agency.'

'But why here?' Dillon persisted.

'You'd have to ask them. Usually something to do with ley lines or burial mounds. They think that King Arthur is about to return and the end of the world is nigh and half a dozen other fairy tales. I wouldn't expect it to make any sense to us mere mortals.'

'So what do you think? Are they for real? Maybe they're anarchists or eco-protestors trying to wind you up.'

'I don't reckon so.' PC Higgs pushed back his cap wearily and scratched at his furrowed brow. 'Sounds like crap, I know, but they seem to believe it. I don't suppose they set out to cause trouble, but they're not on the same planet as the rest of us, that's for sure.'

Dillon looked at the chaos around him. This part of the planet, at least, seemed to be in a bit of a mess. His thumbs were not pricking yet, but he had a bad feeling that something nasty was about to happen. This could be an omen, a portent, or possibly even a harbinger. Somebody ought to do something about it.

He pulled out a pen, then sighed and scribbled a few notes in his faded reporter's notebook. His job prospects were diminishing with every passing minute. All he could do now was wait for inspiration, or possibly Armageddon, to arrive.

2   More News from Nowhere

After a great deal of discussion and some frantic phone calls, the police decided to clear the huge queues of cars stranded on the southbound A1 by diverting them back through the tunnel and the wrong way up the on-slip.

'If you can get through Welwyn Garden City, you can rejoin the motorway at the other side. There's gonna be one hell of a jam, but it's the only way we can get everyone around this shambles,' PC Higgs explained. 'As soon as we have all the cars behind you turned around, you can be on your way.'

Dillon couldn't afford to wait that long. His interview was due to start in just over an hour and even with a clear run, that was cutting it fine. Despite his earlier optimism, he didn't think implausible stories about medieval knights on the motorway would cut much ice with his potential employers. He took a few photos of the chaos and looked around for a better way out.

PC Higgs refused point blank to let him try some DIY road repairs with the digger, so he cast his eyes around the stranded vehicles. At the bottom of the ditch was a Hertfordshire County Council truck, stacked with weathered wooden scaffolding boards and tarnished steel poles.

'Mind if I borrow a couple of those planks?' he asked a beetle-browed council worker who was sitting perched on the tailgate, staring at his phone.

'Help yourself. It was all going for scrap anyway. So is the truck now, I reckon.'

The bored council worker even helped him lug a few of the least rotten planks over to the ditch, and between them, they managed to create a serviceable ramp. Dillon edged the Land Rover carefully over the edge and, after a few nervy moments, reached the bottom of the ditch.

The climb up the other side was trickier and his first couple of attempts resulted in wheel-spinning slides back down into the muddy sump. Finally, he found a navigable route over some broken tarmac and the Land Rover lumbered back onto terra firma. Dillon gave a triumphal toot of the horn and waved to the helpful council worker and the other stranded motorists.

Several intrepid 4x4 drivers immediately jumped into their cars, intent on following him. The first one on to the makeshift ramp was a brand-new SUV, whose loud and pompous owner had been giving the police a particularly hard time. He slithered sideways down the planks until the tyres stuck a slab of tarmac and the SUV rolled slowly onto its roof. A small crowd gathered around the stricken vehicle, all four wheels spinning forlornly in mid-air.

Dillon applied pedal to metal and watched the mayhem disappear in his tiny, cracked rear-view mirror. He patted the Land Rover's steering wheel and smiled. Turning up the radio, he sang along in his best bathroom baritone. He tapped his foot on the pedal in time with the competing rhythms of music and machinery and the ageing engine dipped in and out of key, unlike Dillon, whose voice was flatter than a motorway hedgehog.

After a tedious but uneventful hour's drive, he reached the dark heart of England's newspaper industry, located on the enchanting Isle of Dogs. The newspaper's offices were easily identifiable: a monolithic concrete tower with the motif, 'THE SUNDAY ECHO GIVES YOU MORE' emblazoned across the front in letters, three feet high. More of what, it didn't say. More money or even more job satisfaction would be nice, but he doubted that's what they had in mind.

Dillon checked his appearance in the rear-view mirror and then wished he hadn't bothered. He was the first to admit that he wasn't the most handsome chap in the world but he'd really made an effort to look his best this morning. Now, after his encounter with the Knights of the Wasteland, he looked more like an extra from a disaster movie. He tried out his winning smile in the mirror. His girlfriend, Charlotte said it was his best feature, but in his current nervous state, it gave him the look of a hungry vampire.

Dillon wiped the grisly smirk off his face, prised the lumps of tarmac out of his hair, straightened his tie, and set forth to do battle with the forces standing between him and regular employment. He marched purposefully across the car park and up to the large plate glass door. Just as he was expecting the door to slide open, he noticed the small sign saying 'OUT OF ORDER'. He was still making a desperate attempt to engage reverse gear as his head struck the glass. The impact persuaded the errant door to fly open and he staggered into the foyer under the gaze of a smirking young receptionist. He regained his balance, strode over to the desk and announced himself in his best interview voice.

'Dillon Wright, to see Mr Gladman, please.'

'Do take a seat, sir,' she simpered, gesturing at the row of plush chairs behind him. 'Mr Gladman will be along to see you shortly.'

Dillon sat down and flicked anxiously through some past copies of The Sunday Echo that were strewn over the coffee table. It was a smug, self-opinionated publication. Very certain of itself, and its readers' prejudices. Dillon wondered how people could be so sure about everything. Admittedly, it would be easier to see the world in glorious monochrome. His own writing was often so full of conditional clauses that even he found it difficult to know what he was trying to say.

Still no sign of Gladman. Dillon glanced up at the receptionist and tried his best to smile, but she ignored him. He wondered if she could see the beads of perspiration starting to gather on his forehead. She was quite pretty, if rather snooty, but Dillon didn't feel like squandering his limited supply of chat-up lines right now.

Finally, he heard his name being called from across the foyer. A large flustered-looking woman appeared.

'Amanda Bond, Human Resources,' she said and bustled him along the corridor without further ado. They marched through labyrinthine corridors, up several flights of stairs, through abandoned offices and finally into a small, dimly lit conference room.

Across the battered table sat a slightly built man of indeterminate age, peering at Dillon intently through thick-rimmed glasses. He was sporting a loud pink tie and a brown suit several sizes too big for him.

'Pleased to meet you. I'm Arnold Gladman.' An alarmingly hirsute hand poked out from the end of one sleeve. Dillon reached out and shook it nervously. 'Mr Wright, I presume? How appropriate! Sounds rather like a case of nominative determinism if I may say so.'

Not according to his beloved Charlotte, who seemed to think he should change his surname to Wrong.

'Well, I suppose you could say I'm a bit of a Wordwright.'

'Oh yes, very clever, ha ha!' said Arnold insincerely.

Amanda smiled sweetly at him and wiggled into her seat. She was probably in her late forties, with bottle-blonde hair turning to brunette at the roots. The straining buttons of her tight-fitting dress fought to contain her ample bosom at each gushing intake of breath. There was a brief silence whilst his interrogators appeared to be studying their victim.

'So why are you here?' Arnold gazed at him through thick round glasses, his magnified eyes giving him the look of a second-rate psychopath. Momentarily thrown off balance, Dillon stumbled into a rambling explanation.

'Well, I wrote after a job last year and you said you hadn't got anything for a journalist with my particular skillset, so I was really surprised when you sent me this letter and said maybe you might need somebody after all and I thought…'

'No, no, I mean fundamentally,' Arnold interrupted. 'What are the fundamental qualities you can bring to this paper? What are your strengths and weaknesses? Tell me: why should we give you this job, Mr Wright?'

'Well, I've got a lot of valuable experience of, er, this sort of work, if you see what I mean. I'm very keen to use my experience in a valuable way, you know. I'm sure that as an experienced journalist, I could add a lot of value to the role.'

Realising he was babbling, Dillon took a deep breath and went on the offensive.

'What exactly are you looking for anyway?'

'I'm glad you asked that question, Dillon. That's the fundamental question, isn't it?'

'Er, yes, I suppose it is.'

'We need to be talking the same language, Dillon,' added Amanda.

'Quite,' said Dillon, who thought he might be speaking a different dialect at least.

'We're looking for someone to cover the contemporary religious affairs field, journalistically speaking,' explained Arnold.

'Very sensitive area, religious affairs,' Amanda assured him. 'Couldn't advertise the post without upsetting somebody. We live in a multi-cultural society these days and some cultures, well, they've got a very fundamental approach to religion.'

'Yes, very tricky thing, fundamentalism,' Dillon agreed, trying to appear at least vaguely knowledgeable. 'Perhaps you could explain your definition of contemporary religion. It covers such a broad spectrum, doesn't it?'

'The New Age movement,' said Amanda.

'Neo-pagans,' added Arnold.

'Spiritual Healers.'

'Cults!'

'Sects!'

'Sex?' queried Dillon and then realised his mistake. 'So, this is a new position, is it?' They made a good double act, but Dillon, as desperate as he was for the job, smelled a rat.

'It's an expansion. A whole new full-page feature in our Now! supplement. We're calling it The Cult Report,' announced Amanda.

Arnold Gladman puffed out his chest and gave Dillon his best managerial look. 'Our current affairs department, which I have the pleasure of managing, feels it requires new blood to take on this challenging role in this climate of interfaith intolerance and sectarianism.'

'So, none of your staff fancied the job, then?'

'You just don't get the same standard of fearless, investigative journalist these days,' Arnold complained.

'But it's an important topic,' added Amanda, enthusiastically. 'People are turning away from the conventional religion. There's been a dramatic upsurge in the popularity of alternative faiths. It's a search for the spiritual in an increasingly materialistic world. Our readership is always interested in unconventional lifestyles. We ran a focus group, you know.'

'Of course, there are some risks involved but you would have the full resources of the paper behind you,' said Arnold.

'In a hands-off way, obviously,' added Amanda.

'And the salary would be commensurate with the obligations of the post.'

Amanda leant forward dramatically and laid her cards, and her bosom, on the table. 'Are you a man or a mouse, Dillon?'

Dillon resisted the urge to run off for a bite of cheese. Instead, he leant back in the dilapidated leather chair and thought of his overdraft.

'Well, I have done some investigations in this area, of course.'

'Really?' Amanda seemed surprised by the idea of a reporter carrying out some actual out-of-building research.

'Yes. I spent some time with the Knights of the Wasteland. I'm sure you've heard of them. They're searching for the Holy Grail in preparation for the return of King Arthur.'

It didn't sound very believable, even to him. His audience seemed interested though, so he carried on.

'They've been creating havoc all over the Southeast but it's been kept quiet. I've reason to believe there's an official cover-up. High-ranking police officers may be involved.'

'My goodness! That's just the sort of thing we're looking for,' Arnold enthused. 'These knights, do they have any unusual practices?'

'Apart from dressing up in medieval costume and digging up motorways, you mean?'

'Bizarre rituals? Sacrifices? Orgies?' asked Amanda, enthusiastically.

'Not that I know of,' Dillon admitted.

'Pity. Still, it all sounds very interesting, I'm sure.'

Arnold Gladman gathered his notes together and pushed his glasses firmly onto the bridge of his nose. 'Well, I think we've heard all we need, for the time being,' he said, with an air of finality. 'Someone will be in touch shortly to let you know our decision. Of course, we'll need your references. We wouldn't want to risk employing a crank.' He eyed Dillon with suspicion. 'So, unless you have any more questions, Amanda will show you out.'

Gladman didn't look like a man who wanted to be asked any more questions. Dillon shook him firmly by the paw and followed the stately figure of Amanda Bond back to the foyer, where she signed him out and showed him to the door. Light-headed at his release, he gave the still-smirking receptionist a friendly wave and departed with rather more composure than he'd shown on arrival.

3   The One I Love

The traffic news was full of dire warnings about holdups at the Hatfield Tunnel. Dillon opted to take the scenic route via Ermine Street and his return journey was mercifully incident-free.

As familiar surroundings engulfed Dillon, he sat back and basked in the simple pleasure of coming home. But soon the cares that trailed behind him, like flies following a riding school, caught up with him once again. Dillon had just made himself a cup of tea and slumped into his usual armchair when his peace was shattered by the tuneless burbling of his mobile.

'Hi, Charlotte,' he said, not even glancing at the display.

'Oh, Dilly! How long have you been home? Why didn't you call? I always call you when I've been away, don't I?'

'There's no point. You're always on the phone. I'd never get through, would I?'

There was a hurt silence on the other end of the phone and Dillon felt a little guilty. 'Look, I just got in, it was a long day, I'm really tired, and I would have phoned you later, honest.'

'Don't you want me to come round then?' The tone was bordering on the pitiful.

'Yeah, sure. I don't mind. Whatever. Just give me time to get some food and sort myself out.'

'Don't worry about that. I could cook something over at your place for a change. Much nicer than those terrible takeaways you live off. I'll be right there.'

Dillon glanced longingly at the fridge door, behind which he knew there lay the remains of a Chicken Tikka Masala still in its foil tray. He'd been quite looking forward to some curried comfort eating tonight. Instead, he leafed through the pile of bills that Mark 'Sparks' Munro, his housemate and Lincoln's most frequently electrocuted software engineer, had kindly piled on the table for his attention. He ignored all except those inscribed in bold red lettering and studied those with mounting dismay.

'Sparks!' he shouted up the stairs. 'Are you in?'

'That depends.'

'That was Charlotte on the phone.'

'Usually is.'

'She's coming round to cook something for us.'

There was a brief silence followed by the clatter of feet as Sparks charged down the stairs, pulling on a jacket as he came.

'Sorry mate, I gotta go.'

'Don't you want anything to eat?'

'No, thanks, I told somebody I'd meet them somewhere and I'm late. Ciao!'

The door slammed and Dillon was left to his own devices once again. He knew that Sparks would be heading for the infamous Queen in the Wall. Since the pub was their favourite haunt, it was quite feasible that he would meet someone he knew eventually.

Dillon just had time for a quick wash and brush-up before there was a sharp knocking, and a rattle of the letterbox, as the front door struggled to contain his girlfriend's boundless enthusiasm. He loped over to the door and let her in.

'Hi, Charlotte,' he said, disentangling himself from her embrace with some difficulty.

'Hi, Dilly! How was the drive? And the interview?'

'Eventful.'

'You must be starving, poor thing. I've brought a few goodies with me.'

Dillon peered suspiciously at the carrier bag in her hand. She dived into the bag and pulled out a package in the manner of a department store Santa.

'Look, I got some fresh monkfish from the fishmongers this morning!'

'Great. That'll be nice with some batter on it. And chips.'

'Very funny, Dilly. I brought some beetroot and a few parsnips. They're lovely roasted.'

'Oh, good.'

'And some organic red lentil dahl from Waitrose.'

'Even better. You haven't got any extra-strong toilet paper in there as well, have you?'

Charlotte chose to ignore him, and strode into the kitchen, crunching across the lino as she went.

'Oh, Dilly! You haven't washed up again. There isn't a single clean pan in the place. How am I supposed to cook you a proper meal? There's scarcely enough space to put the bag down.'

Dillon surveyed the kitchen, critically. He had to agree that things had got a little out of hand. He was sure that it was Sparks' turn to wash up but Sparks no doubt considered it was Dillon's turn. The result would have given any hygiene inspector heart failure.

Deciding he had better make at least a token effort, Dillon selected the least revolting work surface and with a sweep of his arm pushed the mountain of dirty pots into an even higher and more unstable pile. He then examined the topmost pans carefully, selected a few to rinse under the tap, and then wiped them dry with a well-used beer towel.

'Why the frying pan?' Charlotte wanted to know, as she watched in horrified fascination.

'You're cooking, aren't you?'

'It's baked monkfish in a dill sauce, not fish fingers, Dilly.'

'You're going to use the oven!' Dillon's tone was disbelieving.

He watched as Charlotte heroically grasped the oven door, opened it, and checked inside for foreign objects. It was pristine. By far the cleanest and least used space in the kitchen. She closed the door, removing several years of grease from the handle, and with a dramatic gesture, turned on the gas. Nothing happened.

'You have to press this button here…' Dillon leaned over and demonstrated.

There was a loud bang and the oven door flew open, catapulting Charlotte across the kitchen into the disused larder, where she lay stunned and singed as Dillon fought with the controls.

'It's OK; I've got it lit. It's a bit temperamental until it's warmed up, but it'll be all right now.' Dillon helped her to her feet and thoughtfully brushed the crumbs and long-dead woodlice from her dress. She stared at the cooker, transfixed.

Reasoning that activity was a good thing in cases of shock, he gently directed her back to the chopping board and went to the fridge for a beer. Before he could bring the bottle to his lips, Charlotte swept it from his grasp and with trembling hands, downed the lot. 'Yuck! How can you drink this stuff?'

'It was cheap. Thirty bottles for the price of twenty. It's brewed in Basingstoke to an ancient Bavarian recipe.'

Acting on instinct, Charlotte prised open the fridge and looked inside. Bottles of beer were neatly stacked on each shelf and upside down in the egg rack. The drawers labelled 'salad' and 'vegetables' contained nothing but a couple of dried-up lemons and a carton of long-life milk. Except for the half-eaten curry, there was not a sign of solid food to be seen anywhere.

'Oh, Dilly! Sometimes I just despair of you.'

'You'll feel better once you've eaten. We could get a set menu from the Chinese if you don't feel like cooking,' he added hopefully.

Charlotte looked at him as if she were an owner whose dog had just peed on the floor. Dillon waited to have his nose rubbed in it.

By the time the meal was ready, Dillon was so hungry that he wolfed it down with relish. He still considered that it would have been better with batter, but he kept the thought to himself. Beer bottle in hand, he looked across at Charlotte with a calculating eye.

Sensing his gaze, she glanced up and brushed back her fringe with a sweep of the forearm. She was bottle-blonde and blue-eyed, with lips that were formed by nature into a permanent pout. For all that, you couldn't say she had an obvious beauty, nothing you could really capture with a photograph, but when she fluttered her lashes and looked at Dillon with those big round eyes, she made him believe he was something special.

As he munched his way through his fish and mushy lentils, Dillon tried to explain about the Knights of the Wasteland, The Sunday Echo, and the whole Cult Report thing. Charlotte was smiling and nodding in that reassuring way that people generally adopt when conversing with lunatics. It did all seem a bit far-fetched now he came to think about it.

'The fish is nice,' he said, changing the subject. 'Even with the lentil slop and all that.'

'Thanks, Dilly. I knew you'd like it. It's just a shame I didn't think to bring a bottle of Pinot Grigio.'

'That's OK. There's plenty of beer left. And you've still got to drive home.'

'I could stay the night if you like,' Charlotte offered, giving him the full big blue eyes treatment.

Dillon was tired and all he wanted to do was sleep, but it wasn't the sort of suggestion a self-respecting young hack could refuse. While

Charlotte was messing about in the bathroom, he washed up a few pots and pans and made a feeble attempt to clear up the bomb site that was their kitchen. When he heard the sound of his bed creaking, Dillon hid the remaining pans in the still-smoking cooker and stomped upstairs. Charlotte was already asleep and making a noise like a small boar on a truffle hunt. With a sigh, Dillon slumped into bed and fell into a deep and dream-filled sleep.

The next morning Charlotte was up bright and early.

'I've decided to spend the whole day helping you spring clean,'

'But it's May. Spring sprung ages ago,' complained Dillon.

'That's not the point. This house is a tip, and if you expect me to come round here more often, you need to make it more homely and hygienic. I'm quite happy to help, you know.'

'Aren't they expecting you at work? I thought you said your boss couldn't cope without you.'

Charlotte worked at the University, but Dillon wasn't exactly sure what she did. He knew she was in accounts and talked about "integrated strategies" and "quarterly budgets", but that was about all. In any case, it seemed like a pretty cushy number to him and paid a lot better than his former employment.

'The University is still in recess, so my department head said I could work from home if I liked. He trusts me to complete the spreadsheets in time for the new term. Most of the managers aren't so good at delegating. Some of them are complete control freaks. Imagine spending your whole day with someone like that!'

Dillon didn't need to use too much imagination to figure out what that would be like. Charlotte marched upstairs to declare germ warfare on the bathroom. Whilst she was out of earshot Sparks, whose knowledge of women was mainly theoretical, tried to offer his friend a friendly warning. 'You realise she's going through that late-twenties biological-clock crisis thing, don't you? You gotta get out of it before she has you pushing a pram up the aisle in a morning suit, mate!'

Privately, Dillon thought that if Charlotte was looking to him as a model husband and father, it was more than just a crisis; it was a Greek tragedy. Sparks had a point, though. Partway through their second date, Charlotte told him that she dreamed of having a big family one day. 'I'm so glad you want children too,' she had added, but Dillon couldn't remember saying anything of the sort.

'Most of the men I've been out with have never really wanted a long-term relationship. They were more interested in trying to get me drunk and take my clothes off! I'm so glad that you're different.'

Dillon had laughed nervously and hoped she was an even poorer judge of character than she seemed. Currently, her mind was on more practical matters. She was looking under the sink to see if there might be a blowtorch or some sulphuric acid to get the muck off the hall floor.

'I literally stick to the tiles every time I come in through the front door,' she grumbled. 'You can have a fifteen-minute tea break first if you like. I brought a couple of filo bakes from the new deli on Bailgate. You'll like these; they're stuffed with feta and fresh figs.'

By late afternoon, they had degunked the hallway, and Dillon was amazed to find that the stone tiles were arranged in a colourful pattern of red and white squares. All the time he'd lived in the house they had been strictly sepia.

They slumped on the couch and Charlotte laid her weary head on his shoulder and sighed. 'Dilly, we need to have a proper talk.' she started, in her best serious-yet-concerned tone.

'Oh, do we? I mean, yeah, righty-ho. What's it going to be about?'

'About you and me, of course.'

'Oh, that talk.'

'You see, I know you're depressed about the job situation and everything, but I think you should consider me a little more. You don't seem to care about the future, about our future together. I'm beginning to think you don't care about me, Dilly.'

'Uh-huh.'

'You do care about me, don't you, Dilly?'

'Uh-huh.'

'You're not just saying that, are you? I want you to be honest with me.'

'Uh-huh. I mean, yeah. I am being honest. It's just, well I don't know, but...'

At that moment, Dillon's mobile rang, and he leapt for it like a drowning man after a lifebelt.

'Hello, Dillon Wright speaking. Yes, that's right. Oh, I see. Just a minute.' He pressed the mute button. 'It's the Echo,' he whispered. 'About the job. I'll be right back.'

Waving crossed fingers superstitiously at his beloved, Dillon shuffled into the kitchen where the reception was better. Through the glass door, he could see Charlotte marching around the room organising books and magazines in orderly piles, rearranging the rows of dead and dying plants, opening cupboard doors and slamming them again in random fashion.

'I'm pleased to be the bearer of glad tidings, Dillon.' Amanda Bond waxed lyrical about the opportunities while Dillon waited for her to get to the point. 'I'm emailing you a contract to sign. Everything you need to know should be in there.'

Dillon thanked her effusively. He put down the phone, gave an Indian war whoop and burst through the door into the lounge, startling Charlotte in the process. He pulled the front of his T-shirt over his head, and punched the air with both fists, sending a battered lampshade flying across the room.

'Yes!' he yelled wildly. 'Ye-es!'

'Calm down, Dilly, or you'll wreck the place.' If she'd paused to look around her, Charlotte might have realised how foolish this sounded.

'I've done it! I've actually gone and done it!' Dillon popped his head out from under his shirt and pulled it back down over his anaemic torso. 'I've got the job. With The Sunday Echo. A weekly feature on contemporary religion in Britain. I get a whole column to myself. Cult Report with Dillon Wright. Me! My photo at the top, and everything. I've just got to sign on the dotted line and here-we-go.'

'The Sunday Echo gave you a job?' Charlotte appeared suitably amazed at this development. 'As a feature writer? I know you said the interview went well, but that's a serious newspaper, Dilly. My parents read it. There must be some mistake, surely.'

'What do you mean "a mistake"? I thought you said you had faith in me.'

'Well, I do, of course,' Charlotte admitted. 'I just didn't think anyone else would.'

Dillon paused for a moment to admire the logic of this and then considered the implications of his new role. 'Of course, it'll be hard work,' he began cautiously. 'There's a lot of research to do in the field before I can start my reports. Mr Gladman wants the first submission by the end of the month, so I'll have to get to work right away.

'I may have to go undercover. Infiltrate these cults. Find out what makes them tick. They can be very secretive, you know. It could be dangerous.'

He waited for a concerned response from Charlotte, but the look in her eyes boded difficult times ahead, even before any religious fanatics got hold of him.

'I'll probably be away investigating for long periods. I know it's going to be difficult for both of us, but you are pleased for me, aren't you?'

Dillon dived for the refuge of his favourite chair and, slumping low to present as small a target as possible, waited for the storm to break.

4   Where Do I Begin?

Starting any new job is always a challenge, and Dillon was finding his first days as a newspaper columnist particularly trying. He was feeling alone and quite unsure of how to begin. He briefly considered calling Charlotte. Her brother was a member of some dodgy religious militia. Dillon disliked the guy intensely, but he might be a useful source of information. Charlotte, however, was in something of a sulk and hadn't called him for several days. Although this was in many ways a relief, it gave him way too much time for introspection.

Unlike his job with the Lincoln Free Press and Advertiser, this one looked like being a very solitary affair. It didn't come with a set of instructions, and there was no one to ask for help. He couldn't even hang around the coffee machine and chat with his colleagues.

Sparks wasn't much help. For one thing, he never drank coffee. In fact, Dillon couldn't recall ever having seen him drink anything but beer and Irn-Bru. And although he allegedly worked from home, Dillon was never convinced that much actual work got done.

He knew there were at least three laptops, a server, and a mountain of other high-tech gear up in Sparks' room, but what he used it all for was a complete mystery. Knowing he was on to a loser, Dillon tried broaching the subject of Internet access.

'Could I borrow your iPad to get on the internet? My laptop's crashed again and I need to do some research for my new job.'

'No chance.'

'Why not?' enquired Dillon, acting hurt.

'Because you're a menace with computers. You're not just a technophobe, you're a human virus.'

'That's rich coming from the man who shorted out the mains supply to the whole street with a tablespoon.'

'I was just testing the UPS. I might have vaporised some cutlery, but I never lost any data. Every time you even touch a computer, you manage to crash the damn thing somehow. If you corrupt my server again, it'll take me hours to get everything straight. And I've got to start work early tomorrow.'

Dillon could be excused for looking somewhat sceptical. He had never seen Sparks get up before ten, and even then he looked half asleep. All in all, he wasn't the epitome of efficient home working.

Dillon was sure he could do better. He was determined to show the doubters such as Charlotte (and pretty much everyone else who knew him) that he could cut it on his own. After all, it was a once-in-a-lifetime opportunity, a real job, and rather a well-paid one at that. If no one was going to help, he would work it out for himself.

Of course, Dillon realised that, as a professional journalist, he would be expected to take a detached approach to the whole multi-cultural spectrum of alternative belief structures. He soon rejected the idea as being too much like hard work. Instead, he planned to scour the country for strange and interesting people with challenging new ideas, and then take the piss out of them.

Early on Monday morning, full of enthusiasm, he ate a cursory breakfast and headed off to Lincoln's Central Library. Even the Land Rover seemed to share his mood and roared into life at the first attempt. The sun was low in the sky, lending a warming glow to the barren stones of the city walls. He weaved his way down Steep Hill, through narrow cobbled streets, crisscrossing the one-way system with reckless abandon.

This labyrinth of ancient lanes was never designed for the motor car, but the Defender was in its element. The suspension was designed for utility rather than comfort and bounced over the rough cobbles, every jolt passing directly from the wheels through the seat and up into the base of Dillon's spine. He resisted the urge to go faster downhill. There was a twenty-mile-per-hour speed limit and he couldn't risk either the fine or the repair bill. He cared too much for his Land Rover, anyway. It was the nearest thing he had to a family heirloom: the only thing his dad had left that wasn't broken or bought on the never-never.

Soon, he passed the final 'Unsuitable for Motor Vehicles' sign and was back amongst the traffic. He crawled through the modern city streets, man and machine coughing and fuming behind the crawling cars, until they stuttered their way along Free School Lane towards the library car park.

All the conventional spaces were full, but the Highways Agency had dumped a mound of loose chippings over the double yellow lines.

The Defender climbed the manmade hill with ease and came to rest at a jaunty angle. Dillon tumbled out of the driver's door skittered down the slope and bounded up the library steps.

Inside, all was clean, warm, and quiet. The high-tech computerised database was offline again due to an unscheduled software update and the Internet portal was firmly closed to all comers. Dillon found a helpful human librarian and explained what he was looking for.

'How interesting,' she said. 'I'm terribly sorry about the technical issues. I suppose we'll just have to do it the old-fashioned way.'

She dusted off her trusty old card index and showed him the relevant results. There were entries for 'cults: apocalypse', 'cults: death', 'cults: misc', and even 'cults: sex'. He picked up a few random reference books to see what might turn up. The pictures in Human Sacrifice in Britain: A Short History sent shivers down his large intestine and he resolved to leave research on 'cults: death' to the very last.

After a couple of hours of note-taking, Dillon had a sore wrist and a much clearer understanding of the role of animist ritual in neo-pagan worship (the pictures of 'sky-clad' female participants had particularly caught his eye). He was, however, no nearer to knowing how to start his quest.

The books were all so depressingly serious. They said things like "celebrants were alleged to use sexual incentives to entice young men to become initiates", but they always left out the interesting details. What sort of incentives, for instance? And how did you get to meet women like that? If he was going to dish the dirt on these cults, Dillon felt he needed to go out and spend some time with them. He needed to check out the incentives in person so that he could disapprove of them properly.

He found an academic book about alternative religion in the UK. It listed some interesting cults, but not their addresses or phone numbers, of course, so he went back to find the friendly librarian, who smiled at him from behind a giant stack of historical romances.

'Excuse me, I know this is probably a really stupid question, but you wouldn't happen to have a contact list for local religious groups, would you?'

She shuffled over to a rusting filing cabinet in the corner and leafed slowly through the bottom drawer.

'Would that be "religions: conventional", "religions: New Age" or "religions: other"?'

'Wow! Well, forget the conventional ones, just New Age and others for me, please.'

'Some of the phone numbers might be out of date,' she warned. 'These fringe groups are terrible for moving on and not telling anyone. If it's not religious persecution, it's the bailiffs or the Serious Fraud Office. Most of them don't even have websites. Keeping track of them all is a full-time job, I can tell you.'

'And is that part of your job?' Dillon wondered.

'Oh, not me. I'm no good with computers. But I know someone who is very interested in alternative religious groups. I'll write down his website address for you. I just make sure the information is available to the people who need it. That's what being a librarian is all about. We're here to help.'

'Well, you've certainly helped me. I wouldn't have known where to start otherwise,' he admitted.

'Are you setting out on a spiritual quest?' she asked with the air of someone who would quite like to come along for the ride.

'Well, sort of; it's more of a search for the truth behind the spiritual,' Dillon replied rather pompously. 'I'm a writer, you see.'

'You write books?' She gazed wide-eyed at the thousands of titles stacked all around her in neat alphabetical order as if realising for the first time that there were people responsible for their creation. 'Gosh! You must be very clever.'

For a brief moment, Dillon felt important and puffed out his chest a little.

'That's so kind of you. You've been a great help. What's your name? I'll mention you in the credits.'

'Dolores Carter.' To make sure he got the spelling right, she pointed to the badge pinned to her left breast pocket.

He waved a cheery goodbye and marched out to the foyer. As he passed through the barrier, a shrill siren sounded and he was seized from behind by an elderly security guard sporting a uniform reminiscent of a military dictator. The guard glared at him menacingly and was about to don the rubber gloves to begin the search for purloined novellas when Dolores burst through the barrier and planted herself between them.

'Stupid, stupid machine! It's always going off. Beep, beep, beep, all day,' she announced breathlessly and shooed the startled security guard back to his desk. 'I don't want you upsetting this man; he's a famous writer.'

'Dillon Wright. Perhaps you've heard of me.'

'Of course, Mr Wright.' The man touched the gold brocade in his cap deferentially. 'Sorry to trouble you, sir.'

On impulse, Dillon pecked Dolores on the cheek before bounding down the steps, three at a time, to the waiting car. She waved faintly at his retreating form and was escorted back to her desk by the strong arms of Security.

Dillon threw his notes onto the passenger seat and leapt in. As he glanced down, he saw a book peeking out at him beneath the pile of paper. He picked it up and glanced at the cover: A Compendium of the Alternative Religions of Britain and Ireland, by W S Chowdary. He felt a little guilty but reasoned that he hadn't meant to run off with it. Anyway, it was at least ten years out of date and to take it back now would be far too embarrassing. He resolved to return the book once his research was finished. Meanwhile, it might come in very handy.

Back home, with his lists and his notes, Dillon settled down at the kitchen table to begin the slow process of elimination. He tried looking up the Knights of the Wasteland in W S Chowdary's book, but there was no mention of them. He was sure they must have been around for a while, so maybe they were just too obscure or too secretive to be included. He added them to the list he got from Dolores, anyway, and began cutting her comprehensive document down to a size that could be managed by a lethargic one-man research unit.

First, he crossed out the groups that were too boring: chanting cults, people who worshipped trees, the Church of England, that sort of thing.

Next, he considered the question of location. A religion, whose only followers lived in the Outer Hebrides, was unlikely to be a realistic prospect for investigation by a penniless English journalist. Amanda Bond had made it clear that The Sunday Echo had a limited budget for travel expenses.

Finally, he noted the groups that were simply too interesting. Some faiths have always welcomed the questioning of deeply held beliefs as the start of the road to enlightenment. Others have welcomed it as a good opportunity to practice their stone-throwing and fire-lighting skills.

Dillon highlighted the ones with obviously low tolerance levels and put question marks next to those that emphasised discipline and obedience. He had a nagging feeling that somewhere along the way he was going to encounter some of these characters. He was equally sure that he wasn't going looking for trouble until it came chasing him down the street with a burning cross.

He needed to start with an approachable group. Something calm and cerebral. No wailing, fasting, or self-mutilation. Preferably in a rural setting, within the Land Rover's normal reliability limits and outside the range of Charlotte's voice. He was pretty sure that she'd want to start talking to him again soon and he would rather not be there when she did.

A shadow fell across the table. Sparks, beer in hand, was peering over his shoulder at the dozen or so remaining prospects scattered in front of him. Dillon was waiting for the sarcastic comments about his handwriting, but instead Sparks picked up a handful of sheets and flicked through them thoughtfully.

'What about this one,' he suggested, waving his selection under his friend's nose.

'Oh yeah? Why that one exactly?' Dillon stared suspiciously at a page, headed The Gnostics of Albion.

'Oh, no reason really. But they're local and they sound harmless enough.'

Sparks was too dozily honest to make a good con man, but for some reason, Dillon thought he smelt another rat. He checked over the notes once more. There was no suggestion that these Gnostics were anything more than unconventional God-botherers. Despite his misgivings, he had to start somewhere. Decision made, he picked up the phone. After a ten-minute phone call, his curious quest was underway.

5   The Prophet Speaks

As he crossed the River Trent, following signs for the historic market town of Newark, Dillon wondered casually why The Gnostics of Albion had chosen to base themselves in a place that was an anagram of "wanker". It was a nice enough town, despite the auto-erotic connotations. The picturesque ruins of the castle provided an obvious marker as he navigated his way through the town centre. On his inevitable second lap of the one-way system, he spotted his turning and followed a narrowing lane down to the riverside.

The more he thought about it, the more he liked the idea of a cult that wanted to meet him in a pub. It's hard to get away with abducting someone from a crowded bar, and it's even harder to subject them to a religious tirade without someone pouring a pint over your head.

This particular pub hadn't let its trendy waterside location go to its head. A sign saying Beer Garden This Way led down to a couple of ramshackle benches on a small concrete platform overlooking the river. He peered over the railings and the scent of ozone and decaying duckweed tickled his nostrils. According to a peeling sign hanging from one hook above the door, the pub was called The Tow Path and the noise coming from inside suggested that it was popular, whatever the state of the decor.

Entering the pub was like a breath of stale air. In medieval times, the ventilation was probably quite adequate, but since it became fashionable to put glass in windows, things had gone downhill. The combination of overheated humanity, real ale and fried food was quite overpowering. This, Dillon thought, is what the Good Beer Guide refers to as 'ambience'. Occasionally, visitors may have mentioned the possibility of ventilation fans or even air conditioning, but this landlord had opted for tradition over mere comfort.

Dillon liked the place immediately. Everything about it had the feel of a genuine English pub: the hand-pulled ales, the tobacco-yellow paintwork, the rustic oak beams and the stone slab floor. In an age when many pubs serve more steaks than pints, and when the décor includes more fibreglass than wood, this was a thing to be treasured.

As he squeezed his way into the narrow lounge, Dillon could see a good cross-section of the town's population enjoying an evening out. There were students, bearded beer-buffs, smartly dressed office workers, and a smattering of hearty country folk. In one corner, a group of businessmen, whose quiet lunchtime drink had gone out of control, struggled with a decreasing grip on reality and the steadily increasing pull of gravity.

At the far end of the bar, an ill-assorted group were staring out at him through the crowd. They looked more like a CAMRA branch meeting than a bunch of religious fanatics, but something about them drew Dillon in their direction. A giant of a man, with a beard any prophet would be proud of, detached himself from the group and strode towards him, parting the crowd like Moses before the Red Sea. The man stuck out an oversized hand and greeted Dillon with a surprisingly gentle grip.

'Ralph Coleman. Pleased to meet you,' he boomed from somewhere in the beams. 'You must be Dillon Wright, that well-known journalist that I've never heard of.'

'Er... yes... How did you know it was me?'

'You have a strong aura, my friend.'

'Is that good?'

'Your aura is a reflection of your inner self. In yours, I see doubt and confusion. You seek after truth, but you do not trust what you find. The depth of your inner turmoil is clear. You are a man in need of wisdom.' Coleman leaned closer. 'You are a man in need of a pint!'

'You can see that in my aura?'

'I can see it in your tongue, which is almost hanging out of your mouth, my friend,' he laughed, in great waves of good humour.

The punters were three deep at the bar, but Coleman simply reached over their heads and plonked a leather tankard down in front of a flustered-looking barmaid.

'Twelve pints of XB please, and one for yourself, Tanya.'

A few of those waiting looked around angrily, but when they found themselves staring into Coleman's chest, they quickly turned their attention back to the bar.

While the beer was being poured, Dillon had a chance to observe Coleman more closely. Even in an old seaman's jersey and open-toed sandals, he certainly cut an impressive figure. Dillon could easily imagine him leading his people across the desert to the Promised Land. Not that his people looked like they would make it without stopping at Ye Oasis Inn for a pint and a pie on the way.

According to Dillon's hurried reading of the encyclopaedia he'd 'borrowed', Coleman had turned to Gnosticism while working as an Oxford college lecturer. Eventually, his unconventional views, or perhaps his dress sense, became too much, even for his liberal establishment.

By then, according to W S Chowdary, he had already made a big impression on those he worked with. When he declared his great revelation to the world, quite a number of his former students and colleagues flocked to his tie-dyed banner. Much to the college's consternation, they were shortly followed by the majority of the refectory staff, leading to the first of several 'brainwashing' accusations.

This fledgling cult under Coleman's divinely inspired guidance became known as the Gnostics of Albion, mainly because they went around in brightly coloured, tie-dye T-shirts with 'Gnostics of Albion' written on the front. As Dillon glanced across the pub, he noticed that one of the group, a rather squat unshaven individual, was still wearing the same T-shirt. Probably, it had been washed since 1973, but he couldn't be sure.

Back in the seventies, the athletic young Coleman apparently had quite a way with the opposite sex, persuading several impressionable and attractive young women to join the merry band. They, in turn, developed an infamous reputation for luring impressionable young men into the clutches of the cult. Dillon suspected that the average adolescent male didn't need much luring. However, looking at the well-rounded figures of the women in The Tow Path, he felt that these sirens had rather lost their edge in the intervening years.

Coleman handed Dillon his pint and ushered him towards the group. He shook hands with everyone within reach, before being grabbed by a statuesque redhead of indeterminate age who clasped him to her ample bosom. Just as he was wondering when he would be able to breathe again, Coleman hauled the woman off with a complicated one-handed manoeuvre, which he managed to execute without spilling any of his pint.

'Oh, Ralph, you spoilsport!' she complained. 'I was only welcoming our new recruit. It's so long since we had any fresh blood in the group.'

'He hasn't joined yet, Gwen, and if you suffocate him, he isn't likely to either.'

'But he will. I sense it in his aura. In his heart, he's one of us already. Aren't you, my duck?'

Dillon opened and shut his mouth several times without finding an adequate response to this.

'Dillon has come to us seeking knowledge,' intoned her leader. 'As keepers of the sacred truth, it is our duty to instruct him, in as much as can be taught to the uninitiated. What he makes of such knowledge is his own concern. We are guides and helpers, not foolish evangelists. We are the instruments of the Messengers of Light, not their soldiers or enforcers.' He turned to direct the sermon at Dillon.

'You may think we are a young group; another of these childish cults that seem to spring from the very air around us. Not all things are as they seem. In truth, we were founded long before the dawn of Christianity. Our roots are in the teachings of the ancient Gnostics and, through them, to the truth everlasting.'

According to Wikipedia, and an inspirational pamphlet Sparks had thoughtfully downloaded for Dillon, at least some of this was true. However, the main link with the Gnostics of antiquity appeared to be a book entitled Understanding Gnosticism from which Coleman had copied his central thesis, almost word for word.

Dillon was quite keen on this approach, having used it for many of his college essays. Coleman was one up on him in this case, since Dillon hadn't understood either the book or the pamphlet. He did, however, understand plagiarism and decided that, on the whole, it was better than homemade hokum.

The main advantage of copying your ideas from textbooks, as opposed to say scribbling them down during a drug-crazed trance, is that they have a reasonable chance of making sense. Coleman's view of the world, while being far removed from mainstream beliefs, was remarkably coherent.

The basic premise went something like this:

a) The creator deity made this world in six days and judging by the state of things, it was obviously a rush job.

b) People say that the world has gone mad. However, the briefest glance at the history books will tell you that it must have always been mad.

c) The most obvious explanation for this is that it was created mad by a mad creator.

The alternative interpretation is, of course, that the observer himself is two psalms short of a testament, but this does not seem to have occurred to Coleman. Instead, he declared that it was the sacred duty of all those in the know (i.e. The Gnostics of Albion) to battle against the mad creator and restore the world to sanity.

At first sight, it would appear to be something of an uneven match: thirty ageing hippies against an omnipotent deity. However, Coleman and his co-religionists were in regular contact with entities from the other side of reality. These Messengers of Light were just biding their time before breaking through to our universe, carting the creator off to the big loony bin in the sky, and suitably rewarding their helpers on Earth (i.e. The Gnostics of Albion, again).

Coleman's six-hundred-page thesis, 'The Albion Codex', (which Dillon had no intention of even speed reading) points out that the great conflict of the Cosmos is therefore not between Good and Evil, but between Madness and Sanity. The whole creation is infected with insanity, but man suffers most from the creator's madness since he is closest to his image.

Fortunately, the Messengers have injected some sanity into the world via the original Gnostics and their intellectual descendants. This means, of course, that the Gnostics of Albion are sane and the rest of the world is just plain crazy. Dillon was pleased that they'd cleared that up for everyone.

'I consider myself a true Christian,' Coleman informed Dillon. 'Though, sadly, most other branches of that faith would call me a heretic. As I explain in the Codex, Christ and the prophets who preceded him were sent by the Messengers of Light to cure mankind's madness. But as you well know, he was killed by agents of the mad creator before he could complete his sacred task.'

Here, Coleman's ideas departed from mainstream Gnosticism (not that Gnosticism has had much of a mainstream in the past millennium).

'I realised after studying the ancient texts that Christ must have told his disciples the whole truth, but it was considered too radical for the average man-on-the-mount, you see. So, naturally, he presented his message in a coded form.'

This insight led Coleman to view the Christian Bible as a giant cryptic crossword. He showed Dillon his latest project: an attempt to decipher the entirety of the New Testament. Dillon was impressed by what he read, and by the way Coleman had manipulated the Gospels to suit his unusual worldview. The cynic in him considered that this was no different from what every religious leader had done throughout history. However, Coleman, being more radical than most, was quite happy to change most of the words as well as crossing out the bits he didn't like.

Somewhere in the dark recesses of the pub, the landlord sounded the death knell for another evening's libations. Dillon was not impressed at having to knock back nearly a full pint of XB, before being herded out of the pub with other reluctant drinkers. He stood aimlessly in the darkness of the unlit lane while the five pints he'd consumed played havoc with his coordination skills. He glanced over at the Land Rover and wondered if the back seat was going to make as uncomfortable a bed as he remembered.

'I thought this sort of pub would stay open a bit later,' he complained, thinking that more anaesthesia would be helpful.

'Such enlightenment has yet to reach our esteemed host. He is one who thinks we have all eternity in which to enjoy his excellent ales. We, who know better, have a keg or two back at the house, which you, my friend, are welcome to share.'

As they weaved their way along the waterside, Dillon plucked up the courage to ask Coleman about a few things that were beginning to prey on his mind. 'So what brought you to Newark of all places? Was it a prophecy or something?'

'Nothing so grand, lad,' admitted Coleman. 'I was brought up here. Due to some rather tedious events back in the early eighties, we had to leave Oxford in a hurry. So I did what any self-respecting penniless bachelor would do and I moved everyone in with my mother. It's a rambling old place and my dear old Mum was far too gaga to complain, I'm afraid.'

Dillon secretly suspected that this tendency might run in the family, but he still pressed on with his questions. 'Do you think the end of the world is nigh? What's going to happen? Do you know something I don't?'

Coleman stopped abruptly, causing several of his less alert followers to cannon into the back of his solid frame. 'I know many things that you do not. I know your calling, your heart's desire, and I know your secret names. Still, I doubt I could make you believe all the things that have been revealed to me. You are on a quest, my son, do you realise that?'

Dillon had a sudden vision of himself, following the Knights of the Wasteland on horseback along the hard shoulders of Britain's motorway network.

'I believe you will find the answers you seek. I have faith in you, Dillon, but you must also have faith in yourself and in your own judgment. Do not let your preconceptions obscure the truth when you find it.

'The world is ever-changing,' he continued. 'Don't assume that just because evil and sorrow fill the world, that it will always be this way. Some prophets speak of the end of the world as we know it, but I believe it will not be the end of all things. The things we cherish will endure and those we despise will surely perish. One day, I hope to show you the truth. One day soon, my friend.'

6 Different for Girls

When Dillon finally got back home, something truly momentous had happened. Sparks had done the washing up.

'It's that Charlotte,' he complained plaintively. 'She's been round here every day. She's harder to shift than the Mormons. I was starting to wonder if she fancied me or something.'

Dillon took a long look at his friend's rustic and uneven features and reassured him that unwelcome female attention was the least of his problems.

'She keeps asking after you, though,' Sparks warned him. 'She's always wanting to know what you've been up to and all that. You ought to tell me where you're going. It's not easy lying when you don't even know the truth in the first place.'

Dillon struggled to make sense of this logic through the haze of a truly world-class hangover. He vaguely remembered accepting an offer to view the Gnostic's inner sanctum, which turned out to be a library stocked with esoteric theological texts and over fifty varieties of single malt whisky. After that, everything became a blur.

That morning, once he had regained consciousness, he had found himself lying on the floor with a weighty tome entitled The Secularisation Thesis as a pillow, and some nagging worries. Had he perhaps agreed to Gwen's plea for him to join the cult? What had he been doing standing on Coleman's shoulders? And most importantly, where were his trousers?

The answers to the last two questions became apparent as he glanced up at the impressive chandelier suspended from the ornate ceiling above. It took some athletic leaps with a broom in one hand before he could reclaim all his missing clothes. Maybe it had been just another party game, or maybe it was part of his initiation into the happy band. It didn't take very long for discretion to overcome curiosity (valour having long since departed). After a couple of strong coffees, he sped home. A strangely clean and tidy home.

'I thought if I looked busy, your Charlotte might go away.' Sparks explained, 'but she just kept on nagging away. I could even hear her over the vacuum.'

With concern etched on his face, Dillon poked his head around the living room door. Sure enough, it was as frighteningly spotless as the kitchen.

'You know, this housework lark isn't so bad when you get into it. You start off with a load of dirt and then after a couple hours of scrubbing and stuff, it's all gone. Just like magic! Maybe if we, like, did a little bit each day and we put stuff away when we'd finished with it, then...'

Sparks broke off, seeing the expression on Dillon's face.

'Well, it was just an idea, like.' He paused. 'Fancy a beer, then?'

'Now you're talking sense.' Dillon pulled two cans from the fridge. 'Hair of the dog!'

'No, piss of the cat,' Sparks corrected him. 'We drank all the good stuff last week, remember?'

Despite its strange aftertaste, the beer had the desired effect. Suitably revived, Dillon decided to write up some of his notes while he still recalled what his cryptic scribblings were meant to convey.

He spent the next couple of hours thinking deeply about religion for the first time in years. It wasn't something he'd considered much since he'd left the Cub Scouts and discovered cynicism. Still, he wasn't actually searching for enlightenment. Like a TV evangelist, he was approaching religion from a very specific angle: he wanted to know how it could make him money.

Dillon had a long-standing distrust of organised religion, which was regularly reinforced by encounters with Jehovah's Witnesses, the college God squad, and the people who stood on the High Bridge every Saturday in headscarves haranguing passers-by. Not to mention TV reports from Palestine, Iraq, Afghanistan, and all the other faith-fuelled conflicts around the world.

Dillon rummaged around the kitchen and rescued his 'project file' from under a neatly stacked pile of plates and cups. So far, it contained the results of several hours of intensive research, culled from Wikipedia, a dog-eared Children's Encyclopaedia, and a copy of The Watchtower. Carefully preserved in a plastic folder at the back, were some imaginative passages he'd dreamed up himself as insurance, in case reality proved to be too boring.

He was convinced that he was on to a winner, here. Everyone wanted to read about people with strange and unusual lifestyles. It was a guaranteed attention grabber. Apart from the obvious prurient interest in oddballs and weirdos, there was the secret hope that maybe there was more to life than this.

Only genuine cranks thought that Armageddon was just around the corner, but there were lots of people who wanted to believe that a cataclysmic event was approaching. Anything would do so long as it shook up their mundane, repetitive lives and gave them a chance to start afresh.

In the other room, Sparks was watching a gardening programme on TV. Dillon was intrigued since his fellow tenant was generally considered to be allergic to fresh air and never even sat in the garden, let alone worked in it.

'What are you watching that for?'

'It's relaxing. I always like to watch something I don't care about when I want to relax. If I was interested in it, I might start thinking about stuff, and then I wouldn't be relaxed, would I?'

'If you see any good ideas, you could try them out in our garden.' Dillon looked out of the window at the miniature wildlife sanctuary that had grown up through the cracked paving slabs.

A loud hammering on the door interrupted the horticultural debate. Sparks gave his friend a long hard look before getting up to answer it. It was a look that clearly said either sort your life out or start looking for a new housemate.

It was immediately obvious that Charlotte was not a happy teddy today. She bustled Sparks back into the lounge and planted her prominent posterior as far away from Dillon as she could manage.

'You never phoned. You never came round. You were happy just to let me sit at home and stew, weren't you, Dilly?'

'There didn't seem to be much point, since you weren't speaking to me.'

'So you were just going to carry on gallivanting around the country without giving me a moment's thought?'

'I only went to Newark. There's not a lot of gallivanting going on in Newark. And I was thinking about you a lot,' he added truthfully. 'You're a hard person to ignore.'

While Charlotte paused to consider if this was a compliment, or not, Dillon pressed home his advantage. 'It's good to see you again, anyway. I hate it when you're angry with me.' That at least was true.

Charlotte, angry was an amplified version of Charlotte, happy. She was hard to cope with in either state unless he employed his favourite form of self-defence: running away.

'Oh, Dilly! I'm sorry, but you make me so mad sometimes.' Her frown melted away as she spoke. 'You just won't face up to things. You never want to talk things through. I know we could sort everything out if we could just talk about it properly.'

Charlotte crossed the room, sat down by Dillon, and patted his hand.

Sparks, who had been staring intently at a feature on composting, took this opportunity to make a break for it. Both Charlotte and Dillon glared at him for different reasons, and he sat down again in a hurry.

'Mark has been really kind to me while you've been away. You can always rely on Mark to be there when you need him.' The object of her praise squirmed in his seat. 'I don't know why you can't get a nice steady job, like Mark.'

Only Charlotte thought Sparks had a steady job. Dillon's fellow tenant described himself as a freelance software engineer, but he was very evasive about who his employers might be. Some of his less charitable friends speculated he was running a porn site or the world's least successful money laundering service.

Dillon, who knew how little money his friend possessed, thought it was something more mundanely embarrassing. IT support for a company peddling dodgy erectile dysfunction solutions, or worse, maybe he was working for one of the social media giants. Charlotte, a certified technophobe, thought that anyone who dealt with computers was a minor genius and she loved the idea of working with all the comforts of home to hand.

'I don't think you should be visiting these dangerous cults by yourself,' she continued, expanding on her theme. 'People like you are very vulnerable, you know.'

'People like me?' Dillon was bemused.

'People who don't have any strong beliefs to protect them.'

'I strongly believe it's all bullshit.'

'They might brainwash you and force you to join them,' cautioned Charlotte.

'You mean like they did with your brother,' he suggested.

'Jerremy has joined a religious group, not a cult. There is a difference, you know. The Defenders of the Faith lead very strict, contemplative lives.'

'They are officially a cult, you know,' Sparks butted in. 'They've been categorised as a religious militia.'

Charlotte and Dillon just stared at him.

'What's more, they're a black hat cult and you know what that means.'

'I don't think we do,' Dillon confessed.

'Well, it's just the symbols they use on the website: there are white hats and black hats. Apollonian and Dio-wotsitian or maybe it's the other way round. Those militia lads are definitely black hats and their leader's got a red flag.'

'He's a communist?'

'No, just red. No hammer and sickle. Like with the old motor cars. "Look out, here he comes." That style of thing.'

'What are you going on about, Mark?' Charlotte demanded in her shrillest voice.

Dillon was wondering the same thing. He wanted to know where Sparks was getting his information from. Perhaps this was the same website that Dolores mentioned. Maybe he could cut and paste some of it for his column.

'Is there something you're not telling me?'

'Yes, but if I told you, I'd have to shoot you,' Sparks threatened unconvincingly.

'You don't have a gun.'

'All right then; if I told you, I'd have to reformat your memory.'

'Shut up, Dillon! I'd like Mark to explain himself,' demanded Charlotte, her voice taking on a sharper, more threatening tone.

'I think I'll probably shut up too if that's all right with you,' Sparks proposed optimistically.

'No,' insisted Charlotte. 'I want to know where you get these ridiculous accusations from. The Defenders of the Faith are a moral, law-abiding, organisation. Otherwise, Jerremy would never have joined them.'

'They sound like the military wing of the Salvation Army to me,' said Dillon.

'That's just ignorance talking. You'd understand these things if you had faith, like Jerremy and I.' Charlotte was beginning to lose patience again. 'If only you'd come to church with me, for once. Reverend Eccleston could have a little chat with you. It's a lovely service: she plays the guitar and we all shake hands—'

'I went to church, once,' Sparks interjected. 'It was a wedding or something. I didn't have a suit, so they put me at the back behind a pillar. And I couldn't get any free wine 'cos I wasn't consecrated.'

'Don't you have any religious beliefs at all, Mark?' Charlotte wanted to know.

'No, I'm an engineer,' he replied, as if that explained everything. 'I put my faith in science. Well not faith, obviously, but something like that, anyway. I read one of those Gideon Bibles once. It didn't make much sense to me. It was full of stuff that could never have happened, like talking bushes and people raising the dead. It never even mentioned the Big Bang once.'

'But don't you ever wonder about the meaning of life?'

'What meaning? If there was a meaning, it would all make sense, and it doesn't. You've only got to look at the lottery. If there was a meaning, poor people with sick kids would win it every week, not some arsehole who's going to blow it all on a superyacht.'

'Maybe the poor people can't afford a ticket,' Dillon suggested.

'Exactly! That's what I'm saying, kind of. It's all random. Meaningless. So there's no point in worrying about it.'

'Have you ever thought of becoming a philosopher?'

'No. It always sounds like a lot of old bollocks. Does it pay well?'

'I doubt it. I wouldn't give up the day job. Whatever it might be.'

Charlotte was clearly losing patience with them both. She turned her back on Sparks and tried to divert her boyfriend onto a different subject.

'What are you going to do next, Dilly? You're not going away again, are you?'

Dillon hadn't planned to leave again for a while, but he considered lying. Unfortunately, Lincoln was a small city, and Charlotte was sure to find him, eventually.

'I'll have to stay and write up my reports for the Echo. They want to see some samples before they publish the first article. Sparks says I can borrow one of his old laptops.'

This was news to Sparks who'd only offered to let him use it while he was down the pub. Since Dillon was always in the same pub, this wasn't an overly generous gesture.

'After that, I'll have to go and do some more research,' he went on cautiously. A fleeting thought passed through his mind. He reached into his back pocket and brought out a beer-stained scrap of paper. On it was a telephone number, and the words 'Magdalene Sisterhood'. He had a vague recollection of Coleman giving this to him and laughing.

'I'm going to visit the Magdalene Sisterhood,' he announced, passing the note to Sparks.

'Aren't they that bunch of man-hating lesbian psychos?' asked Sparks with his usual political correctness.

'Ralph said they believe in the Divine Feminine or some such,' said Dillon, cautiously, wondering how come Sparks had such a handle on the cult scene all of a sudden.

'I heard they cut off some bloke's bollocks.'

'You what?' Dillon was losing enthusiasm for this line of research very rapidly.

'That was never proven,' Charlotte pointed out. 'I remember reading about it at the time. The man who made those accusations was a drunk and a wife-beater and, anyway, he never pressed charges.'

'He's still got no bollocks, though,' Sparks pointed out.

'Perhaps I'll try some other group instead,' decided Dillon.

'Go on. Where's your sense of adventure? You could take Charlotte along. She'd enjoy that sort of thing.'

Charlotte ignored Sparks' insinuation and seized on his suggestion.

'Yes, why don't I go with you? As a woman, I'm bound to have more empathy with a feminist group than you.'

'Why not give them a call?' suggested Sparks. 'Let them have a chance to get everything nice and sharp.'

'Thanks a lot, mate,' muttered Dillon.

Sparks placed the number strategically next to Dillon's phone.

'Make sure you don't get cut off,' he said, with a wicked grin.

'He who hesitates is lost,' added Charlotte.

Dillon stared at his phone. What were the odds of an extreme all-female religious sect agreeing to be interviewed by an atheist male journalist? Slim to none, surely. He picked up the receiver and dialled.

7 Sisters Are Doing It For Themselves

As he drove out of Lincoln, with Charlotte chatting happily in the passenger seat, Dillon silently cursed the Gnostics of Albion and their leader in particular. He wasn't sure whether this was Coleman's idea of a joke or if he genuinely thought he was being helpful. Whichever, Dillon was holding him entirely responsible for his current predicament.

'We were expecting your call,' said the Reverend Mother Sophia Hildegard when he'd phoned the Magdalene Convent. 'You are very welcome to visit us and of course, you can bring your companion. I'm sure you'll both find it a life-changing experience.'

What better way to spend a sunny Saturday, than driving across Lincolnshire with severe castration anxiety, while your passenger rabbits on about her Auntie Audrey, who once met the Pope and took Holy Orders in Scunthorpe?

Auntie Audrey wasn't his concern. Auntie Audrey was in her eighties and was known to be kind to children and to help invertebrates cross the road. In short, she was a real nun, unlike the emasculating religious psychopaths described in W S Chowdary's invaluable compendium. Real nuns helped the poor and needy; they didn't get arrested for carrying concealed weapons.

Dillon promised himself that if he got out of this with all his extremities intact, he would do the rest of his research at home or the library. It was a lot simpler and safer to concoct a story from things he read online or in the mountain of articles that the ever-helpful Dolores had printed out for him.

On the back seat, already for posting, was an envelope containing his first reports for Arnold Gladman's approval. He was very pleased with them. There was little in the way of intellectual pretension, and he felt no compunction to be fair and reasonable. He simply wrote it as he saw it, in the sure and certain knowledge that ninety per cent of The Sunday Echo readers would be on his side.

Gladman might even give him an advance to cover necessary expenses, starting with an urgent replacement of the Land Rover's brake pads, which had been over-stressed during his emergency stop on the motorway.

Amongst the articles packed in the well-padded envelope was one poking fun at the Gnostics of Albion and their idiosyncratic beliefs and another savagely lampooning the Knights of the Wasteland, on the principle that they were unlikely ever to read a newspaper let alone a news website.

Meanwhile, Dillon's road to perdition wound its tortuous way through fields of heavily scented rapeseed and mist-blue flax. An ancient tractor towing an evil-smelling, dung-splattered, livestock wagon edged its nose out of a farm track and paused. The driver waited a few seconds, until he could see the whites of Dillon's eyes, and then pulled out, forcing the Land Rover into another radical braking manoeuvre. He made a few half-hearted attempts to pass the tractor on the busy and narrow road then settled down for a long slow journey.

Dillon considered himself to be an environmentalist, but a short drive through the Lincolnshire countryside could turn him into David Attenborough's worst nightmare.

'Look at this. It's the main road to the coast and we're stuck behind a yokel in a smock using it to drive his swine to market.'

'You should try to relax,' Charlotte advised. 'You won't get there any quicker by losing your temper. I could teach you some of the breathing exercises from our yoga class.'

Dillon wondered if he could get past the tractor if he pushed Charlotte out through the passenger door but dismissed the idea as impractical.

'What we need is a nice big motorway. At least six lanes each way.'

A selective conscience was a wonderful thing. Anyway, he never considered that pesticide-covered fields, belonging to rich twats in Barbour jackets, really counted as part of the environment. Eventually, the tractor pulled off towards Horncastle, leaving the Land Rover to continue its steady progress east. It took the best part of an hour of deteriorating relations between driver and navigator to find the village of Belchfield Magna, where the Magdalene Sisterhood had its headquarters.

'So where are we?' enquired Dillon.

'Just give me a minute, can't you? There's no phone signal and this little map you printed out is useless. You have to turn right. No, I mean left.'

'What do you mean? There's no left turn here.'

'Of course there isn't. You just drove past it.'

Dillon backed the Land Rover up the narrow road at high speed, narrowly missing a dry-stone wall and swung the car into a rough track, overhung by an ancient hawthorn hedge.

'Are you sure about this?'

'Quite sure,' retorted Charlotte, 'unless your directions are wrong.'

Dillon continued to mutter obscenities to himself as the Land Rover bounced its way down the track towards a large ivy-covered house ahead. As he rounded the corner a faded sign announced The Convent of Saint Mary Magdalene. A tall woman in a camouflage-patterned nun's habit motioned them to stop. Charlotte wound down the window and waved.

'I'm Charlotte Chaplin and this is Dillon Wright. We're here to see the Reverend Mother.'

'I know,' she growled. 'I am Sister Charity. You gotta leave your car here. Follow me.'

As they climbed out of the car, Charlotte grasped Dillon firmly by the arm, in case he should be harbouring last-minute thoughts of escape, and they marched in convoy towards the old convent.

The imposing front door was propped open and they followed Sister Charity through dimly lit passages lined with badly painted images of famous women through the ages. It was an odd selection. Dillon thought he recognised Boudicca, Margeret Thatcher, Saint Theresa and possibly Dame Vera Lynn. The panelled wooden door at the far end led into a business-like office where a studious-looking man in his sixties hovered over a younger woman in a more elegant version of Sister Charity's camouflage outfit.

The woman rose to greet her visitors and Dillon held out his hand hesitantly. She ignored him and instead grasped Charlotte by the shoulders and kissed her on both cheeks.

'Welcome to the Magdalene Sisterhood, Charlotte. I am Reverend Mother Sophia Hildegard. I hope you and your companion will feel comfortable in our sanctuary.'

'It's Dillon Wright. I was the one who phoned, remember.'

'You are also welcome here, Dillon. Although we suffer very few men to enter our sanctuary of womanhood.'

'Must be my lucky day. I didn't think you gave interviews to any journalists at all, let alone male ones.'

'It has become necessary for us to attempt to improve our profile in the Press. There has been some unpleasantness with our bigoted local authority. You are fortunate that your request came at the right time.'

'I heard they were going to evict you. Something about planning permission?'

'One of our converts, Sister Agnes, was formerly the Mayor of Scamblesby, our so-called local authority. Since she threw off her chains of office and joined our ranks, the council have been in fear of their pathetic little power games being disrupted. They claim we're not a religious order. They claim we hold women against their will. Soon, the time will come when women rise up against tyrannical regimes such as Scamblesby District Council and sweep them into the sea.'

'Is that right?' There was a messianic edge to her rhetoric that piqued Dillon's professional interest.

'The Age of Man is at an end and the Age of Woman is upon us. Soon, a new saviour in feminine form will step forth, to lead us away from the path of violence and inequality, towards the promised lands of peace, justice, and spiritual harmony. All women will flock to her banner. Men will be seen for what they are, just a step on the evolutionary ladder. They will be tolerated for a while, but their numbers will decline naturally as the years pass until they are nothing but an unpleasant memory.'

Charlotte thought she had spotted a flaw in the argument. 'What about babies?' she demanded. 'If there aren't any men, we won't be able to you-know-what, and even nowadays you need to you-know-what to make children, you know.'

Dillon had some difficulty in following this, particularly as his you-know-what life seemed to be suffering from a bad case of god-knows-when. Reverend Sophia, at least, seemed to understand her meaning.

'Our knowledge of human biology is advancing. Did you know that male sperm count is reducing each year? Some women of science have calculated that it will have reduced to zero within a mere twenty-five years. By then, women will be in control, and science will have made single-sex reproduction possible. It will also enable us to select the gender of our children, and we will choose not to bring forth inferior males into our new world.'

'So, no sex then?' said Dillon.

'There are those here who still entertain lustful thoughts of all persuasions. It is our duty to cleanse them of those urges and prepare them for the coming of the new Messiah. Only through celibacy can we achieve the purity which will make us worthy of salvation.'

Dillon was finding the Sisterhood's philosophy less and less appealing with every new revelation. All this pseudo-science babble was very suspect. There were plenty of things about male behaviour that he wasn't proud of, but could you take the sex out of humanity, without making it less than human? He didn't think it would be a good idea to start that debate with Reverend Sophia, who seemed very keen to cut this interview short.

'Let me introduce you to Professor Frederick Braunschreiber. I'm sure he will be pleased to show you around. The Professor came to us several years ago seeking spiritual growth and enlightenment. To be of service to the Sisterhood, he has put aside many aspects of his masculinity. Are you ready to make such a sacrifice, Dillon?'

Dillon couldn't think of anything to say that wouldn't get him further in trouble. Sophia swept from the room and left her visitors with the Professor, who was more than happy to talk to them. In fact, it was impossible to stop him talking. His straggly beard covered his mouth and he spoke in a dull monotone sermon which appeared to emanate from somewhere near his navel.

'I held the Chair in Comparative Religion at the University of Nottingham for many years,' he explained. 'I had a particular interest in religious symbolism and the role of women in the early Christian church.'

'That's very interesting I'm sure, but...' interrupted Dillon. He wanted to ask Braunschreiber exactly what bits of his masculinity he'd had to give up to join the Sisterhood, but once the professor had started his lecture he was unstoppable.

'Of course, I had long known of the Gospel of Saint Mary Magdalene, but little did I know the astonishing influence that this ancient manuscript was to have on my life. I began to study it in more detail at the behest of Reverend Mother, Sophia. Did you realise that she is one of our country's finest cryptologists? Of course, she is so much younger than I, but I recall there was a certain chemistry when first we met...'

'Well, thank you, professor, but we really must be getting on...' said Charlotte, but had no more success in stopping his flow.

'You will be familiar with the so-called heretical belief that Saint Mary was, in fact, the wife of Jesus, and the mother of his children, and that she was chosen by him to lead his church when he ascended bodily to Heaven. She should have been Pope Mary. Can you imagine that? All the subsequent leaders of the church could well have been women too. Just imagine it!'

'We are trying, Professor, but...'

'Over time, I traced many possible lines of descent from Saint Mary to the present day, and I became convinced that Sophia was one of those very descendants. There were certain symbols hidden within the fabric of Westminster Abbey, Notre Dame, and the Pantheon in Rome, which point irrefutably to a link between the Templar conspiracy and...'

'Looks like a lovely day for a stroll, Professor.' said Dillon, grabbing Charlotte by the arm and edging towards the doors leading into the grounds. The Professor followed them outside, explaining some crushingly dull aspects of religious symbolism and pressed a copy of his latest book into Dillon's hand as they walked.

'It's just a slim volume called, Holy Grail: The Whole Bloody Truth' he explained. 'I think you might find it very illuminating if you get my meaning.'

As they stood in the walled garden, amongst the stone urns and figurines of naiads and dryads, Dillon saw the Reverend Mother lurking behind the greenhouse, looking for all the world as if she was playing hide and seek.

A young fresh-faced nun came charging up the path with an overladen wheelbarrow. When she saw the visitors, she brought it to a staggering halt and bounded over to greet them. 'Hi there, Prof! And look there's Sophie-sweetie behind the tomatoes. Cooee! Have you brought some new friends to meet me?' She hopped from foot to foot, eagerly, her soft round face shining with glee, and her habit straining to contain her enthusiasm and well-rounded figure.

'Greetings, Sister Sharon,' said the professor. 'This is Charlotte Chaplin. She wants to know all about our lives here.'

'Hi, Charlotte it's very nice to meet you.' She enveloped Charlotte in a bear hug. 'Sophie-sweetie didn't tell me we were having visitors.'

Sophie-sweetie looked as if she wished she'd picked a different route or even a different calling. She had the expression of a woman who was planning to introduce a more stringent selection policy as soon as possible. 'I think our guests have to go soon, Sister Sharon.'

'If we asked them nicely maybe they'd stay a bit longer. Do you like gardens, Charlotte? There are some really pretty flowers in our garden. I planted some of them all by myself. We could sit and have a chat in the summerhouse. It's nice and peaceful there. It's my favourite place in the whole garden.'

Charlotte glanced anxiously over her shoulder and gave Dillon an imploring look.

'What's your favourite flower, Charlotte? I like daffodils. It's too late for daffys, but I could pick you Chrysanths from the greenhouse. They smell really nice. You've got a nice smell, too, Charlotte. Just like a pretty flower.'

Sister Sharon's persistence and incessant chatter were clearly throwing Charlotte off balance. She didn't have many close female friends and sometimes seemed to find the workings of the female mind as much a mystery as Dillon did.

'It's a lovely garden,' Charlotte said, 'but I've got to go.'

'Don't you want to be my friend, then?'

'I'm sorry.'

'You can't go unless you give me a kiss.'

Charlotte closed her eyes and timidly offered a cheek in the manner of a Jane Austen heroine. Sharon grasped her face between her hands and kissed her full on the lips before running off between lines of fruit-laden trees, her habit billowing in the wind. Before Dillon had a chance to say anything he might have regretted, Charlotte ushered him out of the walled garden. As they passed through the stone arch, the arresting figure of Sister Charity appeared from nowhere to escort them from the premises.

A brooding silence engulfed the Land Rover as they drove away. After a few futile attempts at communication with his passenger, Dillon lapsed into a gloomy trance. Even the radio sounded dull and muffled. As they dodged the parked cars, strewn randomly outside the pretty stone cottages along Belchfield Magna's one and only street, Charlotte finally broke the spell.

'What dreadful people. And you just left me to deal with that silly Sister Sharon. You could have done something. As for that awful Reverend Mother, who does she think she is, pretending to be a leader of a religious order?'

'She's not really a Reverend Mother. She's a man-hating, fundamentalist in a wimple. There is a difference. And anyway, I wasn't the one who kissed a nun.'

Charlotte gave Dillon a furious glance, then folded her arms across her chest, and stared fixedly at the far horizon for the remainder of their interminable journey back to Lincoln.

8 Spirits in the Material World

The next morning, Dillon came slowly back to consciousness with a fuzzy head and birdcage-bottom throat. It took him a while to remember exactly how he'd got into this state.

He and Charlotte had got back quite late after losing their way again in the Lincolnshire countryside. He'd dropped Charlotte off at her apartment in Burton Waters and she'd got out of the car without a word or a backward glance.

He and Charlotte had got back quite late after losing their way again in the Lincolnshire countryside. He'd dropped Charlotte off at her apartment in Burton Waters and she'd got out of the car without a word or a backward glance.

With unusual perceptiveness, Sparks had noticed, straight away, his friend's sour mood. Maybe it was the natural empathy between old friends or, more likely because Dillon had nearly taken the door off its hinges as he came in.

There are few words for situations such as these and none at all in Sparks' vocabulary. He silently placed a can of bitter in Dillon's hand and put on AC/DC at high volume, hoping that their uncomplicated approach to relationships might help. Many beers later, Dillon had fallen into a drunken stupor, with a can still clutched firmly in his hand.

How he'd got to bed, Dillon wasn't sure, but this morning, he found himself under the duvet, still wearing most of his clothes and one shoe. He crawled out from beneath the covers and attempted to stand, but the sudden movement was too much for his fragile brain and he slumped back onto the mattress. With much pathetic whimpering and clutching of the temples, he finally made it to the bathroom to survey the damage.

Dillon was normally an optimist as far as his own appearance was concerned, but today he was definitely not looking his best. He licked his palm and tried to tame his alpaca hairstyle. Blood-flecked eyes stared out from sunken sockets at a pallid, careworn face. Today was a good day to stay at home.

He staggered downstairs to be greeted by the smell of frying bacon. Sparks was nominally in control of a large frying pan and was trying to damp down a small fire, which had broken out in the middle of his breakfast. Dillon's stomach did a couple of flips, and he sat down heavily at the kitchen table.

'Best thing for a hangover,' Sparks declared, breaking another egg into the greasy melange. 'Here, eat this.'

Dillon found himself holding several rashers of bacon and a runny egg between two slabs of bread. Deciding on a kill-or-cure approach, he stuffed the sandwich in his mouth and munched away. A stream of yolk dribbled off his chin onto the table. He absent-mindedly mopped up the mess with his fingers and shoved it back in his mouth with the rest. His stomach, which had come to equate cholesterol with contentment, settled down.

With the help of more strong coffee, his head stopped spinning, and he felt able to start work. He couldn't face writing about the Sisterhood just yet and turned instead to some of the more bizarre cults his research had previously uncovered. He was particularly fond of a group calling themselves the Seekers of Light, who were obsessed with the idea that the Messiah had arrived a few years ago without anyone noticing. He found them busily harassing people on the High Bridge in Lincoln as they tried to form an impromptu search party. They were issuing everyone with copies of a "psychic" drawing of a man who looked rather like a young Richard Branson.

There was also his interview with an assistant manager at the McDonald's in Grantham, who claimed he was descended from an illicit union between King David and the Queen of Sheba. He was planning to lead the world into a new era of tolerance and enlightenment just as soon as he paid off his student loan. Unfortunately, the lad had made Dillon promise not to publish until he got a job with some street cred and a nicer uniform. Anyway, Dillon wasn't sure that you counted as a cult until you got someone to believe you.

By late afternoon, with still no sign of Charlotte, Dillon's mood had lifted considerably. He sat in the garden amongst the dandelions and nettles, slumped in an old striped deckchair. A notebook rested on his lap, and his pen hovered over the blank page in suspended animation.

The warm spring sunshine was beginning to disappear behind the monolithic water tower when Sparks made one of his rare sorties into daylight. He was sporting a shapeless khaki sun hat, and his body was protected from the offensive sunlight by a black sweatshirt several sizes too large for his racing-snake physique.

'So, what are you going to do next?' he wanted to know.

'I dunno,' Dillon admitted. 'Something will probably turn up. Something less stressful this time, I hope'.

'Why don't you try Glastonbury?'

'The festival?'

'No, the town. The festival is taking a year off to stop the cows going deaf. Everyone is going to Cornwall for Lizard Live! instead. Maybe your paper could wangle us some tickets. Though I don't suppose your crappy old Land Rover would make it all that way.'

'I don't suppose it would. And I don't think the Echo approves of music festivals.' Dillon wasn't sure what The Sunday Echo did approve of, apart from the royal family, and cake-baking competitions. 'Anyway, why should I want to go to Glastonbury? It's full of hippies and weirdos.'

'There's bound to be plenty of wacky cults around, isn't there? You ought to get some good stories.'

'Do you want to come along?'

'Are you taking Charlotte?'

'I don't think she'd fancy another trip like the last one.'

There was a crunch of approaching footsteps on the gravel path and, as if summoned by the speaking of her name, Charlotte's head appeared over the top of the wooden gate. Her brow was furrowed and she was wearing her most serious expression. The sun, struggling to break through a watery sky, lit up the blonde halo of her hair and gave her the appearance of a particularly vindictive avenging angel. Dillon opened the gate and Sparks scuttled frantically back into the house, like a woodlouse whose stone had just been upturned.

'Just because I've come to talk doesn't mean I've forgiven you, Dilly.' Charlotte paused to gather her thoughts. 'If we don't talk about it, I'll never get you to understand how I feel. I simply can't believe you could be so insensitive. I've never been so humiliated. I hope you're pleased with yourself.'

'Sorry.'

'Is that it? Is that all you can say?'

'But I really am sorry.' He meant it, though he was also feeling sorry for himself and partly sorry that Charlotte had come back. 'I didn't mean to upset you. I was angry with the Sisterhood; not with you.'

'Well, they were very strange nuns,' Charlotte agreed. 'I hope you're going to be brave enough to tell the truth about them in your article.'

Dillon looked down at what he'd written in the margins of Professor Braunschreiber's book. It looked as if he was going to be either very brave or very stupid. As for the truth, few journalists consider that to be an absolute concept. He had a good idea of what people wanted to read about the Sisterhood, and he was going to give it to them.

'I hope you're not going away again,' said Charlotte.

'Sorry, I have to visit Glastonbury next week to check out some more religious groups. I don't suppose you'd want to come along.'

'I've never been to Glastonbury. Is it nice?'

'It's full of hippies and weirdoes.'

'I've always fancied seeing Glastonbury Tor. It's supposed to be a place of ancient mystery and wonder.'

'It's probably closed. To keep all the weirdoes out.'

'I'll come with you if you promise to be on your best behaviour.'

Glastonbury really was full of hippies, goths, freaks and a variety of new-age tourists searching for their inner selves. Many of their outer selves were oversized and the loudness of their clothes was matched only by the volume of their voices. Quiet meditation didn't seem to be on the spiritual shopping list. Outside a shop specialising in herbal remedies and palmistry, a young Rastafarian was playing the didgeridoo to a middle-aged couple in matching kaftans.

'Hey, is that thing for real?' the woman wanted to know.

'It's a genuine aboriginal instrument.'

'Are you a real aborigine?'

'No, I'm from Wolverhampton.'

'Say, can you play that song again? I didn't quite catch the tune.'

The young man obliged, setting up a pulsing drone that rose and fell with the wind in the trees and the distant traffic noise. Dillon stood listening to the rhythms as they mingled with the sound of the crowds bustling by on the busy street. Eventually, Charlotte tired of window shopping and pulled him away. He wondered if liking didgeridoo music was an indication of spiritual development or an early sign of madness.

A man wearing an old diving suit and wellingtons, all sprayed with silver paint, handed him a leaflet explaining how Christ was an astronaut and the pyramids were built by aliens.

'You forgot the bit about the landing strips for alien spacecraft in the Andes,' Dillon pointed out helpfully.

'Everyone knows that a Neolithic civilisation made those markings in the desert,' the DIY spaceman explained. 'There was a documentary about it on the Discovery Channel. Of course, the real mystery is why they weren't engulfed by the tidal wave when Atlantis sank.'

A small group had set up a market in the courtyard of a derelict building. One of the stalls was selling a variety of pagan and New Age books. Dillon picked up a prophetic pamphlet claiming to foretell the coming of great tribulation in England's once green and pleasant land. Dillon couldn't be bothered to wade through all the gobbledegook so he wafted the pamphlet under the nose of the dreadlocked gent minding the stall.

'What's all this about Armageddon in Cornwall?'

'You don't know? The prophesy, man. TEOTWAWKI and all that.'

'The TWATTY-what?'

'The End Of The World As We Know It, of course!' We're raising a new stone circle; there's a festival, druids, everything. You've got to be there. We still got room in the van.'

So, Sparks wasn't the only one keen on going to Lizard Live! Maybe he really could get the Echo interested. They printed plenty of nonsense in the slow summer months. Surely, they could spare a few column inches and an expense account for their new up-and-coming feature writer.

9 Avalon

Dillon was in the process of buying another pamphlet and a book featuring some very eye-catching sky-clad Wicca women when Charlotte returned to interrupt his research.

'I'm hungry, Dilly. Let's find a nice tea shop.'

They wandered along the High Street, past a couple of interesting-looking pubs until their progress was halted by a crowd of people gathered around three men in medieval dress.

'Oh look, Dilly, a pageant!' Charlotte exclaimed excitedly.

Dillon pushed his way through the crowd. One of the men looked suspiciously familiar to him.

'Our liege lord, King Arthur was brought here to the Isle of Avalon in years long past,' the knight was explaining to the expectant audience. 'The Tor at Glastonbury is all that remains of the Sacred Isle since the angry sea receded. And it is from there that the Once and Future King will return to reclaim his realm.'

'When will he return? Is it soon? Won't King Charles be upset?' cried his eager audience.

'When we have uncovered the grail of our saviour, King Arthur will walk again upon the Earth. This is our quest. To this, we have dedicated our lives. We shall succeed before this millennium passes. I, Sir Kevin de Bord-Foss pledge this.'

'Hi there, Kev,' Dillon stepped forward through the crowd. 'You probably don't remember me. I was one of the people you nearly killed in Hatfield. Are you planning to dig up any more main roads today?'

Sir Kevin was unmoved. 'You have nothing to fear from us. We come in peace, to pay homage to our High King at his last earthly resting place.'

'Could I just get a picture of you with the wife?' enquired a thin-faced man in his thirties with a whining nasal voice. 'That's it. Right up by the big horse. Great! You don't mind if my little boy gets in the saddle, do you? Up you get, Harry. Don't kick the nice horsey, he don't like it. I'll just pop little Beatrice up next to you. Smile everybody.'

Sir Kevin tried his best to intervene, but the crowd was pressing in on him and his sword arm was pinned by a dozen eager hands.

'Me next! I want a ride on the horsey, Daddy.'

'Where's Merlin? I like Merlin the best. He's got a magic wand and he can turn you into a fish.'

Dillon was being pushed in all directions by the crowd. He managed to get a couple of photos before escaping the chaos. He felt a tug at his sleeve.

'Stop bothering those street theatre people, Dilly. I've found us a lovely place to have lunch.' Charlotte pointed towards a medieval building with a hand-painted sign hanging above the door. 'It's called the Sword and Stone. It's supposed to be the oldest pub in Glastonbury. And they have lots of vegan options on the menu.'

Dillon could hardly believe his ears. Charlotte wanted to go to a pub? Their trip to the Sisterhood must have traumatised her more than he thought. As they stepped off the pavement, there was a rush of wind, and a large grey horse came galloping by. Perched precariously on its back was a small boy, howling with distress.

'Waah! I didn't mean to do it. Nice horsey. Make it stop, Daddy, make it stop!'

Checking carefully for further hazards, Charlotte guided Dillon down the street and into the sanctuary of the Sword and Stone. As the warm beery air hit Dillon's face, he relaxed visibly and strode to the bar with renewed purpose.

Before he had a chance to attract the barman's attention, a booming voice cried out from the far side of the room.

'Dillon Wright! As I live and breathe!'

Dillon peered across the dimly lit bar and saw the larger-than-life figure of Ralph Coleman waving at them. He grabbed Charlotte by the hand and dragged her over to meet the tall, bearded figure, and his ill-assorted companions.

'Hi Ralph! Hi everybody! Good to see you all again.'

Coleman clasped him by the hand and shook it firmly. 'Well met, Dillon! It seems our fates are intertwined,' he suggested enigmatically. 'And this must be the fair Charlotte,' he declared, barging several locals out of the way and steering her by the shoulder towards his happy crew. 'It's an honour to meet you; I have heard so much about you.'

Dillon wondered what he'd said in his drunken state in Newark. He thought it unlikely to have merited such a gushing welcome.

'Does she know?' Ralph enquired of Dillon, in a conspiratorial tone.

Dillon wondered what was coming next. What exactly had he got up to at the Gnostic's HQ? It seemed unfair to be blamed for something he couldn't even remember.

'You, Charlotte, are fated to play a great role in the events to come.'

Dillon relaxed. If Coleman was going to spout one of his mumbo-jumbo prophesies, he was in the clear.

'Your actions will shape the lives of thousands of people and your name will be remembered for generations. That is both an honour and a burden, Charlotte, for how you are remembered will depend on how you act. Think on that most carefully in the days ahead.'

'Are you a clairvoyant?' she asked, with a wistful hint in her voice.

'No, he's a Gnostic,' Dillon explained.

Charlotte looked impressed. 'I've never met a Gnostic before. It sounds fascinating. Yesterday, my horoscope said I would meet a tall stranger who would tell me something life-changing.'

'You and all the other Pisces in Britain,' muttered Dillon.

'Scoff all you want, Dilly. I believe in fate, but it's important to choose the right fate, of course.

'I too believe your future is predestined, Charlotte, but I cannot predict your fate,' said Ralph. 'Instead, I see the choices which will define our destiny. Both of you will have difficult decisions to make, which will affect the lives of many. You, Charlotte, have a calling. Are you ready to accept the challenge?'

'I don't know. It's a lot to ask. I mean I always try to make the right decision, but sometimes it doesn't work out how I expected. What happens if I get it wrong?'

'Then your future will be different. The Cosmos does not judge what is wrong or right. What you do changes nothing, but yourself. The Divine still exists in this emptiness; the Unknown Father still awaits you in the fullness of existence. As it is above, so it is below.'

'Amen!' chorused the other Gnostics.

'I cannot tell you what is good and what is evil. May Sophia and the Christos, the logos of the True God protect and preserve you. I will pray that you walk in wisdom with us. May the light of the aeons; interior, invisible and universal, liberate you from the corruption of the world.'

Ralph's voice became louder and more sonorous as he spoke. By the time he paused for breath, he had the attention of the whole pub. Dillon was impressed and a little overawed. Maybe he ought to take the Gnostics a bit more seriously. Taking the piss out of people who were bigger, louder, and had a more impressive aura than him was asking for trouble.

Before Ralph could continue, there was more commotion from the street outside. Through the window behind him, Dillon could see a riderless horse galloping back up the street pursued by several Knights, and some anxious-looking tourists.

'Did you like my article, then?' asked Dillon, hoping to deflect Coleman from his sermon.

'You made fun of us.'

'Well, yeah, but—'

'And you held our beliefs up to ridicule.'

'I didn't mean to—'

'But it brought us all a great merriment,' Ralph's stern expression returned to its usual genial state. 'Humour is a great weapon in the battle against madness and evil. You wield it well. Perhaps we are not what we once were.' He inspected his motley crew with a critical eye. 'We have aged. It is one of the woes that the Demiurge has inflicted upon us, and we are not immune from such things. When our spirits enter Pleroma, we will be renewed, the dead shall rise, the sick shall be healed, and perhaps our clothes will even come back into fashion. Now, that would be a miracle. What would you write on that great day, Dillon?'

'I'd probably still take the mickey, but maybe the joke would be on me,' he admitted.

'Could all that be true?' wondered Charlotte.

'It would be nice to think so,' replied Dillon. 'I like a happy ending. It's just that I don't really believe in them. Everybody dies in the end. That's what happens. Every story ends in tragedy. No amount of talking about faith or miracles can change that.'

'We don't ask for your faith, Dillon,' Ralph assured him. 'As long as you are true to yourself and follow the Path of Wisdom, you will come to the truth in your own way. You can start on this path this instant if you choose to do so.'

'How, exactly?'

'Well, you can begin by shedding yourself of your base hyletic constraints. Reach deep within and buy the next round.'.

10 Eton Rifles

Charlotte paused to check her make-up in the rear-view mirror. 'I'll never understand why you don't like Jeremy. He and I are so much alike. Everyone says so.'

'Uh-huh.'

'I'm glad we brought my Kia, aren't you?' said Charlotte, swerving briefly into the outside lane before continuing her intimate relationship with the hard shoulder. 'It's so much more comfortable than that dreadful old Land Rover of yours, don't you think?'

'Uh-huh.'

The intermittent drone of the rumble strip was beginning to get to Dillon. He gripped the door handle and pressed on the imaginary brake pedal once again.

'With the money from The Sunday Echo, you could buy a decent car. Martin, our Assistant Manager, got himself a lovely hybrid SUV on zero per cent finance. It's ideal for the family, Martin says. I saw a lovely yellow one the other day. Martin says yellow is the safest colour because then everyone could see me coming and get out of the way. Are you listening, Dilly?'

'Uh-huh.'

As Charlotte swivelled in her seat to check that her boyfriend was paying attention, her baby-blue Kia wandered back out into the fast lane, forcing a young sales executive to test his ABS in a real emergency. He flashed his lights and made an obscene gesture, but it was wasted on Charlotte, who had returned to her original theme.

'Everybody admires Jeremy. Mother and Father are so proud of him, you know. He's terribly clever, but he's not at all big-headed. He always makes such an effort to help people out with their problems. Look how he helped you with that piece you were writing at Christmas. Taking all that time to explain about grammar and punctuation. And you never even thanked him.'

'Hmm.'

'I'll bet Jeremy could have been a successful writer if he'd wanted. Everything he turns his hand to is a success.'

'What about the Marines?'

'Trust you to bring that up, Dilly. Mother explained it all to you at Christmas. Sometimes, he's just too clever for ordinary people. I don't think the Marines were ready for someone like Jeremy. They just didn't understand him. He tried to show them how they could do things better, but they wouldn't listen.'

'He'd only been there for three months,' Dillon pointed out. 'He never even finished basic training. I'm not surprised they were pissed off.'

'If you're destined to be a senior officer, you have to show initiative.'

'You're also supposed to know when to shut up,' Dillon suggested. 'They only let him join in the first place to please your dad.'

'That's simply not true,' Charlotte's voice rose half an octave. 'Of course, they like to take men with a military background, but Jeremy got there on his own merits, and you know it.'

'So, what made him join the Onward Christian Soldiers instead?'

'It's called the Defenders of the Faith, Dilly. I think you ought to remember that when we get their HQ,' she responded, earnestly. 'I don't think they'll appreciate you making fun of them. They're a serious religious organisation, not like your funny friends in Glastonbury.'

'The Gnostics are serious too, but they've got a sense of humour. The two things aren't mutually exclusive.'

'Anyway, when Jeremy decided to leave the Marines, he met an old school friend who introduced him to some of the Faithful. Since he joined them, he's never looked back. I think he's found a real purpose in life. That's very important, you know, Dilly.'

Dillon thought he had a perfectly good purpose in life. It involved having a good time and staying out of trouble. He wasn't sure why he had agreed to visit the Defenders of the Faith, since they didn't meet either of these criteria. Even WS Chowdary, who was normally impartial, had described them as 'militaristic in nature and hostile to criticism'. It might have had something to do with Charlotte's relentless nagging, or perhaps Gladman's requests for more probing articles had finally got to him.

So here they were, playing dodgems on the M5, on their way to a fun-packed weekend with a bunch of belligerent religious fanatics in the middle of the Wyre Forest. As they pulled off the motorway and headed down the main road to Kidderminster, Dillon wondered if it was too late to leap from the car and make a run for home.

'It's a shame you don't have Jeremy's outlook on life, Dilly. I know you can't be as clever as him, but you could try and make something of yourself, you know.'

'How come you never joined the forces? I thought it would appeal to you,' Dillon asked, trying to divert the conversation away from her brother's questionable merits.

'I was in the cadets for a while, but Daddy never really approved. He thought the fighting should be left to the men. I suppose I agreed with him really, Dilly. You wouldn't want to see me get shot or anything, would you?'

Dillon reserved judgment on this.

'But I did enjoy it; the weapons and the uniforms and the marching up and down. They let me try one of those big guns that can blow a hole the size of a dinner plate in a man's chest. It was lots of fun.'

'So that's when you decided to take up accountancy?'

'I wanted an interesting career like Father's, but without the danger, and all that crawling around in the mud,' Charlotte informed him, without any trace of irony.

'The strategies, the ruthless corporate battles, the power dressing. Explains it all, I suppose.'

Charlotte lapsed into an indignant silence. This pleased Dillon, since it gave her a better chance of concentrating on driving. He wasn't sure if his nerves could stand many more miles of this.

'Are we nearly there yet,' he asked, sounding like a small child on his way to the seaside.

'Oh yes, very close. I'm sure we'll see the turning soon.'

Half an hour later, they reached an imposing gatehouse. A large sign informed the unwary that this land belonged to the Defenders of the Faith and trespassers would be persecuted. Dillon couldn't be sure he'd read that right; he still had one eye closed, following a close encounter with a combine harvester.

Sensing the car slowing down to a safe speed, he opened his other eye and was reluctantly impressed by the gleaming paint, smart brickwork, and manicured lawns surrounding the courtyard. The Faithful's grounds had the appearance of a country estate or an affluent golf club. The only indications that this was something more sinister were the immaculately dressed guards and their very real-looking weaponry.

Charlotte pulled up at a barrier and applied the handbrake. Dillon breathed a sigh of relief until he noticed the guard was pointing a gun at his left ear. Startled, he jumped up, cracked his head on the roof, and slumped back down with a thump. Charlotte, though, was completely unfazed.

'Cooee! Don't worry, it's only me!' she cried out as she searched around for the button to operate the electric window. The guards were beginning to look decidedly agitated. Eventually, she managed to get the passenger window open and Dillon was faced with a bombardment of questions.

'Who are you? What are you doing here? Don't you realise this is private property?'

Charlotte leaned across the car and gave the guard her sweetest little girl smile.

'Don't you recognise me? I'm Charlotte Chaplin, Jeremy's sister. I remember you. You won the archery competition when I was here last Easter. You were very good.'

The man stepped back and saluted smartly. Dillon fully expected him to tug his forelock as well.

'Terribly sorry, Miss Chaplin. You are expected, but we didn't know about your friend here. There's been a lot of snoopers around. Press types and the like. Can't be too careful, ma'am.'

Charlotte gave him a regal wave and parked up by the security hut.

'We have to get our passes first. I shouldn't tell them you're a journalist, Dilly. They're not very happy with the press since that awful God's Militia article in The Mirror.

'You mean you haven't told them why I'm here?'

'Shush, silly. Of course not. You're just here as my special friend. When you get to know them a better, you can ask them for an interview. If you promise to say nice things, I'm sure they'll agree.'

Once inside, a uniformed woman with her hair in a fist-tight bun glowered at them until they had filled out the appropriate forms. Under the section labelled "Profession", he wrote "Cynic". She presented them with badges in the form of a target which Dillon considered rather ominous.

A driver arrived in a smart new Range Rover and whisked them away down the lane towards the main complex. They passed rows of low barrack-like buildings before crunching up a broad gravel driveway to the entrance of a grand manor house.

Dillon thought the building looked more like some kind of financial institution than the headquarters of a psychotic cult. He supposed that was the idea.

'This is the HQ,' Charlotte explained, 'and that's where Jeremy and the other officers live.' She pointed towards a pleasantly converted stable block across the courtyard.

Charlotte's brother, the model soldier and literary genius, came out to meet them. He appeared fit and tanned. Militia life obviously suited him. His short-cropped blond hair and steely blue eyes gave him the Hitler Youth look, but up close, the resemblance to Charlotte was quite marked. The same rustic features, the same stubborn chin, and the same unflinching gaze. He embraced his sister and shook Dillon by the hand, with all the enthusiasm of someone greeting a plague victim.

'You're in luck, sis,' Jeremy declared in an accent borrowed from a 1950s war film. 'Marcus wants to see you up at the parade ground. I think you made a big impression on him last time. Especially when you reversed that tank over his hat, haha!'

Dillon didn't like the sound of this at all. The thought of Charlotte in charge of a tank sent a shiver down his spine. Nor did he like the idea of Charlotte being so pally with Marcus Hardwick, the founder and 'Commander-in-Chief' of the Defenders of the Faith. He was reputed to be a charismatic leader, handsome and dashing, with a ready wit and repartee. Dillon was quite looking forward to meeting him so that he could hate him in person.

Dillon had tried to make an honest attempt at proper research before visiting the Defenders of the Faith. He'd read some press cuttings, all of them negative, including an article in The Guardian by a left-wing atheist denouncing Hardwick as the Antichrist.

Hardwick's mistrust of the press was well known, but in truth, they had done him something of a service over the years. Vitriolic attacks, particularly by leftie liberal journalists, lent him a kind of reflected respectability in certain quarters. In their attempts to demonise him and his followers, the papers had given him the kudos and the publicity he needed to draw the disaffected and disillusioned into his fold.

Hardwick himself was something of an enigma. A career politician, he had been one of the Conservative party's golden boys and one of the few to hold on to a marginal seat during the party's wilderness years. As one of the few Tory MPs with no known skeletons in his closet, he was immediately tipped as a future leader.

Despite this, and to the amazement of all concerned, he quit his seat a year later, on a question of principle. Dillon considered this to be a very unlikely motivation for a politician, but Hardwick insisted he had received a "message from God" and that his life now had a "divine purpose".

Of course, his former colleagues considered him a complete crank, and he was universally shunned. There, his career might have ended if it hadn't been for a chance meeting with the anti-immigration campaigner and international arms dealer Sir Douglas Reynard. Reynard was still reeling from a near-death experience after picking the wrong side in a West African coup and he was wide open to Hardwick's inspirational message.

The vision Hardwick communicated to Reynard was of a fundamentalist Christian Britain, run by men of moral purpose such as themselves, battling against the insidious evils of Islam, Atheism, Homosexuality and Socialism.

Reynard immediately saw the light and decided to throw his not-inconsiderable financial weight behind Hardwick's vision. It was a marriage made in megalomaniac heaven: Reynard had the money, the contacts, and the illegal arms cache, while Hardwick had the vision and the personality to entice followers into the cause.

If they expected to persuade other Tories to follow them in droves, they were sadly mistaken. The offer of financial security, and the chance to play soldiers, tempted some young reactionaries, but precious few others. Many of their early recruits came from former members of the armed forces. There were plenty of traumatised and disaffected young men, ripe for conversion to Hardwick's aggressive cause.

That these included the likes of Jeremy Chaplin, who never made the grade in the first place, worried them not at all. It was God's function to sort the wheat from the chaff, not theirs, and for the time being, establishing credibility required quantity not quality.

Like most survivalist cults, the Defenders of the Faith was a male-dominated organisation. Hardwick believed a woman's role was to raise children and support their menfolk. He laid no great strictures on their dress or behaviour, beyond those explicitly demanded by the Bible, but made it clear that men, particularly his men, were in charge and would stay that way.

Women could work in the house or the fields. In extremes, they might be expected to beat their breasts and hurl their babies at the oncoming forces of evil (he did a good line in messianic doom-mongering) but they would have no part in deciding when this was necessary.

11 Lords of the New Church

Jeremy led Dillon and Charlotte across the quadrangle to where the Commander-in-Chief was standing with a few of his men. After all he had read about him, Dillon felt a sense of anti-climax.

Hardwick was a short, tousle-haired man with roundish, slightly chubby features, and a fixed smile that never quite reached his eyes. He was sporting camouflage fatigues a size too big for him, and when he saw visitors approaching, he perched a khaki army cap precariously on his oversized head. All in all, Hardwick looked far more like a failed politician than a charismatic, religious fanatic.

Charlotte, it seemed, didn't share Dillon's viewpoint. She waved excitedly at Hardwick and trotted across the tarmac, leaving her brother and boyfriend trailing in her wake.

'Hello there, Commander Hardwick. It's me: Charlotte Chaplin. It's so good to see you again. Such an honour to be here. I don't know what to say.'

Hardwick ignored the obvious nonsense of her last statement, clasped her warmly by the hand, and kissed her on the cheek.

'Charlotte! Good to see you. Are you well? You must call me Marcus, you know. We don't stand on ceremony here.' He paused for comic effect. 'Except of course when we *are* standing on ceremony. Ha ha!'

He delivered the punchline with the characteristic politician's timing and snorted with mirth. Everyone, except Dillon the party-pooper, joined in. He was used to being ignored. He decided to take the direct approach and strode forward with his hand outstretched.

'Hello, Marcus. I'm Dillon Wright. Pleased to meet you.'

He thought he saw one of the bodyguards reaching for a weapon, but Hardwick smiled, looked Dillon straight in the eye, and shook his hand with the firm grasp of a sales rep.

'Hello, Mr Wright. We haven't met, have we? Splendid. Glad you could make it.'

Hardwick turned off the charm and turned back to Charlotte. 'Do you ride, Charlotte? Skelton has just gone to fetch my horse. You could join me in a gallop if you like.'

'Oh, I'd love to. I haven't been riding for simply ages.'

'I once went for a donkey ride on Skegness beach,' Dillon recalled, but no one seemed to be listening.

A placid-looking grey mare called Pendle was fetched for Charlotte. Hardwick helped her up into the saddle with a little too much of the hands-on-arse approach for Dillon's liking. He resigned himself to being a spectator and mooched around with his hands in his pockets, looking for something to frighten the horses with.

Charlotte and Marcus rode off up the lane without so much as a backward glance. The sounds of merry laughter drifted through the warm evening air, then faded away, leaving an uncomfortable silence in the quadrangle.

'Well, I must be off,' said Jeremy finally. 'Things to do. Can't stand around here chatting all day.'

He saluted and marched smartly back towards the barracks, leaving Dillon in the care of the self-proclaimed messiah's minders.

'Turned out nice again,' Dillon ventured.

One of them grunted noncommittally.

'Anywhere around here you can get a beer?'

'Alcohol is forbidden. It clouds the mind and poisons the body.'

'I bet it's a barrel of laughs here on a Saturday night.'

There was no response. Somehow, Dillon had known it would be like this. He had the feeling that the Faithful had been drawn entirely from the ranks of people he'd spent his life avoiding: the school bullies, the college God squad, the office bores, he thought he recognised them all. He pulled out his notebook, scribbled down a few pithy observations and waited for somebody to object. It was going to be a long evening.

The sun was beginning to set behind the tall pines, and Dillon had long since given up trying to provoke the Faithful, or the Hateful as he had privately started to call them. Instead, he began poking his nose around the compound, mainly to see if anyone would stop him. He was in the mood for a good stand-up row.

The women he saw on his travels were mostly glimpsed briefly through windows and soon disappeared. One young girl passed him in the corridor. He tried to stop her, to ask the way to the kitchens, but she scurried past quickly with her head bowed. He was beginning to get desperate. No beer and no one had even offered him so much as a mug of tea and a chocolate biscuit. Staccato bursts of gunfire and muffled explosions were going off all the time, but they didn't seem to be aimed at him and eventually, he stopped noticing them.

Just as he was considering hot-wiring Charlotte's Kia and making a dash for it, she and Marcus Hardwick finally returned. Dillon heard her piercing voice and the clatter of hooves well before they came into view. Charlotte's eyes were alive with excitement, and she waved to him with both hands, nearly losing her balance in the process.

'Oh, Dilly, you'll never guess what happened.'

'How many goes do I get?' he glanced meaningfully at Hardwick, who was sauntering into the courtyard with an unpleasant smirk on his face. Dillon was fair-minded enough to admit that this wasn't very significant. Hardwick had probably been born with an unpleasant smirk on his face.

'We were having such a lovely ride along by the river, but when we got to the bridge there was this huge great bang!'

Dillon nodded vaguely. He'd hoped that the last loud explosion had been Hardwick straying into a minefield.

'Poor little Pendle was scared to death and she bolted. I didn't know what to do. I just hung on and hung on and I thought I was going to fall and be trampled to death. Then suddenly Marcus was there with his great big stallion, Halifax. He galloped alongside, grabbed hold of the reins and made her stop. He was terribly brave and he's such a brilliant horseman. I wish you'd seen it, Dilly. He saved my life, you know; he really did!'

Hardwick's smirk became even wider and smugger.

'We have to look after the ladies, don't we, Mr Wright?'

'Some of them can look after themselves,' Dillon muttered. He spent a pleasant few seconds wondering what might happen if the Hateful and the Magdalene Sisterhood were ever put in a confined space together. Maybe he could sell tickets.

Hardwick clapped his hands, and various flunkies came running out to unsaddle the horses.

'Charlotte, why don't I show you to your room,' Hardwick offered gallantly. Dillon was about to walk with them until the leader waved a hand in his direction. 'Oh, Skelton, can you take our young gentleman to the main dormitory? I'm sure we must have a spare berth somewhere.'

Charlotte forestalled any objections. 'Don't forget this is a strict Christian establishment, Dilly,' she pointed out.

'Oh, yeah…No sex please, we're homicidal religious maniacs,' he muttered. Dillon was beginning to get quite good at insulting people under his breath. Not that anyone seemed to be listening to him.

Once inside the building, Dillon found the foyer particularly impressive: all smoked glass and designer lighting. The intention presumably was to overawe lesser mortals, such as journalists and local government officials, who would then slink away with their tails between their legs, having been assured of the Defenders of the Faith's professional standing and financial clout.

The stairwells were covered with photographs and diagrams of the cult's activities, each one carrying a veiled threat or inducement. They included shots of Marcus Hardwick meeting various VIPs, artistic shots of the Faithful, armed only with ploughshares, marching through rural England, and an unpleasant mural of souls in torment in the fires of Hell (the Devil resembling a former socialist leader). 'Don't mess with us,' they said, in a nasty symbolic way.

At the top of the stairs, Hardwick took Charlotte by the arm and led her away down the corridor. 'If you'd care to freshen up now, Charlotte,' he suggested, 'I'll escort you down to the dining hall later for our evening banquet.'

Dillon started to follow but was pulled back by Skelton. 'Your room is this way, sonny,' he said.

If Charlotte was going anywhere near the bathroom, they would be late for the banquet, thought Dillon, glumly. As it happened, he had misjudged her. Either that or hunger had forced her to cut short her routine. A mere twenty-five minutes later, Charlotte appeared, shiny and clean, with her hair moulded into an unstable pyramid.

'Come look at my room, Dilly. It's lovely!'

Dillon glanced around the dormitory.

'Come look at my room, it's shit,' he reflected, ungratefully. 'The bunk beds must have been lifted from some derelict youth hostel. They creak even when there's no one near them.'

Charlotte was halfway down the corridor by now. Dillon trudged after her, radiating a total lack of enthusiasm.

'Yeah, nice room. I like the pink bits. Did they run out of other colours? There are more frills on that bed than on a ballerina's bum.'

'Oh, Dilly! Do you have to be so coarse?' she protested.

'Yes, I think I do.'

'Look, it's nearly dinner time. Why don't you wait here until Marcus comes for us?'

Dillon had no intention of leaving, anyway, and he was pleased to note Hardwick's discomfort when he appeared shortly afterwards.

As they entered the large dining hall, the three of them were ushered towards the top table, and a place was thoughtfully cleared for Dillon at the far end. The set-up reminded him vaguely of a posh wedding breakfast, with the plebs lined up in rows, and a dozen or so important people out front, where everyone could gawp at them in their finery.

The rank and file rose as Hardwick entered the room, and sat down again when he did, like a well-rehearsed 'rent-a-crowd'. If Dillon had been a bit quicker, he might have considered sneaking around the table and pulling the leader's chair away, but the opportunity passed before any suicidal urges could be put into practice.

Dillon cheered up somewhat when the food arrived. He wolfed down the starter, which consisted of tinned mushrooms floating in garlic, and gave a resounding belch of which he was quite proud.

'Excuse me!' he apologised to the elderly gentleman on his left. This officer had the look of someone with a permanent bad smell under his nose. Any more garlic and Dillon felt he could reinforce that impression.

The next course could have benefitted from some of that garlic to disguise the taste of the meat. Both it and the accompanying vegetable mush appeared to have been boiled for several hours. Dillon prodded at the unappetising green mass then looked suspiciously across at the others, to see if he was missing out on anything edible.

'Got any tomato ketchup?' he asked an emaciated-looking officer with a pencil-thin moustache.

'Certainly not! We pride ourselves on eating a healthy and nutritious diet. Our Lord's bounty from the earth, enriched with our own sweat and blood, is sufficient for all our bodily needs. We have no need for processed food or genetically modified abominations.'

'Sounds just like The Good Life, except for all the guns, of course.'

'We are creating a paradise on earth, here, my man. We have to defend it against the heretics and heathens that our current government is so keen to invite into our country. When Satan comes knocking at our gate, you don't suppose he will come unarmed, do you?'

'I didn't know he was coming at all.'

'Oh, he will come. Believe me. Or even better, believe Marcus Hardwick. He has seen it all. In his visions. He's a great seer is Marcus. Remarkable!'

'I wonder if he's foretold next week's lottery numbers,' wondered Dillon, softly.

'I beg your pardon?'

'Doesn't matter.'

It was funny how all these seers were never any good at predicting the lottery numbers or the winning horses. Dillon was quite prepared to follow a useful kind of oracle like that.

After the dessert, which appeared to be Sticky Tofu Pudding, the detritus of the meal was cleared away and a couple of the 'chaps' got out their acoustic guitars. It occurred to Dillon that hadn't seen an electric socket anywhere, yet. He wasn't quite sure what to expect. Folk music? Rugby songs? Hymns? After much tuning and discussion of keys, they broke out into an off-key medley of popular tunes from the seventies. Dillon made his excuses and left.

He had hoped to get his head down before any champion snorers turned up in the dormitory, but already there were low rumblings from one corner. As more and more of the men turned in, this grew to a cacophony, interspersed with the creak and ping of bedsprings. At midnight, someone switched off the lights, and the last few music lovers found themselves stumbling in the dark. Each one, in turn, crashed into Dillon's bed as they passed, swearing, and apologising in the same breath. Eventually, the noise in the dormitory achieved its natural rhythm and his snores joined in the greater chorus.

He awoke in a confused state in the small hours of the morning. The urgings of his bladder were too strong to allow him to fall back to sleep, so, reluctantly, he crawled out of bed and felt his way to the door.

He found the Gents on the second attempt. But when he returned to the corridor, his subconscious registered something amiss. At the far end, were the officers' quarters and a few guest rooms. Charlotte's door was the second from the left. It was ajar.

All the way along the corridor, common sense was telling him to turn back. If she was there, she could quite rightly accuse him of paranoid jealousy. If she wasn't, then he didn't want to know. Except that, now he had to know.

The thought of Charlotte being unfaithful had never crossed his mind before today, whereas, the thought of him running off with other women occurred to him almost daily. But he hadn't, had he? He'd stayed true to Charlotte, despite all temptations. Because, deep down, he respected her and cared for her. Because he didn't want to see her hurt. And because those other women had always turned him down.

He padded up to the door, pushed it open ever so gently, and peered into the moonlit room.

The bed was empty.

12 Stay With Me

Dillon awoke with a start and looked at his watch. It was six o'clock in the morning and somebody was playing a trumpet. He peered out, bleary-eyed, from under the bedclothes to see people rushing around pulling on uniforms and polishing stuff.

'Oh God, it's Reveille,' he groaned and hid back under the covers.

He was surprised to find he had been asleep at all, what with the snoring, the creaking, and the mental anguish. The mental anguish being the worst to deal with since you can't cover your emotions with a pillow.

The thought of Charlotte with someone else, especially that arrogant fascist tosser, made his stomach tighten into a sickening knot. He'd considered leaving Charlotte often enough, but that didn't give anyone else the right to sneak in and take his place. This was probably all a direct insult to his manhood. His subconscious certainly seemed to think so, and on that basis was currently giving his self-esteem a good kicking.

He understood that several Shakespearean heroes had come to a sticky end from making such rash assumptions based on limited evidence. Perhaps she had just got up to go to the bathroom, or to get a glass of water. It would be best if he let things take their course when he saw Charlotte again. He could confront her with his suspicions and deal with the situation like a man. Or he could pretend it hadn't happened and brush the whole thing under the carpet.

When he did see Charlotte at breakfast, she was full of smiles and chatted away happily to him about the usual trivia. He could find nothing in her demeanour that suggested anything untoward. Either she had more guile than he credited her with, or there was nothing for her to feel guilty about.

He munched away at his bowl of taste-free muesli, absentmindedly picking the more stubborn bits out of his teeth with his fingernail as she planned the day ahead.

'Marcus has promised to show us around the whole place. It'll be so exciting, Dilly. They're totally self-sufficient, you know.'

'They whittle their own weapons, do they?' Dillon enquired sarcastically.

'Well, some things are donated by well-wishers, like that nice man Sir Douglas Reynard. I met him at Henley once. He's ever so generous. He donates to all the big charities for orphans and landmine victims, and that sort of thing.'

Before Dillon had a chance to marvel at the irony of it all, Hardwick and his entourage arrived to begin the guided tour. They started with the schoolhouse. It looked remarkably like a genuine village school. Dillon wondered what it was doing in the middle of the Wyre Forest.

'This was my old school, you see,' Hardwick explained. 'We brought it here brick by brick and rebuilt it.'

'Gosh, I bet that was a wizard wheeze! How long did it take before they noticed it was missing? Personally, I always fantasised about burning my school down.'

As a former politician, Hardwick was used to dealing with fatuous questions. He smiled unctuously and led them inside. There were two classes with a wide mix of age groups in each, about thirty children, in all. They all looked bored stiff, and they all stood to attention when the tour party entered their classroom. Hardwick motioned them to sit, and the teacher carried on with the lesson.

They listened to the little cherubs chanting out their times tables. It was all very impressive. Dillon checked it out with the calculator function on his phone a couple of times to see if they were getting the right answers. This didn't go down too well with the goons, one of whom nudged him sharply in the ribs.

'Wassa matter?' Dillon hissed.

'It's forbidden. Computers are instruments of the Devil.'

'He's certainly got a lot of instruments. He ought to start an orchestra.'

Dillon glanced around the room. There were several inspirational notices and a lot of things seemed to be banned. There was also a robust-looking cane hanging up behind the teacher, to reinforce the point. He wished his trendy teacher friends could be here.

When they were back outside, Dillon quizzed Hardwick on his aversion to technology.

'I know computers are a bit annoying, but banning them is a bit over the top, isn't it?' he suggested.

'God has given each of us the power of thought and reason. To put such divinely inspired powers into something man-made is a great evil. The forces of darkness want to replace humans with machines. Automatons who would march to the tune of anyone who commands them. They will never be drawn to God's light in the way that we humans are. And they have the temerity to call it artificial intelligence!' He virtually spat the words out.

'So where do you draw the line? Are pocket calculators OK? What about heat-seeking missiles or satnavs?'

'It is a very valid point, Dillon. I'm glad you asked me that question,' Hardwick replied, stalling like a good politician. 'It may be that some electronics are harmless, but the Devil is very cunning, and we must exercise perpetual vigilance. That is why I have decreed that no microprocessor technology is permitted at all in our sanctuary.'

'That must make things a bit difficult. There are computer chips in most things these days,' Dillon suggested.

'I'm afraid that's true. There are machines that talk for men, walk for men, and even think for them. It is weakening the manhood of our great country. It is destroying our free will.'

They walked on, past the main buildings and out along a paved track. Hidden behind a high earth wall was a firing range where several Defenders of the Faith were getting in some early morning practice.

'All men and boys over the age of fourteen are expected to train here at least twice a week,' Hardwick explained.

'What about girls?' Charlotte wanted to know, 'Can we fire guns too?'

'Of course you can, Charlotte. You can do anything you wish. Though when it comes to conflict, we don't expect our womenfolk to fight. That is man's work.'

A column of militia in combat fatigues came yomping down the forest track, towards the firing range. They seemed to be having some difficulty in keeping together, and one or two of the stragglers looked ready to drop. Their leader was endeavouring to boost morale with a marching song. Several of the men tried to join in, but no one seemed to have much breath to spare.

Dillon watched their arrival with interest. It was just like Full Metal Jacket only with much worse singing. They were a mixed bag: a few bodybuilders whose uniforms struggled to contain their overblown muscles; some ageing couch potatoes, and several young men who looked as if they'd gained all their fighting experience online. Their leader appeared to be the only one built for running around the countryside with a heavy pack, and he was expending most of his energy shouting at his reluctant charges.

Dillon wondered if anyone was taking bets on the outcome of Armageddon. If this was the best the Defenders of the Faith had to offer, he fancied a few bob on Satan. To be honest, if they ever did get into a fistfight with the Sisterhood, he was betting on Team Nun.

Next stop on the grand tour was Home Farm, a grand farmhouse on the edge of the forest, where George Mallett, the farm manager and his family lived. There were also some Nissen huts which provided temporary accommodation for non-combatant members of the Faithful who had "volunteered" to work on the farm. Looking out over the fields, Dillon couldn't help but notice that most of these hardy sons of the soil were in fact, daughters. Somehow, he hadn't expected the Hateful to beat their swords into ploughshares, but he thought they might have dipped into the pockets for some more modern equipment.

'It's all traction control and electronic power steering these days,' complained the militia corporal who seemed to be in charge of proceedings. 'We have to make do with what we've got. It's either that or shackle up the horses like in the olden days. Not that I'd mind, but some of the lasses might complain. You know what they're like,' he added, conspiratorially.

Dillon nodded wisely. He knew he should be making notes of all this 'colour' as his editor liked to call it, but it didn't seem advisable in the circumstances. Every time he reached for a biro, somebody with a gun got nervous. You could almost believe that the pen was mightier than the machine gun. He could make it all up later. In fact, the paper seemed to prefer it that way.

The corporal was keeping the party entertained with a few amusing stories about silage, so Dillon slipped away and had a closer look at the farm. He'd expected to see a few bits of rusting machinery, but here, everything seemed to be rusty. Regular maintenance didn't appear to be part of the Great Plan. Perhaps it wasn't surprising if you thought the world was about to end, but a lot of this gear would never make it that far. All around the farm, gates were hanging off their hinges, walls were down, and weeds were rife. Even in the fields, the crops were growing in irregular patches, and there were large areas of bare earth.

Whoever was in charge didn't seem to know much about farming. Dillon wondered if they might have been at the same college as him. The Agriculture students he'd met spent most of their time at the bar, pissing their grant away. At least, they were always in the bar when he was, which amounted to the same thing. Whatever the reason, if the Defenders of the Faith wanted to be self-sufficient, they had better go out and find some real farmers or start tightening their belts.

On his way back, he had a look inside the farm buildings. In white-tiled sheds, women were washing clothes in a barrel with a peggy stick. Others were churning the butter by hand and patting it inexpertly with wooden implements. It reminded him of the Beamish Open-air Museum. The Defenders of the Faith could probably charge admittance, if they were prepared to admit anyone, of course.

When he returned to the group, their guide was just finishing off his favourite hand-up-the-cow's-arse tale, which got a good laugh, even from Charlotte who always complained about Dillon's scatological jokes. Hardwick clapped the man heartily on the shoulder and motioned the group to move on.

As they walked back in the direction of the main buildings, Dillon heard the sound of machinery for the first time since he'd entered the compound.

'This is the Power House,' announced Hardwick, pointing in the direction of a low brick building.

'So you don't believe electricity is an instrument of the Devil, then?' Dillon asked.

'Of course not,' Hardwick replied. 'Whatever gave you that idea? Electricity is a natural phenomenon which man has merely harnessed for his own purposes. You must think we're living in the Dark Ages, Dillon.'

'I wouldn't dream of suggesting such a thing.'

'As in all things here, we are self-sufficient in electrical power. We try to minimise electricity consumption since our resources are not unlimited. We have solar panels on all the new buildings and we do not need to rely on the vagaries of the National Grid because in here we have our own gas turbine.' Hardwick threw open the door dramatically to reveal an ancient piece of machinery mounted on a sturdy iron skid.

'So where do you get the gas from?' Dillon enquired.

'Biomass,' said Hardwick

'Charlotte looked confused.

'It's the technical term for shit,' said Dillon. 'Cow shit, presumably, by the smell of this place.'

She wrinkled her nose and scurried away.

'So, what happens when the turbine breaks down?' asked Dillon.

'It's very reliable. Hardly requires any maintenance. If there is a fault, we light our candles and we fix it. It's as simple as that.'

Dillon wandered over to the machine with his fingers in his ears to block its whining roar and saw Ruston TA1250 and an address written on the nameplate.

'Hey, this thing was made in Lincoln!' he shouted across to Charlotte. She didn't seem impressed.

The turbine had an agricultural look to it, certainly. There was a large dustbin-like combustor, a fly-ball governor, lots of hand wheels and dials, and the whole thing looked as if it could withstand a major earthquake. Dillon liked it. He liked machinery, whatever Hardwick might say. Perhaps the world would be a better place if machines did most of the thinking and left the humans to argue over the small stuff.

The noise was getting too much, even for him. He went outside and found Charlotte talking animatedly to Hardwick under the shelter of an ancient oak. As he approached, she broke off their discussion and came over.

'We ought to have a little talk, Dilly. I have been thinking over a lot of things since we got here…'

'Shouldn't we be on our way? It's getting late.'

'That's what I want to talk to you about.' Charlotte paused to collect her thoughts. 'I love it here, Dilly. They're my sort of people. They're dedicated, hard-working, and disciplined, and they have a real sense of purpose. Don't you feel it?'

Dillon grunted noncommittally. He could see what was coming.

'I think that's what has been missing from my life: that sense of purpose. Marcus has given these people a mission, a divinely inspired one. God has shown him the way. I really believe that, don't you?'

'What are you getting at, Charlotte?'

'I think we belong here, Dillon. Why don't we stay? We could join the Defenders of the Faith. They would welcome us with open arms.'

'We?'

'Yes, of course. Both of us. I want you to stay here with me. You just drift along, living from day to day, without any moral compass. Becoming one of the Faithful would change all that. It would give your life meaning. Without that, everything you do is a waste of time. A waste of life, Dillon.'

Now, Dillon was really confused, and being confused made him angry. What made it even worse was that Charlotte was saying all the right things. She wanted him to stay here with her. He would have rather stayed with the Sisterhood, but that wasn't the point.

He wanted her to tell him she was leaving him because he lived like a slob and farted in bed. He could accept that. Or because Hardwick was so clever and brave and handsome. Then he could go and kick the shit out of the slimy little twat. He wondered what would happen if you hit a messiah. It would certainly be one way to find out if he was for real.

'This is all a sham, Charlotte. It's all a big ego trip for lover boy over there.'

'Dilly! You're talking about a godly man. How can you suggest…?'

'If God talks to Marcus Hardwick, then He must be desperate for company. The man is psychotic, Charlotte. Maybe he believes what he says, but it's all bullshit. He just wants to take over the world like every other power-crazed maniac. Look around you,' Dillon swept his arm across the compound. 'This place is a shambles. The women are treated like serfs. Everything that's not a weapon belongs in the scrapyard, and the leaders don't know the first thing about running a community. This is what the whole country would be like if this bunch of Sandhurst rejects had their way.'

'You just don't see it, do you?' It was Charlotte's turn to be angry now. 'You think that because people start talking about God, and morals, and religion, that they must be mad or stupid. Not everybody thinks like you, Dilly. Some of us are prepared to commit ourselves to a worthy cause. We're prepared to work for what we believe. You may not be able to understand it, but I have faith and that's good enough for me. You can stay or you can go, Dillon. I don't think that I care which anymore.'

Dillon could feel himself shaking inside. He took a deep breath and forced himself to speak quietly and deliberately. 'I'm going to walk out of here now and I'm not coming back. Not for you, not for anybody. I don't think you realise what you're letting yourself in for, Charlotte. If you've got any sense, you'll come with me now, before it's too late.'

He spun on his heels and walked very slowly towards the gate. No one ran after him. No one called him back. He kept on walking until the Defenders of the Faith and all their works disappeared into the gathering gloom.

13 Mystic Mile

As a dramatic gesture, Dillon thought it had gone quite well. Unfortunately, like most dramatic gestures, it had its drawbacks. He'd left most of his belongings behind. All he had with him was a jacket and his wallet, which contained an overdrawn bank card and enough cash to buy a bag of chips and a cuppa.

He only had the vaguest idea where he was heading. e was in the middle of a forest, miles from anywhere, and it was getting dark. As if to complete his misery, it started to rain. As he was looking for shelter, he heard the sound of hooves on tarmac. For a moment he thought it was Charlotte coming to apologise, but there was more than one horse behind him. Maybe the Defenders of the Faith had come to give him a whipping with their riding crops for insulting their leader's new girlfriend. He moved off the road and secreted himself behind a small Norwegian Spruce.

Whoever it was, they were making a lot of noise. In addition to the clatter of several horses approaching, there was the rumbling of a heavy and slow-moving vehicle and an erratic, rolling drumbeat.

Dillon was still trying to figure out what it reminded him of when the Knights of the Wasteland came trotting around the bend in all their finery, followed by an authentic-looking medieval wagon. For once, he was mightily pleased to see them. He stepped out from behind the tree and hailed their leader.

'How's it hanging, Sir Kev?'

Sir Kevin de Bord-Foss brought his weedy steed to a sharp halt and wheeled round, drawing his sword in a surprisingly fluid motion and pointing it directly at Dillon's chest. 'Who goes there?' he demanded.

'It's only me!' Dillon announced himself as cheerfully as he could manage in his current sodden and emotional state. 'Dillon Wright. Remember Glastonbury and the Hatfield Tunnel? I see you got your horse back.'

'Sir Dillon? I recall you now. Well met! The hand of fate is at work here, I'll warrant. Methinks you are inextricably bound to our quest.'

'Somebody else said that to me, recently. He wanted me to buy him a pint. What do you want?'

'We ask no favour from any man, save that he does not gainsay us in our holy venture. But from your bedraggled mien, I would hazard that it is you who would seek our aid.'

'Well, I wouldn't mind a lift. Where are you headed?'

'We must travel the length and breadth of this fair land, to places no mortal man has trod in millennia. But first, we will rest and provision in the ancient city of Shrewsbury.'

'Is there a railway station there?' asked Dillon.

'Such things lie outside our domain, though it is my belief that we crossed the Iron Road when last we came hither. Perchance, it still serves the town.' Sir Kevin furrowed his brow as if recalling some ancient history. 'If you wish, you may ride in the wagon with Althred.'

Althred turned out to be an elderly man of few words, whose clothes appeared to date from the days when knights were a common sight on the road. He grunted and nodded to Dillon, who nodded back.

'We're a long way from Glastonbury. How did you get here so fast?' Dillon enquired, half seriously. 'Have you got a Chinook hidden away somewhere?'

After much thought, Althred replied, 'It is not always them as hastens, what arrives soonest.'

They certainly weren't travelling fast. The horses were moving at little more than a steady walk and the wagon, pulled along by a single massive Shire the size of a small elephant, had no trouble in keeping pace. The drumming of dozens of hooves, as they plodded down endless forest roads, lulled Dillon gently into slumber. It had been a long day, full of anguish and unpleasantness. He felt his head, weighed down with fatigue, nodding towards his knees.

It seemed for a long while that they were riding along the edge of a steep escarpment. Dillon awoke long enough to see, far below, a grey patchwork landscape dotted with the lights of isolated homes and farms.

There was a dreamy quality to this panorama. A mist was hanging in the valley, and it was impossible to judge the distance they covered. It was all so unnaturally quiet. No background roar of traffic, no planes in the sky. Only the soft patter of hooves broke the silence, as the horses trotted along the grassy track.

Gradually, the mist rose to meet them, blotting out the world with its damp embrace. How long they travelled like this, it was hard to say. Eventually, a wan shaft of moonlight cut through the gloom, and the mist began to clear. The ridge had disappeared, to be replaced by rolling hills and moorland. Then, as the moon sank over the far horizon, they entered an ancient forest, crisscrossed by rough tracks and deserted lanes.

Dillon was roused from his stupor by the light of a streetlamp cutting through the gloom. He prised open his eyes to find himself being driven down a tidy suburban street with its manicured gardens and identikit houses. He stared down the road in puzzlement. 'Where are we?' he asked Althred.

'Yon will be the city of Shrewsbury if it be anywhere at all,' his companion declared.

'No way! I can't have been asleep for that long.'

'Forty winks are as good as a nap, I always say,' said Althred.

Dillon looked at his watch, but the digital display was blank. He shook his wrist to get the electrons moving and a row of eights appeared.

'Bugger! What time is it?'

'Time?' Althred said. 'It is night-time.'

'Yeah, right. I'd noticed that. How long before it gets light?'

'That is indeed most difficult to say since the sun is presently hidden from our view by the great bulk of the Earth.'

'Are you really stupid, or are you just taking the piss?'

'Stupid be as stupid thinks, they say.'

Dillon shook his head, thoughtfully, and tried to read the addresses on the 'For Sale' signs as they passed. They just couldn't have reached Shrewsbury by now. It was at least fifty miles. It would have taken them all night and most of the next day at this carthorse pace. More to the point, they hadn't seen a single car or passed through a single village on the whole journey.

It was only when they crossed the English Bridge and began to piece their way through the maze of cobbled streets that Dillon accepted the truth of his situation. His mind was still too full of the night to think of an explanation or even a sensible question to ask Althred.

The old man glanced over at him. 'It's a long journey that has no ending,' he pointed out, helpfully. 'I have travelled here many times, by many roads, and each time I have found myself in the same place.'

'It's been an education travelling with you, Althred. We must do it again sometime.'

The wagon pulled up by the main entrance to Shrewsbury Castle. The gatehouse loomed up menacingly in the darkness; the portal baring its iron teeth at the intruders. At this late hour, Dillon was surprised to find the gates thrown wide open and the courtyard beyond illuminated.

Sir Kevin dismounted and steered his horse back along the train of wagons to where Dillon sat, rubbing the sleep out of his eyes.

'Follow me,' he instructed Dillon, helping him down from the wagon and leading him into the courtyard.

Waiting to meet them was an old man, sitting hunched in an ancient and highly decorated oak chair. With some difficulty, the man looked up, his head seemingly weighed down by the heavy golden chain around his neck.

To Dillon's untutored eye, he looked near to death. He kept clutching at his stomach and wincing in pain. Dillon wanted to ask what was wrong with the old man, but it seemed a bit rude. He didn't even know his name. Maybe this was the Lord Mayor or something; though, in truth, he looked far more regal than that.

In the courtyard beyond, there was a soft glow, which seemed to come from everywhere and nowhere at the same time. Figures were moving in the light, several women all dressed in white by the look of it, but Dillon's tired eyes couldn't make out if they were performing some ceremony or out for a stroll.

As Dillon approached the chair, there was an expectant silence and the Knights appeared to be watching him rather too closely for comfort. Dillon felt an urgent need to say something to the old man, anything to break the silence.

'Er, I'm very honoured to meet you, sir. I have to get back to Lincoln. Could you tell me how to get home?'

The old man held up a wavering hand and pointed in the general direction of Wales. This wasn't the sort of detailed directions to the railway station that Dillon had been hoping for, but he muttered his thanks.

Sir Kevin was standing behind him, shaking his head sorrowfully. 'Do you have nothing else to ask of the Lord Pelles?'

'I don't think so. He doesn't look very well. I don't want to bother him.'

Reluctantly, the knight took hold of Dillon's arm and led him to the gate. 'Alas, here we must part,' he announced. 'I wish you a safe journey. May God be with you.'

'And with you,' said Dillon. 'I expect we'll be running into each other again, soon. Thanks for the ride. If you ever want a lift in the Land Rover…'

The Knights filed through the castle gates, which closed slowly behind them. All was dark and silent once again.

It took Dillon a little while to work out his bearings. The narrow, cobbled lanes zigzagged their way down the hill without ever giving him a clear view of where he was heading. Eventually, he came out in an open area bounded by darkened shop fronts.

A forest of black iron signs directed him to various historical wonders, but more usefully, to the main station. He followed the signs for some way before they abandoned him by the river. There being no one around to give directions, Dillon hugged the riverbank until he sighted a railway bridge and followed the line to his destination. The station was deserted, so he sauntered onto the nearest platform, made himself uncomfortable on a slatted wooden bench, and waited for a train to arrive.

It was with a stiff neck and bleary eyes that a dishevelled Dillon Wright boarded the early morning commuter special to Birmingham. His unkempt appearance earned him enough space to lie down, but they reached the outskirts of the city before he could drift back to sleep.

The remainder of the journey home was slow and tedious, on trains that stopped at every potting shed and bus shelter. After changing at Derby and Nottingham, he finally arrived home in the late afternoon, slid thankfully into his favourite armchair, and closed his eyes.

He was awoken from a fitful slumber some hours later by the sound of Sparks crashing through the door in his usual genteel manner. 'How do, mate? When did you get back?'

'A while ago. I'm not sure. I've been asleep. It's been a long day.'

'Where's Charlotte?' Sparks looked around nervously. 'Did those nutters decide she was a witch and burn her?'

'Not quite. I...well...she...' He began again. 'She's given me the push. She's joined God's Militia, and I had to walk home, and it started raining.'

Sparks completely ignored the note of despair in his friend's voice. 'Brilliant!' he exclaimed. 'I thought you'd never shake her off. Let's celebrate.'

He handed Dillon the last bottle of Budvar from out the back of the fridge.

For some reason, Dillon didn't seem to be in a celebratory mood. Sympathy and understanding weren't Sparks' best points, but he tried his best.

'It's just a shame she beat you to it,' Sparks suggested.

'How do you mean?'

'Well, you were going to ditch her anyway, weren't you?'

'Right, of course I was,' Dillon lied. 'I was just waiting for a good moment. I didn't want to upset her.'

'I've heard about these cults. They're always brainwashing people and coercing them. Somebody as dumb, I mean as vulnerable, as Charlotte would be easy prey. Not much you could do about it, I suppose.'

'I tried to tell her what she was letting herself in for, but she wouldn't listen. There's only so much you can do.'

'It'll be a bit strange not having her around, especially for you. Might take a bit of getting used to.'

'Yeah,' Dillon admitted.

'Still, you've got to look on the bright side. We could get a Chinese takeaway.'

'Or a curry. I haven't had a good curry in ages.'

'Then we could go down The Queen in the Wall and get completely rat-arsed.'

'Yeah! Great idea!'

Things were never as bad as they seemed. Except when they were worse, of course. It was just a question of perspective.

'I wonder if that new barmaid, Debbie, is working tonight,' Dillon pondered.

Sparks handed him the beer and fetched a dog-eared menu featuring a sketch of the world-famous Taj Mahal.

Coriander, cumin, cardamom. After two days of army rations with the Defenders of the Faith, even the very names of the spices sounded like heaven to Dillon.

14 Another Brick in the Wall

It was early evening when Dillon and Sparks wandered into The Queen in the Wall. The lounge bar was relatively quiet. There was no sign of Debbie. Ed, the gap-toothed and dishevelled landlord, said she might be in later. It was still light outside, though it made little difference to the gloom in the pint-sized pub. A few residual tourists were seated around the bar, recovering from their historical fact-finding mission.

'So where did the name come from?' A man in calf-length trousers and a pink polo shirt was asking Ed. 'I mean, have you got royalty bricked up in the bathroom, or what?'

'Well, you see, it's like this,' Ed explained for the umpteenth time that week. 'Back in the day, there were five pubs in the city all called The Queen's Head. The queen's army was on the rampage in the city. In them civil war times you had to pick the side you think is most likely to win, get a sign made, and then stand by with a pot of paint, just in case.

'Anyway, once the dust settled and they put the fires out, we still had three pubs within half a mile with the same name. Their landlords didn't want the punters getting confused so they played conkers for it, and two had to change. The one on Bailgate became The Queen's Legs since the landlord was sorely lacking in imagination and we became The Queen in the Wall because we're up against the castle.'

'So which queen are we talking about again?' a large woman in an ill-fitting sundress enquired politely.

'That would be Queen Matilda; the Nearly Queen they called her. She were the daughter of Henry I and that other Queen Matilda. The one who changed her name from Edith. Our Matilda should have been crowned queen, but she was beaten to it by that usurper, King Stephen.'

'So, she was never a queen, really,' the woman pointed out.

'Ah, well, her first husband was the Holy Roman Emperor, so that makes her an empress by rights. She had King Stephen by the short and curlies here, back in 1141. That was the famous Battle of Lincoln.

You young 'uns wouldn't remember that one, I suppose. But you're right. She never made it to the throne.

'Those barons didn't like the idea of a woman in charge, you see, or maybe they couldn't work out which Matilda was which. In any case, old Stephen wasn't exactly what you'd call a ladies' man if you get my drift, so her son became king, after him. She was more of a Queen Mum really.'

'Gawd bless her,' muttered several of the regulars, instinctively.

'There's no queen in these walls, though legend has it that there was a local woman bricked up in the cellar by the clergy,' said Ed, concluding his lecture.

'You mean the Whore of Lincoln? I could tell you a few things about her,' offered a wizened-looking man at the bar, glancing meaningfully from the tourists to the empty glass in front of him.

'There weren't no whore o' Lincoln, Cecil. There were just some slapper from Skegness,' countered another local historian.

The discussion was interrupted by the arrival of more regulars, including Tanya, owner of probably the loudest voice in Lincoln.

'Calling that poor woman names just 'cos she had natural urges,' she complained to the pub in general. 'What was she supposed to do with her husband away at the crusades and 'im probably at it with every woman between here and Jerusalem?'

'Nothing wrong with whores anyway,' explained Cecil, who had given up on getting a free drink out of this lot. 'I knew a very nice whore in Calcutta back in my army days. I offered to marry her, but she went and joined that Mother Teresa instead.'

'You know, that reminds me of a joke I heard a while back,' said Cecil's pal. 'There's that bloke they've got for Pope, the Italian fella. Well, one day he pops out of the Vatican for a packet of fags, and he sees this lass standing on a street corner in a right short skirt. Well, it's a bit windy innit, and he says…'

The rest of the joke was drowned out by the creaking of the ancient wooden door as the visitors exited in haste. They even left some of their beer undrunk, which was about as big a sin as you could commit in The Queen, short of assaulting the bar staff or attempting to buy a packet of crisps with a credit card.

Dillon was about to give up on ever being served by Ed when he was joined behind the bar by the dependable Debbie.

'Electrocuted yourself lately, Sparks?' she asked.

'I got hit by lightning if that counts. I took a shortcut across the golf course, and when I bent down to pick up a stray ball...zap! I've got the scar to prove it.'

'Ooh, just like Harry Potter! He got a lightning scar on his forehead and you got one on your arse.'

'Want to see it?'

'I wouldn't ask you to take your pants off if they were on fire.'

Dillon was getting thirsty and decided it was time to break up the banter.

'What's the guest beer?' he asked, trying not to stare down Debbie's cleavage.

'Landlady Best,' she informed him, reaching for a couple of cleanish pint glasses. 'Or there's ZXB, but it's six per cent, and Ed says you're not to have more than a pint.'

'Are you saying we can't hold our beer?' Sparks exclaimed with mock anguish.

'It's not the beer I'm worried about. Last time you were trying to hold all sorts of things that didn't belong to you.'

'Two pints of Landlady then, please,' Sparks cut in, before her accusations could get too detailed.

The two friends sat themselves down in a corner of the bar and mulled over recent events as they waited to see where the evening would take them. Based on previous experience, it was unlikely to take them very far. It might bring a few people to see them and it was always possible that those people might buy them a beer. However, in all likelihood, they would still be sat in the same place when Ed finally remembered to call time.

'I'm going to give those bastard Onward Christian Soldiers a real oven roasting. Who does that bastard Hardwick think he is?' ranted Dillon, from somewhere on the road to oblivion. 'Self-righteous, smug little prick.'

'You want to be careful with that lot,' warned Sparks. 'They've got friends in high places, and some very low places, too.'

'What do you mean?'

'Oh, nothing. Just something I read somewhere. You ought to talk to that Ralph Coleman first; I reckon he knows a lot about that sort of thing.'

'He's nothing but trouble is that bloke, setting me up with those man-hating nuns and all that,' complained Dillon. 'There's something strange about him. I reckon he knows more than he's letting on.'

'That's what I just said, wasn't it?' said Sparks, who wasn't exactly sure if it was.

'Well, yeah, but I doubt it's anything I want to know about. I can't see that's a good reason for calling him up again. I'm going to deal with Hardwick my own way. It's about time someone stood up to him, the little runt.'

'I'll drink to that,' agreed Sparks, finishing his pint quickly as he spied friends approaching the bar. They looked sufficiently inebriated to be persuaded into buying a round for them both. After all, the night was yet young and full of promise.

It had been a good night from what Dillon could remember of it. The world seemed a better place when it was full of friendly faces, beer, and general bonhomie. The next morning it seemed less good. He had a fuzzy head again and a sick feeling in his stomach, which wasn't entirely due to the amount of beer he had consumed. Visions of Charlotte in sexual congress with Marcus Hardwick flitted through his unconsciousness.

Partly to banish such thoughts, but mainly because another deadline was approaching, Dillon sat down at the dining table to write out his experiences with the Defenders of the Faith. His two features on the Sisterhood had been a great success. The paper had received a whole sackful of complaints from feminist and religious groups, plus a suspected parcel bomb which turned out to be a commemorative wall clock. Circulation was up again for the third successive month.

Dillon considered asking for some more money, but, by now, he suspected the paper had a whole department dedicated to making excuses why he couldn't have any.

He opened his pad at a blank page and stared at it thoughtfully as if expecting the words to appear of their own accord. He was still staring half an hour later. Until now, Dillon had always felt a certain empathy with the cults he'd described, even the Sisterhood. They were generally sincere in their beliefs, however crazy they might be, and he understood where they were coming from. It made it much easier to take the piss out of them.

The trouble with the Defenders of the Faith was that he simply didn't like them at all. They had no redeeming features as far as he could see. They were a bunch of power-hungry sad-cases, who might just be funny if they weren't so obviously dangerous.

Dillon decided to concentrate on their leader. He, at least, he thought he understood. He wrote down the words 'arrogant, psychotic, upper-class twat' then crossed out 'twat' and wrote 'arsehole' instead. Sometimes, the paper censored his swear words, and sometimes not. There may have been some editorial policy at work, but Dillon liked to think it depended on whether they were listed in the sub-editor's spellchecker.

He was in full flow now, his pen virtually dripping with malice. He postulated the concept of 'negative charisma'. Since all these people had been drawn to this unappealing religious leader, Dillon speculated that it was because they were so terminally lacking in personality themselves. He went on to wonder whether, if you put enough of his followers together, you would create a charismatic black hole, which would suck all the charm out of the world.

Once he had exhausted this topic, he phoned up the Echo's farming correspondent for a few agricultural double entendres. He was planning what he considered to be an amusing comparison between Marcus Hardwick's farm and George Orwell's. By mid-afternoon, Dillon felt he had the basis of several good articles. Just as Dillon was about to press send, Sparks wandered downstairs.

'Did you put my bit in?' he wanted to know.

'Which bit was that?' Dillon thought he remembered most of last night, but the only one of Sparks' gems that stuck in his mind was the punchline of some joke about the Pope.

'About them being so close to Wales that they needed to mount a twenty-four-hour guard on the sheep...'

'Oh yeah, that bit. I remember. Yeah, I, erm, put it in, but I don't suppose they'll print it. The editor won't want to offend the entire Welsh nation, it might affect sales.'

'Some people have no sense of humour,' Sparks complained. 'What about my two-nuns-and-a-bar-of-soap joke?'

'Probably a bit too intellectual for the Echo, I'm afraid.' Dillon suggested. 'To be honest, I wasn't sure why the Archbishop of Canterbury would be in a bath with two nuns anyway.'

'Fair point,' Sparks admitted, 'I think you're sort of meant to suspend disbelief. Those jokes never work so well when you're sober.'

Once his friend had left, Sparks went upstairs and surveyed his room. When they'd first rented the house, Dillon had suggested that Sparks take the biggest room, since he'd be working from home. He'd then suggested Sparks paid a tenner more than him for the privilege. Sparks had suggested he pissed off, explaining carefully the problems of cash flow commonly experienced by small businesses.

Perched on a rickety wooden desk sat his pride and joy: a black military-spec laptop, virtually bursting with processing power, capable of operating at speeds many gigahertz faster than Sparks' first-generation brain. This expensive toy communicated with a hub that had more flashing lights than the Blackpool Illuminations, which was plugged via a long tangle of wires into three remote monitors, one of them a huge affair, hanging from the far wall.

Sparks bought the biggest screen he could afford so that he could view it far away from the malignant influence of electromagnetic radiation and other nasties. This mild psychosis resulted from an episode of Doctor Who, in which alien beings had beamed death rays from television screens during the ten o'clock news. It had taken him until his late teens to get over the need to watch the TV from behind the sofa.

In the opposite corner was a small, yet perfectly formed hi-fi, and a bookcase containing row upon row of CDs. The rest of the room bore all the signs of a man who'd had no female visitors for some time. Books with such exciting titles as The Linux Bible and Practical Cryptography for Engineers were scattered liberally across the floor. Yesterday's meal plate fought for space on the dressing table with a row of crushed beer cans.

Against the far wall, a humid pile of used undergarments steamed slightly as if approaching critical mass. Sparks kicked at it to show who was boss, then sat down, plonked the wireless keyboard on his lap, and leaned back on the chair, until it came to rest precariously against the wardrobe. He booted up, logged on, and set to work.

Displayed on the screen was a user interface, not unlike the one used by Dillon's tame librarian, Dolores. He opened a directory labelled, '001_CultReport_Network' and frowned. There were an awful lot of new entries and data to be cross-checked.

'Why can't people just download the information in a standard format?' Sparks wondered.

He considered this sort of work to be far too mundane for a man of his advanced intellect, so he set about writing a macro that would do the job for him; searching for keywords and sorting them into some kind of order. It almost certainly took him longer than it would have done to sift through the data manually, but that wasn't the point.

Soon, he was doing what he was good at, breaking problems down into smaller and smaller chunks and expressing them unambiguously in the simple language of machines.

Human problems he found more difficult to deal with. He wanted to help Dillon, for example, but there didn't seem to be much he could do. The absence of Charlotte lifted his own spirits almost as much as it had dampened his friend's. If only he could share this feeling of relief without depressing Dillon even further.

Sparks tried sketching the solution out as a simple flow diagram, but soon became locked in an endless loop. Sometimes he felt that life, like the latest Windows operating system, was continually on the verge of another crash. Sparks turned back to the screen, in time to watch it turn blue, flash twice, and then freeze. He pressed Ctrl+Alt+Delete and waited for his world to reboot.

15 Watching the Detectives

As part of his research, Dillon took to collecting 'omens and portents' cuttings from the newspaper. In Berkshire, there was a plague of weasels; the River Tees at Stockton flowed red with blood (or possibly noxious chemicals), and fear stalked the Lincolnshire Wolds in the shape of a giant wolf. This beast was seen to devour livestock whole, as witnessed by two farmers who had recently taken out a rewilding insurance policy.

Finally, of course, there were the prophecies of the Mad Woman of Pau, recently unearthed in a rather smelly cave in the Pyrenees. These included the usual predictions of Armageddon, Tribulation, and Rapture, with particular emphasis on the very nasty things that would happen to fornicators, adulterers, and people who were rude to elderly women with solitary lifestyles.

In amongst these crazed ramblings, however, were some pretty specific predictions, including the date and location of the Second Coming, and the exact place where apocalypse-spotters could park their deckchairs for a good view of the last battle between good and evil.

The prophecies, which were written over a thousand years ago, talked about a place known as 'The Hill of Fools' that lay across the sea from her native France, where men talked to the stars. The location and a liberal interpretation of the text led some researchers to conclude this was a reference to Goonhilly in Cornwall. This, it was said, was where the righteous should gather if they fancied a good punch-up with the forces of darkness. If further proof were needed, believers pointed out that the original satellite dishes at the Goonhilly Earth Station were named Arthur and Merlin, and that the station was now a centre for deep space communication.

So impressed was one of the researchers, Dr Fanny Cruikshank, with these findings that she wrote an extremely speculative and alarmist book, which naturally, went straight to the top of the best-sellers list in several countries.

Since the Mad Woman of Pau's handwriting was unsurprisingly not of the highest quality, many experts cast doubts on the exact location and date of her prediction. Not Dr Cruikshank, who categorically stated that it would all take place in Cornwall at the summer solstice that very year. 'The sun will never rise on the fateful day' was her rather dubious translation of the old woman's scrawl. Though this would obviously put some limitations on the longevity of the book sales, her publisher rightly felt that this gave it an immediacy that would produce very handsome short-term gains.

With the date for Armageddon set, a few 'End of the World is Nigh' headlines started appearing in the papers. The Cornish Tourist Board, stung by their failure to monetise the previous millennium's eclipse, was reluctant to jump on the bandwagon, but a few enterprising companies began offering Doomsday Tours to the curious and deranged.

Of course, to most people, it was seen as just another load of silly season ravings, or maybe, even a clever scam to part them with their hard-earned cash. However, as the date drew nearer, the consensus of scepticism began to wear a little thin.

'What if the doom-mongers are right?' people wondered. 'Why is my local hardware store stockpiling sandbags?' and 'How come my insurance company won't answer the phone?'

Answers to these and other queries were hard to come by, and leading politicians began making excuses to avoid appearing on Question Time until after it had all blown over.

Panic finally set in when Ladbrokes started taking bets on the end of the world. The company promised to 'make every effort' to pay out in the event of global destruction, but whichever way you looked at it, they were on to a winner. The big surprise was that there were quite a few takers amongst the more gullible punters.

Not everyone was concerned by this doomsday scenario, of course. In the Lincoln home of Dillon and Sparks, a healthy reservoir of cynicism was still to be found. That evening, with the two friends sprawled in their usual battered armchairs, a thunderstorm broke overhead. Torrential rain washed the dust from the pavements and cars and replaced it with a fine layer of Mablethorpe sand. Lightning split the sky and kettledrum thunder rattled the windows.

'It's probably an omen. Or a portent,' suggested Sparks, who wasn't quite sure of the difference.

'What sort of omen?' Dillon wanted to know.

'A bad one, definitely. The gods probably didn't like that last article you wrote. You'd better be careful when you go out.'

'Why should I want to go out in this?'

'Because we've got no beer. It's either that or we drink the home brew Pete left behind last week.'

'Why can't you go?'

'You know what happened the last time I went out in a thunderstorm. Do you want me to show you the scar again? Anyway, I've got a medical condition: I'm allergic to high voltages.'

There was no arguing with Sparks' logic. The rain was easing off and the thunder reduced to a grumbling in the distance when Dillon ventured out of the door. By hopping from doorway to doorway, he managed to arrive at the off-licence only slightly damp and maximised his chances of survival on the way back by following a tall chap with an umbrella.

For a few days, the omens had seemed good. Arnold Gladman, from The Sunday Echo, phoned Dillon up personally to congratulate him on his latest offering, Debbie from The Queen in the Wall said she might consider going out for a meal with him once her acid reflux settled down, and the bank made an error in his favour.

It didn't take long for things to deteriorate, of course. Shortly after his third article on the Defenders of the Faith had appeared in print, Dillon received his first death threat. He found an old picture frame and carefully hung it in pride of place over the mantelpiece.

Sparks was impressed. 'They've even spelt "disembowelled" right. I don't think they like you very much, Dillon, old son.'

'I'd better call the police, I suppose.'

'I heard that lots of policemen have connections with the Defenders of the Faith. Or it might have been the Masons. Or both,' Sparks warned, helpfully.

The young police officer that came round promised that the matter would be taken very seriously, but without any firm evidence that the threat came from the Defenders of the Faith, there wasn't much he could do. He made some notes and took the letter away for forensic examination.

It seemed that Gladman's postbag at the Sunday Echo contained a letter in a similar vein. He phoned again later, sounding extremely nervous, and suggested to Dillon that he moderate his articles. 'Let's face it, we don't want one of these cult wallas declaring a fatwa on us,' he joked, with a laugh that sounded more like a death rattle.

Dillon didn't think that was particularly funny. The Defenders of the Faith might not bother with a fatwa. They might just arrange for him to be accidentally run over by a tank. He promised Gladman that he would be more careful in future.

'Did you really mean that?' said Sparks.

'Of course not. I think it's about time Cult Report went and did some actual reporting. I'm going to go back to the Wyre Forest and see what the Defenders of the Faith are up to. You could come too; you know a bit about surveillance, don't you?'

'I'm not saying I do, but I could stay here and try hacking their email system if you like. I don't do fieldwork.'

It was a long drive, but Dillon decided to risk the Land Rover. He shunned the motorways and took the scenic route, barely getting above fifty most of the time. He parked in a lay-by just north of Kidderminster, pulled on his hiking boots, and loaded up a rucksack with his notebook, binoculars, and provisions. He was determined to catch those militia bastards doing something dodgy, even if it took all week.

After an uneventful afternoon of cult-watching, Dillon decided to give up for the day. He trudged back to the Land Rover, dragged his old canvas Force Ten tent out of the boot, and looked for an unobtrusive place to pitch it in the forest. He finally found a small clearing about half a mile from the car. Not only was it impossible to see from the road, but it was also only a few hundred metres from the Who'd a Thought It Inn, which advertised rooms, real ale, and home-baked pies.

It wasn't until lunchtime on the second day, while Dillon was munching on a stale Cornish pasty, and spying on the Defenders' camp, that anything of significance happened. A couple of Shropshire police officers arrived at the gatehouse to have a quiet word with Marcus Hardwick. The great leader came out to apply his famous political skills to the situation. Judging by their expressions, it wasn't a great success. Hardwick's attitude appeared to have rubbed them up the wrong way, as did his henchmen who were making very little attempt to hide their weaponry from the police.

Dillon sneaked a bit closer under the cover of some particularly spiky holly bushes. Both sides in the dispute were starting to raise their voices, and it wasn't difficult to hear what was being said.

'Why don't you calm down, Mr Hardwick?' said the taller of the two policemen. 'All we want is to take a look around and clear up a few paperwork issues: gun licences and the like. I'm sure you understand.'

'No, I don't understand at all,' shouted Hardwick, who had turned a healthy shade of pink. 'This is a deeply religious community; a place of reflection and prayer. I can't let you barge in here and disturb our sanctuary on the say-so of some jumped-up newspaper busybody.'

Dillon assumed that was a reference to him. If so, it was very gratifying, and at the same time, rather worrying.

'I'm afraid we have to insist. We have a warrant, Mr Hardwick. We're coming in whether you like it or not.'

The older, stocky officer thrust a piece of paper towards Hardwick who brushed it aside.

'I'd like to see you try!' he scoffed and beckoned to the two gate security guards. They came marching towards the police with rifles lowered, ready for action.

'Put those guns down, lads!' shouted the tall policeman, as they both scuttled away towards their car. His colleague was already radioing for backup as they slammed the doors and drove off at speed.

Dillon waited for a while, but there were no sirens and no sign of any more police on their way. Once he managed to disentangle himself from the holly, he decided to walk the perimeter to get the circulation back into his legs and to see if there were any weak points in the Defenders' defences.

He hadn't gone more than a hundred metres when he stumbled upon a group of half a dozen men in dark jackets hiding behind a rhododendron bush. They were as surprised to see Dillon as he was to see them.

A man in a black peaked cap with a scar down one cheek grabbed him by the arm and pulled him to one side, out of view of the Defenders' main gate.

'What are you up to, sonny?' the man wanted to know.

'I could ask the same thing,' replied Dillon, once he was sure no one was pointing a gun at him.

'Detective Sergeant Fiskerton, National Crime Agency,' said Scarface, reluctantly relaxing his grip. 'And who might you be?'

'Dillon Wright, National Union of Journalists.'

'The Cult Report bloke?' asked another NCA officer with a ginger goatee beard. 'We have a right laugh reading your stuff. Passes the time while we're watching these knobheads ponce about.' He waved towards the Defenders' sentries who were now marching up and down in front of the gatehouse.

'Wow, that's great! I didn't think the police took the Defenders of the Faith seriously enough to send NCA. Are you here because of the death threats they sent me?'

'Death threats? No, nothing as lame as that. We're more interested in Douglas Reynard and what he's done with all the cash the Nigerian insurgents gave him for safekeeping. We're here unofficially, so keep it under your hat. Counter-Terrorism wanted to take over, but this lot have been too crap to terrorise anyone. So far, anyway.'

'Shut up,' hissed DS Fiskerton. 'It's supposed to be a secret operation. I haven't even told the Chief yet. I don't want him reading about it in the Sunday papers.'

'I won't tell anyone, I promise. I want to help you lock up that bastard Marcus Hardwick more than anyone.'

'Yes, well, I think we'd all like to see that little shit taken down a peg or two. As for locking him up, though, I think you might have to wait a while on that one. Unless the local plods wind him up so much that he shoots them.'

'You mean they don't know you're here?'

'What part of secret operation do you and Officer Muppet here not understand? The boys in blue will be off eating doughnuts somewhere right now, wondering why they've been ordered to back off.'

Dillon thought that rather unfair on the Shropshire police; at least they were doing something. This lot might as well be on a picnic for all the intelligence they were gathering. One of the officers was clutching a large packet of fruit scones and a pot of clotted cream.

'You better clear off as well, laddie. And keep your gob shut, all right? Leave this stuff to the professionals. This lot might look like toy soldiers but I don't reckon those are toy guns.

16 Inspection (Check One)

That evening in the Who'd a Thought It, Dillon was reviewing his notes over a pint of Spotted Dog Ale, when two men in dark suits, carrying numerous bags and cases of equipment, staggered up to the tiny reception desk at the end of the bar and asked to check in to their rooms. For a second, he thought it might be the NCA lads again, but he'd made a point of ensuring they weren't staying here before he ordered his beef and stilton pie with savoury potato wedges.

Dillon made an unscheduled trip to the Gents so he could take a crafty peek at the hotel register. There was a booking for two single rooms: a Mr Bird and a Mr Beard, from the Department for Environment, Food, and Rural Affairs.

It wasn't long before the two men returned to the bar and began studying the menu. Dillon sidled up to them and introduced himself. 'My name's Dillon Wright from The Sunday Echo. I think it may be my fault that you've been sent to the Wyre Forest.'

'Cult Report?' enquired the shorter of the two, who was sporting a bushy moustache that seemed to move independently of his lips as he spoke. 'My name's Bird, and this is Beard.'

The clean-shaven Mr Beard shook Dillon by the hand and suggested he joined them at their table. 'Not sure you're entirely to blame for dragging us out here. However, we did spot a few things in your reports that set alarm bells ringing. And your sheep jokes kept the lads in the office amused.'

'We did our own checks, of course,' said Mr Bird. 'If they are grazing as much livestock on their land as you say, then most of it must be unregistered and possibly illegal.'

'We tipped off HMRC as well,' added Mr Beard. 'And they couldn't seem to find any records of the farm paying its taxes in the last ten years.'

The DEFRA men seemed mostly concerned about the evils of foot-and-mouth disease, bird flu, and Atkinson's dropsy, and felt duty-bound to check out this potential source of contamination. They could smell another cull smouldering just over the horizon.

'You ought to come along,' suggested Mr Bird, his third pint of scrumpy making him more convivial company. 'Get a bit of a scoop, like. We could use some good publicity. Nobody ever writes about us in the papers unless we're burning cows.'

'I'm not sure the Defenders of the Faith would be too keen to see me again,' said Dillon regretfully, since it sounded like an otherwise excellent idea.

'We have a spare DEFRA cap you could wear. And you could carry our bags for us. Nobody ever looks at the bag man. We had to bring half the lab with us, and those trolley cases get stuck in the mud as often as not. We'll need all the help we can get.'

It wasn't the best sale pitch Dillon had ever heard, but it was the only way he was likely to get into the compound without being spotted by Hardwick, or even worse, Charlotte.

The next morning, the Men from DEFRA picked up Dillon from the lay-by where his Land Rover was parked and drove up to the gatehouse demanding to check the Defenders of the Faith's livestock records. They were not greeted with enthusiasm.

The gate guards viewed their credentials with suspicion. They ignored Dillon who had his new cap pulled down over his eyes. They were more concerned about Mr Bird and Mr Beard who they instantly suspected of being atheistic state officials come to harass honest God-fearing farming folk. It took a long time before Bird could convince them that they had no connection to the police and only wanted to check their farming procedures. After a flurry of phone calls, an escort party arrived to take them to see Mr Mallett, the farm manager. He met them in his plush office suite in the converted manor house, wearing a tatty tweed jacket and cloth cap.

Mallett was no more pleased to see them than the guards were. He listened to their demands with increasing impatience, accusing them of being sent here as part of a vendetta against him by unspecified political organisations. Eventually, after subjecting them to an hour-long, part lecture, part rant, he agreed to let them have a look around the farm.

They weren't impressed. It seemed as if the entire set-up had been deliberately designed to flout every regulation in the DEFRA book. Everything from the feeding of the livestock to the state of the milking pails filled the officials with horror.

Both sides were starting to get very edgy. Every time they wrote something down in their notebooks, Mallett became flustered and wanted to know what it was they were saying about him. Eventually, he became aggressive and started pushing them out of the barn when they criticised his milking methods.

'Don't tell me how to do my job! I've been a farmer for thirty years. I was farming when you college boys were still in short trousers. How dare you tell me how to do my job? I won't stand for it.'

'Ah, yes, Mr Mallett,' said Mr Beard. 'Would you be the same George Mallett who ran High Grove Farm near Church Stretton?'

'I might.'

'Am I right in thinking you were warned on seven separate occasions for unsafe practices and inhumane treatment of livestock? In fact, were you not banned from keeping animals for several years?'

'How's a man supposed to run a dairy farm with no cattle? That farm had been in our family for generations. I had to sell it to some land-grabbing Taffy, all because of your pettifogging regulations. You lot have had it in for me from day one, and now here you are, trying to mess up my life again. Well, I tell you, you've bitten off more than you can chew this time. I've got God on my side and Marcus Hardwick behind me, so you'd better look out.'

A few of the militiamen, hearing all the shouting, wandered over to see what was going on. With a group of hot-headed former squaddies involved, the argument soon descended into a pushing match, during which, Dillon and most of the DEFRA equipment, ended up in a drainage ditch.

Mr Beard hit the panic speed dial on his mobile, which put him straight through to the duty officer at DEFRA, who in turn alerted the police. Meanwhile, Mr Bird helped drag Dillon back up the slippery bank. He told Mr Beard to abandon the lab gear, and all three started legging it across the fields with the militiamen in leisurely pursuit, lobbing the odd mangel-wurzel at them as they went.

As they approached the gatehouse, Dillon peered hopefully down the lane for the NCA team. It seemed they were not about to break cover to rescue a couple of civil servants. Instead, the same local patrol car that had caused so much friction yesterday arrived, sirens blaring and lights flashing. This time, they were accompanied by a large, wire grill-covered van full of more officers in riot gear.

Dillon and the DEFRA men heard the sirens and ran towards the sound. The gatehouse guards were shouting and waving their guns at the police and didn't notice the three panic-stricken runners until it was too late. All three hurdled over the barrier and were safely behind the police cordon before the Faithful had a chance to stop them.

The riot police backed away, their commander having decided that the priority was to get out of there, and away from all those guns and short fuses. They scooped the escapees into the van and drove off at speed, with the patrol car close behind.

Back at the police station, Mr Bird and Mr Beard were offered coffee and comfy chairs, while Dillon was ushered into a small interrogation room and left alone with DS Fiskerton.

'You really know how to cause trouble, don't you?' said Fiskerton. 'Now the Chief's made it official and we have to liaise with the local plods. Have you any idea how much of a ball-ache that's going to be?'

Dillon said nothing. He had broken no laws as far as he knew, but lately, trouble seemed to be following him around like a bored sales assistant in a furniture shop.

'Those Defenders of the Faith tossers have a serious persecution complex,' Fiskerton continued. 'They've been preparing themselves for a siege, all year. Now you've given them an excuse to put up the barricades. How are we supposed to get in there and find out what Hardwick is up to now? I've half a mind to push you back in there on the end of a long stick and see what happens.'

DS Fiskerton motioned to his colleague who grabbed Dillon by the shirt collar and hoicked him out the door. Mr Bird and Mr Beard were escorted into an unmarked police car by a jolly-looking female officer.

'Wait for me!' Dillon shouted and jumped into the passenger seat.

The policewoman offered to drive them all to the Who'd a Thought It, but with DS Fiskerton's threats in mind, Dillon asked her to drop him off at the lay-by and the safety of his trusty Land Rover. He shook hands with Mr Bird and Mr Beard and then scurried off into the woods to pack up his tent and get out of there.

The tent proved hard to find due to the amount of branches and leaves he'd strewn around for camouflage. Eventually, he managed to gather up everything in the groundsheet and bundle it into the back of the Land Rover. He turned the key in the ignition. There was a soft click as the starter motor engaged, but that was it.

'Bollocks!' he cursed and banged his palms on the steering wheel in frustration.

He sat there for a while and considered who he would rather ask to help him push-start the car: NCA or the Defenders of the Faith. Neither option seemed particularly attractive, so he tried to roll the Land Rover down the gently sloping forest track. It took a lot of effort to get it moving, but finally, it started picking up speed.

Now, it was just a question of getting back into the driver's seat before the car disappeared down the hill without him.

17 Firestarter

Spring had been unseasonably warm, rousing woodland creatures from their hibernation several weeks early, and now with summer approaching, there was a cold snap. Sparks, whose mother had often complained that he had 'fish shop vinegar' running in his veins instead of blood, was not happy.

With Dillon away on Cult Report duties, Sparks was left wearing three jumpers and had no idea how to deal with the idiosyncratic central heating system.

It looked simple enough. There were only three buttons, a dial, and a limited number of permutations and combinations. How difficult could it be? But after an hour's fruitless fiddling, he was beginning to lose patience.

'Bloody archaic manual; bloody controls,' he complained to the empty air. 'This whole house needs a digital upgrade. If only there was Bluetooth, we'd be up and running in no time.'

He thumped the thermostat, but it failed to respond. As he squeezed his protesting arms, already cocooned in several layers of clothing, into the sleeves of his winter jacket, he had an inspiration: last Christmas, Charlotte had made Dillon buy some coal for the open fire in the lounge.

'It'll be so romantic,' she had said at the time, but Dillon had been unable to get the fire going at all. The only rosy glow that Christmas had been from Dillon's cheeks, due to all the huffing and puffing.

Sparks, true to his name, was sure he knew how to start a fire. He turned his collar against the below-seasonal-average air and wandered out to the shed. All the essential items were there: a box of kerosene firelighters, several back issues of the Lincoln Free Press and Advertiser, the remains of the dead Christmas tree, and a large bag labelled, 'Smokeless Fuels. Industrial Grade Coke (approved for blast furnace use)'.

Sounds like good stuff, he thought, warmed already by fiery visions of molten steel. After a quick review of the principles of combustion, Sparks rolled up several entire newspapers and made a small paper mountain in the centre of the fireplace. He then piled a lopsided tepee of wood on top. In between the branches, he stuffed the entire box of evil-smelling firelighters. Finally, he went back to the shed for the coke, dragged the filthy bag inside, across the carpet, and proceeded to tip a good armful into the fireplace.

Once he was happy with the aesthetic look of his creation, Sparks struck an extra-long match and offered it up to the nearest exposed firelighter. To complete the combustion process, he blew hard into the grate and was pleased to see flames begin to flicker and dance over the paper as they consumed an article on pig farming with Dillon's name at the top. With the onset of hypothermia postponed, Sparks went back upstairs to fetch his laptop, so he could curl up next to the roaring fire while he read his emails.

Of course, the laptop was busy completing an update of some software he'd never used, and there was an unfinished game of solitaire running on his tablet. By the time he'd finished, it had become pleasantly warm in his room. There was even a faint wisp of smoke drifting under the door.

The fire must be properly roaring by now, he thought. Probably needs more oxygen. Perhaps I need to blow on it some more.

Sparks reached for the doorknob and that seemed quite warm as well. He pulled back the door. More smoke poured in, accompanied by small pieces of burning wallpaper. The carpet appeared to be melting, and the whole stairwell was like the inside of a factory chimney, with smoke and flames surging upwards and along the landing.

Sparks quickly slammed the door shut and reviewed the situation. He wondered if he might have used a few too many firelighters. There was no fire extinguisher in the house. All he had to hand was a half-empty Stingray water pistol and a small can of Red Bull. He manoeuvred the pile of used socks on the floor until it blocked the smoke seeping under the door, but the socks started to smoulder and the paint on the door began to blister.

Sparks wasn't one to give in easily, but it was time to abandon ship. He wrapped an old towel around his face and forced open the sash window. Without pausing to unplug the maze of wires, he ripped his precious laptop from its nest, tucked the tablet under his arm, and climbed out of the window. From there, it was a gentle slide down the outhouse roof, and a short drop to the garden below, where he landed, in a heap, next to the wheelie bin.

Once through the back gate, and with unaccustomed urgency, Sparks broke into a jog and made his way down the street, past the shops, past the bright red phone box, and into the taproom of The Queen in the Wall. Here, his cries of distress elicited immediate help in the form of a phone call to the fire brigade and an offer of free beer.

The excitement was all over by the time Dillon returned from Shropshire. The fire engine had done its work and departed, leaving the remains of his home smouldering in the watery, evening sun. A solitary policeman was there to greet him as Dillon approached the charred front door.

'Would you be Mr Wright?' the officer enquired in his best 'bad news' voice.

Dillon could only nod as he peered at the devastation through the window. 'Where's Sparks? Mark Munro, I mean. Is he all right?'

'Your friend is a little shocked. He was in the house when the fire started. But he's being well looked after.'

'Is he in hospital?'

'No, he refused to leave the pub. We thought it best to keep him there until some other arrangements can be made for you both.'

Dillon was more than a little shocked. He'd often joked about some cult or other burning his house down. If he'd genuinely thought it would happen, he'd have been a bit more careful in his choice of words. In his heart, he always believed that people were basically reasonable and could take a bit of a joke. Things like this shook his faith in human nature. 'The bastards. I didn't think they'd stoop to this. They could have killed Sparks.'

'I'm sorry, sir. Who are you referring to?'

'The Defenders of the Faith. Marcus Hardwick. My bloody girlfriend. Ex-girlfriend,' Dillon corrected himself. 'It's hard to believe they'd be stupid enough to think they could get away with it.'

'Are you sure they were responsible, Mr Wright?'

'Well, who else could it be? You're not suggesting we burnt our own house down, are you?'

'Certainly not, sir, but could it not have been an accident?'

'If it was an accident, why does the place stink of kerosene?'

The police officer saw the logic of this. 'I have to say that I wasn't overly impressed with your friend's account of the incident, Mr Wright. However, I don't suppose he would be that foolish, now would he? He does claim to be some kind of engineer, after all.'

The officer escorted Dillon to The Queen in the Wall, where he found Sparks sitting in the back room of the pub, being ministered to by a couple of guardian angels, in the shape of Debbie the barmaid and PC Rosa Burkitt of the Lincoln constabulary. Despite the company, he was looking pretty miserable and, as Dillon entered, he began apologising profusely.

'Hey, I'm the one who should be sorry,' Dillon protested. 'I got you into this. I left you to face those maniacs on your own. There wasn't anything you could have done. I should have known they'd try something like this. Did you see them?'

'No, you see I went down the shed and…'

'They may have dropped some kind of incendiary device down the chimney,' the policewoman butted in. 'Part of the roof was destroyed and the fire seems to have started in the lounge. It could have been a petrol bomb or something more sophisticated. We're not sure yet.'

'I was feeling a bit cold, like, so I thought it'd be a good idea…'

'Are you OK, Sparks?' Dillon asked in a concerned tone.

'I'm feeling a bit woozy,' he offered, waving his fifth pint around for emphasis. 'But I managed to save my laptop and the iPad and a couple of me old LPs.' He patted the pathetic pile of belongings on the table in front of him and appeared to be about to burst into tears. Debbie clasped him even tighter to her ample bosom and PC Rosa Burkitt patted him on the head.

'Where are you both going to stay tonight?' PC Burkitt asked in a concerned voice.

'I'm open to offers,' suggested Sparks, optimistically.

'There's a spare cell at the station, or we could drive you over to the Salvation Army hostel.'

Dillon, having a rather more practical outlook, wandered into the busy lounge bar and scanned the crowd for a possible saviour. Soon, his patience was rewarded as the door opened to admit Steve Mathews, demon darts player and sole owner-occupier of a three-bedroom house on the nearby Carline Road. Dillon intercepted him as he approached the bar and offered to buy him a pint.

'What are you after?' asked Steve. 'I'm not buying you another pint. I've only popped in for a swift one.'

'Haven't you heard about the fire?'

'I heard the sirens. Are you telling me that was your house? Sparks been doing more rewiring?'

'Yeah, something like that. There was a problem with the heating. Burnt the place to the ground.' Dillon carefully omitted any mention of angry cults or arsonists, in case Steve considered such things to be infectious. 'We're temporarily homeless.'

'Shame. I'll buy a Big Issue off you.'

'We just need somewhere to stay for a couple of days,' Dillon pressed on.

'There are lots of hotels in Lincoln. It's very popular with tourists, you know.'

'And I'm going to be pretty broke for a while until the insurance comes through.'

'My heart bleeds.' Steve looked long and hard at Dillon as if calculating the risks. No one who'd seen how he and Sparks lived was ever likely to consider them ideal houseguests. 'One night and that's all. Just the two of you. No lasses, no pets, no smoke-damaged whatnots and you keep Sparks away from my electrics. If anyone even goes near the wine rack, you're both sleeping in the shed.'

'Thanks, Steve; I knew we could rely on you. You know what they say: a friend in need…'

'Is a pain in the arse. I know.'

It took a lot of persuasion to convince Sparks of the wisdom of this idea. He was especially unhappy at having to buy rounds all night to keep Steve sweet. However, the nice policewoman was long gone and no one else seemed keen to accommodate a couple of lightly charred ne'er-do-wells.

When Ed finally bade them a fond farewell with the toe of his boot, the three of them staggered along beside the castle walls, admiring the twinkling lights of the Tritton Road Trading Estate, far below.

Steve's house was spotless. Dillon and Sparks took their shoes off in the hall and hung around the lounge door, scared of contaminating the deep, cream carpet and the white leather chairs.

Dillon retreated to the kitchen to see about making a cuppa and Sparks followed. It was the tidiest kitchen they'd ever seen. Polished copper pans and gleaming steel utensils lined the walls. The worktops could have been used for surgery and there wasn't a cobweb to be seen anywhere. Sparks picked up the toaster, turned it upside down, and shook it. Not a single crumb fell out.

'Do you think he actually lives here?' whispered Dillon, filling the kettle from the multi-functional water dispenser.

'I dunno. I've seen cosier-looking show homes.'

From the hall came the low drone of the vacuum cleaner.

'It reminds me of that time when I had to work in the semiconductor clean room,' complained Sparks. 'I keep expecting someone to hand me a hairnet.'

'Shall I make a cuppa, Steve?' Dillon called out over the drone of the vacuum.

'Yeah, thanks. Use the blue cups, not the china, and be careful with the teapot: it was handcrafted in India.'

Steve reappeared shortly in his Marks and Spencer's carpet slippers and guided them into the safety of the dining room with its hardwearing parquet floor. Then he kindly fetched the biscuits, two each, laid out on matching plates.

'Do you get many visitors, Steve?' Dillon wanted to know.

'God, no! They do me head in, visitors. Takes forever to clean up afterwards.'

'Yeah, I know what you mean,' agreed Sparks, who was now regretting his wasted attempt to clean the house with Charlotte.

'Me folks come sometimes,' Steve added, not wanting to appear completely anti-social. 'And there's all the girls of course,' he added quickly. 'Lots of them, like. Well, a few, anyway. I prefer to play away from home, me. You know how it is.'

'Women make a lot of mess, don't they?'

'Too right. Handbags and shoes everywhere, your bathroom full of make-up and stuff. I can't be doing with it, me.'

'It's a very nice house, anyway, Steve,' declared Dillon, politely. 'You ought to invite the lads round sometime. We could have a great party here, loads of room.'

Steve looked horrified. 'No way! Absolutely no way! I had a barbecue here for the crowd from work once. They trampled all over the lawn, even though I put up signs about it, and then someone went and puked up in the rockery. They kept wanting to come inside for a piss and stuff. With their shoes on. Can you believe it? What a nightmare.'

'Well, it's good of you to put us up like this,' Dillon reiterated, though Steve's whining was starting to give him a headache.

'No problem, mate. When do you think you'll be leaving?'

'Oh, soon. Very soon, I'm sure.'

Dillon's phone buzzed. He held it gingerly up to his ear, expecting more bad news. There was a familiar voice on the other end.

'Hello, Dillon. I understand you have been experiencing some difficulties.'

'Ralph!' he exclaimed with some surprise. 'How the hell did you know?'

'I have my sources. Particularly amongst the connoisseurs of fine ales.'

Dillon bobbed and dipped his head in an effort to get better reception, but the crackle on the line merely turned into a whooping howl. He was genuinely pleased to hear from Coleman, but he was equally suspicious as to his motives.

'Did you know this was going to happen? Is it a sign?' Dillon wanted to know.

'If this was truly the work of the Defenders of the Faith, I am as surprised as you. This was never indicated. They may be dangerous, but for all their posturing, they rarely venture from their strongholds. Are you sure you haven't been upsetting anyone else, lately? A loan shark perhaps or an angry husband?'

'Definitely not!'

'Then I'm afraid we can come to no other conclusion. No good will come of this, of that you can be sure.'

'I thought you might say that. No good has come of it already. Our house has burnt down, my girlfriend's left me, and we're stuck here with Mr Ideal Home Exhibition.'

Their reluctant host could be heard in the kitchen, loading up the dishwasher.

'Got any bright ideas?' said Dillon.

'Indeed I have!' Coleman boomed down the phone. 'And I think, for once, that you will like this suggestion. Are you feeling adventurous?'

'Adventurous? Is that another way of saying heroic, or suicidal?' Dillon wondered.

'Not at all. No physical courage is required, though a certain mental resilience may prove necessary...Tell me, Dillon, have you ever heard of a group called the Wild Things?'

'Wow! I read about them in Prof Chowdary's book. I remember hearing some crazy stories about them when I was at college, but that was years ago. Are they still around?'

'Good cults never die, unless they commit mass suicide, of course,' Coleman corrected himself. 'Like our good selves, they are not quite what they once were. However, they still know how to enjoy life to the full. I can give you a telephone number. Once you have recovered sufficiently, why don't you call my good friend, Sheryl Keane?'

'What gives?' Sparks whispered in Dillon's other ear.

Dillon cupped his hand over the receiver. 'It's Ralph Coleman, the Gnostic bloke. He's fixed us up with somewhere to stay. Sounds pretty wild.'

'Nice one,' Sparks conceded. 'Steve will be pleased.

18 Walk on the Wild Side

Breakfast at Steve's turned out to be Shredded Wheat and a mug of de-caff. By nine o'clock, Dillon and Sparks were in the Land Rover waving farewell to their host. Dillon parked the Land Rover in his usual spot next to the Central Library and the homeless and hungry duo went in search of a hearty breakfast. They wandered around the pedestrianised streets for a while past fast-food joints and generic coffee shops. Eventually, they found a welcoming café at the top of the High Street and spent an enjoyable hour scoffing bacon butties, drinking tea and reading the papers.

The café had a crumbled copy of the previous day's The Sunday Echo, featuring a full-page article on the shenanigans in the Wyre Forest. It didn't mention Dillon's part in the proceedings, fortunately, but it did refer to Cult Report several times.

It was days such as these that justified Dillon's whole limited career in journalism, he felt. You could champion a worthy cause for years and never achieve anything, but occasionally, a chance word in the right place could start a story snowballing.

Dillon liked to think he wasn't a vindictive man, but anyone who could steal his girlfriend and make him get up at six in the morning deserved everything that was coming to them. Even if his writing never made a major contribution to world peace or the elimination of poverty, he could retire happy in the knowledge that he had introduced a little misery into the life of that odious little shit, Marcus Hardwick.

Feeling ready for the next challenge, Dillon decided to visit the Central Library for some essential research on the Wild Things.

'Forewarned is forearmed,' he explained to Sparks; adding hopefully, 'Two heads are better than one!'

'And too many cooks spoil the broth,' countered Sparks, heading for a nearby electronics superstore to check out replacements for his charred computer hardware.

The library was having a quiet Monday morning and Dolores was happy to scurry around looking for references to the Wild Things in her archives.

After a little while, she came back with a couple of dog-eared books, a loose-leafed folder of newspaper cuttings, and a dusty DVD, which covered the subject in a fair amount of detail.

'It's a bit provocative, isn't it?' said Dillon, 'Calling yourself the Wild Things. Just asking for trouble.'

'Oh, that's not their proper name,' Dolores explained. 'Officially, they're called the Cult of Eternal Joy, though it's hard to imagine the Wild Things doing anything officially.'

'Interesting. They're the only cult I've come across so far that actually calls itself a cult. I like that.'

Dillon leafed through a couple of interviews with the group. It seemed that this perverse honesty came naturally to them. With any luck, he would be able to tell the Wild Things' story without needing to burn up too much of his creative imagination.

The Wild Things was a nickname coined by a journalist who infiltrated the cult in the early eighties for a feature in Rolling Stone magazine. From the article, it sounded like he had a very wild time indeed. Unlike the majority of cults, who might have responded to this sort of intrusive behaviour with heavy threats and maybe a few burning crosses, the Wild Things refused to invite him to the next party. This, they seemed to consider, was sufficient punishment for any right-thinking individual.

'Here's something about Sheryl Keane, their founder,' said Dolores. 'She was a blues guitarist, but I don't think she was very successful. The music business is so very male-dominated, you know. She said she heard the voice of God speaking through her TV. I think she might have been taking drugs at the time.'

Dillon thought that was a near certainty. Judging by the size of Keane's book, kindly loaned to him by Delores, it must have been a long TV show. Either that or she made most of it up later on. Dillon had no intention of reading all his rambling scribblings, but the gist of his message was nothing out of the ordinary for a drug-addled cult leader. Apparently, the world would come to a sticky end sometime soon. Sheryl was advised not to worry too much about this, since a band of angels would appear at a suitable dramatic eleventh hour and carry the good guys bodily into Heaven. A heaven, by the way, which was a lot more earthly in its delights than the conventional biblical depiction.

Left behind would be all figures of authority, such as the police, government officials, and other likewise unpleasant characters. Right-minded people, such as Sheryl and her friends, were already "saved" and they could look forward to the big day with a clear conscience.

The new messiah saw this as an excuse to party on into the afterlife. With a philosophy like that, she didn't have too much trouble recruiting disciples. Soon the good times began to roll. Admittedly, God hadn't set up Sheryl with the music career she'd always wanted, but she quickly realised that religion was the next best thing. All the fun, without the need to toady up to slime-ball record company executives.

The Cult of Eternal Joy soon attracted a reputation for crazy parties and fast living. The police repeatedly raided the house in South London they were using as a base. Warrants were issued and Sheryl Keane decided it was time to move on. She still treasured childhood memories of a family vacation in Derbyshire. After a few false starts, God led his chosen few to the appropriately named village of Hope, where they purchased an old, abandoned station building and proceeded to turn it into a comfortable home from home.

Any antipathy that the local residents might have felt towards their new neighbours was soon dispelled by their exemplary behaviour, outside their own grounds anyway, not to mention the amount of money they spent in the local pubs. According to Dolores' records, their numbers had stayed pretty constant. One or two of the Wild Things got bored and wandered off every year, but there was a steady trickle of deranged and curious new members keen to take their place.

Dillon noticed that Dolores had turned away from her screen and was staring over her shoulder with a quizzical look on her face. He spun around and saw Sparks slouching towards them.

'Are you done researching yet? They chucked me out of Silicon World because they said I was being a smart arse. I was only trying to help. It's not my fault they employ a bunch of dimwits who don't know anything about computers. Or the outside world for that matter.'

Sparks was staring thoughtfully at Dolores. 'Your face looks familiar. I'm sure I've seen your profile somewhere. Heh, are you Guardian of Nineveh?'

'Yes, it's me! Call me Dolores. And you must be Divine Spark. Fancy seeing you here. I heard you were based in Lincoln, but I've never seen you in the library before.'

'Most people call me Sparks. I don't deal with hardcopy much.'

'Now come on,' said Dillon. 'You have to be kidding me. You two know each other?'

'Online,' explained Sparks. 'Not in the flesh, so to speak. We're Dataheads. "Information is Power", you know.'

'Well, that explains the geeky nicknames, I suppose. Divine Spark? Wait till the lads in The Queen hear about that.'

'Of course. Silly me. I should have realised!' exclaimed Dolores, fanning herself with her hands. 'That means Mr Wright is Sir Perceval, doesn't it?'

'Yeah, kind of,' admitted Sparks turning to Dillon. 'It's just a kind of online tag I gave you. No big deal.'

'It's because you are on a quest,' explained Dolores. 'Sir Perceval was the Grail Knight. The Perfect Knight.'

'Or the Perfect Fool,' said Sparks.

'Sir Perceval was a great warrior: matchless with lance and sword.'

'With zero control over his own destiny.'

'He was an innocent. Only the pure of heart could find the Holy Grail.'

'Ignorance is bliss, I suppose.'

'Oi!' interrupted Dillon. 'Are you talking about me, or this Perceval character?'

'Both,' said Dolores.

'Neither,' said Sparks. 'Can we go now,? I want to party on down with the Wild Things. Do you think we ought to bring a bottle?'

'By the sound of it,' said Dillon, 'that really won't be necessary.

19 Come As You Are

By a strange coincidence, Dillon and Sparks were following the same route that the Cult of Eternal Joy took on their flight from persecution, some twenty years previously. As they circumnavigated Sheffield's Park Square roundabout for the second time, they passed the very spot where a sacrilegious traffic warden had stuck a parking ticket on the cult's van.

Dillon opted to park legally in the Ponds Forge multi-storey car park. He and Sparks desperately needed to replace essential items lost in the fire. Neither of them enjoyed shopping, especially for clothes. They skurried through the department stores in the Fargate shopping precinct with the speed of an experienced shoplifting gang and returned to the car with several bags of ill-fitting monochrome garments.

After an unscheduled lap around the Bramall Lane football ground, they found the road to Ringinglow. The urban sprawl gradually gave way to the rough moorland of the Peak District National Park. It was a bright day with just a few wisps of cloud gathering on the hills. The road twisted its way over the moor tops then rounded a sharp bend, presenting a spectacular view over the village of Hathersage and the Hope Valley beyond.

Dillon consulted the directions as best he could with one eye on the road. It was not much use asking for Sparks' help. His directional sense was only slightly more evolved than his dress sense.

'Where did you say we were going?'

'Hope,' Dillon said, for the third time that day.

'As in "abandon all"?'

'Yeah.'

'Is that west of here?'

'Do you know where we are?'

'No.'

'Then it's definitely west,' said Dillon.

Sparks sat back, happy in the knowledge that someone knew where they were going, even if it wasn't him.

Just before they reached Hope itself, Dillon swung off the main road. Protesting loudly, the car climbed up a tiny road, past the cement works and into a secluded and steep-sided dale. There, nestling beneath a rocky outcrop, was a long, low building with a rusty iron plaque reading 'Pindale Station'.

'By this sign, you shall know us,' Sheryl had said when he called her earlier. 'We used to have one saying Cult HQ, but the National Park made us take it down.'

Dillon parked the Land Rover next to a couple of beaten-up vans and a row of rusty bicycles. There was no one around, nor was there any response when they knocked on the door of the old stationmaster's office. The two of them sat down on the platform edge, dangling their feet over the gravel track where the railway had once run.

It was a pleasant spot to sit and think. The sun was beating down and even Sparks felt obliged to remove his jacket.

Behind them, there was the rattle of a catch. A window opened and out climbed a dark-haired woman in her late twenties wearing nothing but a long T-shirt and hiking boots. She blinked in the bright midday sun then staggered past them uncertainly. At the platform's edge, she knelt as if in prayer and promptly threw up violently into the bushes below.

'Are you alright?'

The woman broke into a minor coughing fit and then rolled over on her side clutching at her head and moaning pathetically. Dillon delved into his pocket and passed her a paper napkin.

'Thanks,' she squinted up at him as if noticing his presence for the first time. 'I guess we shouldn't have tried to finish off the barrel. There were a few chewy pints at the bottom.'

She wasn't currently looking at her best, but Dillon was prepared to be generous in the circumstances. Lying there, propped up on one elbow, she had the appearance of an extra in one of Rubens' lesser-known masterpieces: Drunken Madonna in Boots possibly. She smiled up at them sleepily and allowed Dillon to help her to her feet.

The two of them led her gently back to the house, taking a more conventional route through the old waiting room door. Sparks rushed into the kitchen to get her a glass of water.

Dillon was happy just to act as her support. She had one arm around his waist and was resting her head on his shoulder. He had to admit, this was a far better reception than the one he'd had from the Defenders of the Faith.

'I'm Dillon, by the way,' he said, thinking that introductions were probably in order.

'Rachel.'

'Sparks,' said Sparks, in case anyone was interested.

'I'm here to see Sheryl Keane,' Dillon added, hoping to establish his credentials. 'I made an appointment.'

'Why?' Rachel gazed up at him with a quizzical expression. 'Life's too short for appointments and schedules. Sheryl might want to talk to you. There again, she might have thought of something better to do. Meantime, you've got me.'

'That's, er, great. Why don't we go outside? You could tell me all about the Wild Things; your philosophy on life, and all that stuff.'

'Later,' Rachel stretched out her free arm and stifled a yawn. 'That's far too serious for this time of the morning. Right now, I'm going back to bed. Are you coming?'

Dillon nearly choked. There were few things he would like better than to go to bed with Rachel. From what he could see and feel, beneath her billowing T-shirt she was all curves and contours. Definitely his kind of woman.

He'd been looking forward to chatting to her, getting to know her better, then maybe plying her with drink and subtly suggesting that he should stay the night. No woman had ever propositioned him at two o'clock in the afternoon, having just met him. Come to think of it, the only women who propositioned him at all were those whose livelihoods depended on that sort of thing. It was quite a scary concept for someone of his limited self-confidence.

Rachel blew a kiss to Sparks, led Dillon off to her room, and closed the door. It was rather cramped, with a rickety pine bed taking up most of the available floor space. She helped him out of his jeans, giggling all the while, then ushered him under the covers, kissed him lightly on the lips and snuggled up to him, resting her head on his chest. He combed her locks vaguely with his free hand and waited for the next move. Soon her breathing became slower and a gentle snuffling sound came drifting up from beneath the spread of her rich chocolate-brown hair. A feeling of déjà vu overcame Dillon, but he wasn't sure whether to be relieved or disappointed.

Meanwhile, Sparks wandered about the station house disconsolately. No one else seemed to be up. Eventually, he found his way back to the kitchen and helped himself to some chocolate chip ice cream from the freezer. He was sitting, perched on a stool like a guilty garden gnome with spoon and tub in hand, when in walked an anaemic-looking couple.

They were both in their thirties, and both looked severely hungover, but there the similarities ended. For a start, the woman was wearing a long floral dress buttoned to the neck, whereas her friend was wearing nothing at all. He didn't seem embarrassed, or even surprised to see Sparks.

'How do?' he said, absent-mindedly scratching his left buttock.

'Not so bad,' replied Sparks, waving his spoon around, apologetically. 'I got a bit peckish. Sorry.'

They didn't seem concerned. The woman said nothing. She simply stared at him blankly, her big brown eyes seemingly fixed on a point somewhere on his forehead. Sparks stared back.

She was small, slim and, to his eyes, quite pretty. Her jet-black hair, hanging down in tangled waves, only highlighted the extreme pallor of her skin. She looked like a girl who didn't get out much during daylight hours, Sparks thought. She looked as if she needed cheering up. He pulled a face and stuck out his tongue. She attempted a smile, but her mouth was permanently turned down at the corners and it took a considerable effort for her even to look non-committal.

Sparks wondered how to get the conversation going. 'I'm from Lincoln. My name's Sparks, what's yours?'

The woman looked across at her companion.

'This is Megan,' he explained in a thick, Derbyshire accent. 'She don't talk. It's just a thing. You get used to it after a while. I'm Boz, by the way. From Sirius.'

'I had a friend who was mugged in Damascus once,' offered Sparks, keen to share experiences.

'Not Syria, you daft bugger. Sirius. The bloody Dog Star. It's about three hundred light years from here.'

'Oh, I see.' Sparks was unsure of how to respond. 'No, I've never met anyone from there before. Do you get back much?'

'I've been stranded on Earth for over two hundred years. In Bolsover mostly.'

'I'm sorry to hear that.'

'I were trying to build a communications device, but Earth technology isn't up to it. The Wild Things passed through the town on their way here and I decided to join 'em. Sheryl said the world was going to end and, on that day, a craft from my home world would arrive to take me back home.'

'Are the rest of your people expecting a spaceship? My mate Dillon said something about a band of angels coming to pick you up.'

'They've all got their own beliefs and myths and the like.' Boz counted off names on his fingers. 'Drax is Atlantean, Joy is from Alpha Centauri, and Denise is a quarter Martian on her mother's side. Oh, and Danny claims to have come from the subterranean Kingdom of Num, though Sheryl reckons that means he worked for the coal board.'

'You don't say?' said Sparks.

'Doesn't matter, really. The point is, we all believe in the same fundamental truths,' Boz went on. 'Each soul must find its own path to salvation. All these other religions, what think we should behave like clones, don't have a clue. Life is for living, man. Enjoy yourself. You're only here for a short span, so make the most of it. Let's face it, if God thought all the cool stuff was evil, he wouldn't have made it so much fun, right? The ways of the Lord aren't as mysterious as some would have you believe.'

'Sounds reasonable to me,' agreed Sparks. He was all for a life of unrestricted pleasure, but it would take more than a change of attitude to achieve it.

'Now then lad, you need to start by chilling out. You're much too tense.'

'I'm pretty chilled already, to be fair,' he replied, looking around for his sweatshirt.

'You've got to learn to unwind, shed your inhibitions. You can do it, Sparks. I can show you how.'

'I'm not doing any of that yoga stuff. I can't even sit cross-legged without dislocating my knee.'

'It's much simpler than that,' Boz assured him. 'The solution is all in the mind, but first, you need to shed the trappings of civilisation. Get naked, Sparks! Free your body and free your spirit!'

'Get stuffed! Nobody's going to get me to take my clothes off in public. I might catch me death of cold and somebody might see me, and...'

Megan winked at him and began to unbutton her dress slowly and provocatively. Sparks froze. He stared at her in wide-eyed fascination. After the fifth button, she stopped and coyly motioned for him to follow suit.

'Oh, bugger it,' he protested. With a sideward glance at Boz's un-aesthetic nakedness, he pulled his fleece over his head. There was a crackle of static that made his already wayward hairstyle take on gravity-defying properties. Then with an air of great ceremony, Sparks removed his shirt and folded it neatly on the side.

Megan stepped towards him and inspected his hairless chest with great interest. Sparks wasn't particularly proud of his body. He wasn't ashamed of it, though. It was just a body. It never gave him any trouble, and in return, he never asked it to do stupid things like exercise or sunbathing. Megan picked a couple of spoons out of the drawer and mimed the playing of a xylophone on his ribs.

'Yeah, very funny. But this is as uninhibited as I'm going to get. I'm as cool as a brass monkey. I'm not getting any cooler, whatever you might say.'

Megan turned her back on him and continued to unfasten her long robe. Glancing round to check he was still paying attention, she slipped the dress off her shoulders and onto the ground. She was wearing nothing underneath but a pair of white silk knickers and she had Sparks' total and undivided attention.

As he considered his options, Megan folded her arms and tapped her bare feet on the cold stone floor. She watched him remove his shoes and socks and then his jeans to reveal a pair of frayed Wallace and Gromit boxer shorts.

'Happy now?' he asked, rather peevishly. She shook her head. Sparks took a deep breath and discarded the last shreds of his dignity.

Megan clapped her hands and spun around. Sparks gave up all pretence of being cool and covered his private parts with his hands. He was desperately trying not to stare at her breasts. They were tiny but perfectly formed, and he wanted to examine them more closely. But not in public.

'That's the way,' Boz assented. 'You feeling relaxed now, man?'

The Perfect Fool

'Relaxed? Not exactly. No.'

'You'll be OK when we get outside and start phase two.'

'Outside! I'm not going outside and showing me knob to the world. It'll get sunburnt.'

Firm hands guided him to the door and ushered him out into the garden. If it hadn't been for the glare of the late afternoon sun, he might have spotted the bicycle coming up the lane. As it was, the smartly dressed postwoman clutching her bundle of letters was upon him before he could hide his embarrassment behind a convenient bush.

Sparks gave a panic-stricken squeal and ran back into the house, closely followed by his two companions. The postwoman, who had seen a few naked men before, calmly waited for the door to close so she could make her delivery in the conventional manner.

Inside, Sparks was hurriedly gathering up his clothes. He was mightily embarrassed and was naturally responding by making a fool of himself. In his haste, he put on his boxer shorts back to front and then rammed both feet into the left leg of his jeans. He hopped about for a short while before slowly and inevitably toppling to the floor.

Megan looked down at him with hands on hips. From somewhere deep inside there came a low chuckle, which built into a staccato laugh. Soon she was shaking with laughter and tears were running down her cheeks.

Sparks saw himself reflected in her eyes. He was a pitiful sight. In such circumstances, a man could skulk away and sulk, or he could try and laugh it off. Sparks chose the latter, partly to cover embarrassment, but mainly because he was starting to see the funny side. He was lying on the floor, stark-bollock naked, with his trousers round his ankles. Humour didn't get more basic than that.

He groaned in mock distress until Megan and Boz helped him to his feet, then joined in as they re-enacted the scene between bursts of hysteria and incoherent shouting.

20 Just What I Needed

Dillon resurfaced a couple of hours later, as the smell of cooking drifted along the disused platform. Someone had set up a makeshift barbecue beneath an ancient beech tree at the far end, and rows of juicy sausages were already sizzling over the glowing charcoal. He followed his nose past the colourful hanging baskets and the overflowing flower tubs. Every spare inch of the old brick building was festooned with plant life, some of it cultivated and most of it decidedly wild. The whole station was bursting with life and colour as it inexorably returned to nature.

Dillon sidled up to the taciturn chef and snaffled the first of the food before anyone could object. It was a long time since his last meal and he was truly starving. The sausage he'd picked up was charred and piping hot, forcing him to toss it from hand to hand until he found a bread bun to put it in.

Next to the barbecue was a collection of half-empty bottles of spirits from around the world and a couple of barrels of beer. Dillon filled a pint glass from the nearest tap and checked it for clarity and taste. It tasted pretty good, in fact, so he downed the rest and helped himself to another, just to be sure.

Soon, Sparks arrived, attracted by the same greasy aroma. He was still clad in his Wallace and Gromit boxer shorts and looked terminally confused.

Dillon handed him a pint and shook his head in amazement. He wondered if this was the same Sparks who only ventured outside after dark. A man who was so averse to cold weather that he was known to sit in front of the fire wearing a down jacket. 'How's it going?' Dillon enquired, cautiously.

'Not so bad,' Sparks replied. 'I've met a right interesting bunch of folk already. They're all pretty cool, this Wild lot. Some of them are from Mars and stuff, but they're OK when you get to know them. It's good fun here. I'm really enjoying it.' He paused for reflection. 'Oh, and there's this lass called Megan. She's a bit of all right, she is, and she seems keen, even if she doesn't say much.'

Dillon was impressed. He tried to pick out this paragon of womanhood from the crowd of hungry cultists heading towards him. None of them exactly fitted his idea of what a "bit of all right" might look like, but he let it pass. 'Do you think you're in with a chance there?'

'Maybe. Maybe not.' Sparks weighed up the prospects with a twist of the hand. 'She got her kit off without me even asking, but she hasn't actually said anything yet so it's hard to tell.'

Unlike Sparks, Megan had the good sense to put her clothes back on. She left the approaching posse, skipped up to Sparks and waited for him to introduce his friend. Dillon took in her pasty complexion and her funny-serious expression and decided that she and Sparks were probably made for each other. She gave him one of her upside-down smiles and prodded Sparks in the stomach.

'Yeah, I am pretty hungry, like. What about you?' Sparks asked her.

She licked her lips and sniffed the air.

Sparks nodded knowingly. 'It looks like sausages or nothing at the moment. Boz is bringing the steaks along in a minute and those chicken's whatnots. Did you fetch the marshmallows?'

Megan held up a multi-coloured bag for inspection.

'Great. They taste like pink goo to me, but some people must like them. Fancy one, Dillon, mate?'

Dillon was temporarily lost in his own thoughts. 'What? Oh, no thanks.'

Rachel was strolling down the platform behind the crowd. They hadn't exchanged many words since waking up together. He wasn't sure where exactly he stood, or what he was going to say to her. Sparks raised an eyebrow.

'Yeah, it's like you said,' Dillon admitted. 'Not sure where I stand, to be honest.'

He had considered lying about the afternoon's events, but there was no point with people like these. At any moment, they might break out into displays of openness and honesty. Dillon thought that perhaps he should just let things take their course. Things tended to work out better if they were allowed to happen in their own good time. He could even tell Rachel how he felt, once he'd worked it out for himself.

'Hi there!' said Rachel.

'Hi. Fancy a sausage?' It wasn't much of a line, but Dillon was trying his best to stay on safe ground.

'I think I'll wait.' She eyed up the blackened remnants. 'But you better have one. You'll need your strength for later.'

She slipped her arm around his waist and Dillon felt the ground returning to its normal booby-trapped state. Boz arrived, bare-arse naked and carefree as ever. Dillon felt obliged to be embarrassed on his behalf. It reminded him of one of his bad dreams where you turn up for work with no trousers on and nobody notices until the boss walks in. Well, everybody had those dreams, didn't they?

More people were arriving. Soon, thirty-odd Wild Things and two Mild Men were standing along the platform munching on various burnt offerings. Dillon scanned their new friends. Most were well past the first flush of youth. Not that this seemed to worry the Wild Things; they certainly felt no need to cover up the effects of the ageing process. A few, like Boz, were sky-clad. The rest were dressed for an exhibitionist's outdoor, fancy-dress party, with no particular theme.

One shortish, balding man of indeterminate age was wearing what appeared to be a real goatskin, complete with head. He was waving a burger and talking animatedly to two women who were modelling fur bikinis. Further on, an Amazonian woman with most of her extremities pierced was comparing tattoos with the alleged Atlantean, Drax. He was wearing nothing but a biker's jacket and boots and had patriotically painted his genitalia red, white, and blue.

Joy, from Alpha Centauria, was kneeling on a bench with her ample thighs wrapped around one of her fellow cultists. His body was hidden by her wild fan of jet-black hair and only his knobbly knees were visible.

Dillon tried not to stare. Perhaps they were just chatting, or something. He decided it was a good time to find out what Sparks was up to. Megan had borrowed some woad dye from the friendly giantess and was painting an intricate pattern around Sparks' pale body, giving him the appearance of a Pictish Mr Puniverse.

Dillon looked down at his faded jeans and grey T-shirt. He felt like someone who had turned up to a black-tie function dressed as a chicken. He started to edge away, to find an unobtrusive place from which to observe the proceedings, but Rachel intercepted him and pulled him back into the bosom of her adopted family.

Several of the group had brought musical instruments of an ethnic and tuneless nature. Once most of the food had been consumed, this impromptu band struck up with a weird wailing chorus. Some of the audience started a low humming, which rose and fell with a slow pulse. Others began a chant to an entirely different tune and rhythm. The overall effect was surprisingly pleasant, all things considered, and even Sparks tried his best to join in.

'It's a traditional Native American song of thanksgiving for the bounty of the land,' explained Rachel.

'I think I'd better stick to humming,' said Sparks. 'You can't go wrong with humming.'

Megan deliberately hummed a few bum notes to prove him wrong.

A tall, elegant woman was walking towards them along the disused railway line. Compared to the rest of the cultists, she was very conventionally dressed, but all eyes were on her as she climbed up the steps and onto the crowded platform. Dillon recognised her from the news articles Dolores had given him: Sheryl Keane, the spiritual leader of the Wild Things. The tempo of the music increased. She began spinning and dancing around like a drunken dervish, her sun-bleached hair fanning out as a golden halo until she came to a halt facing the two visitors.

'Alesh asheena alakra! May divine love shine upon you, bless you and keep you. We have strangers in our midst. Shall we welcome them to our home?'

There was some incoherent clamour, which Dillon took to mean yes.

'Then they should declare themselves. How shall we know you, strangers?'

Still firmly clutching his beer glass, Sparks was hauled up onto a wooden picnic table amid much laughter and shouting. He staggered slightly and motioned for quiet with his free hand.

'Thanks for having us. My name's Mark Munro, but everybody calls me Sparks because of my electric personality. I was living in Lincoln with Dillon, here, which was nice until the house burnt down. I'm a software engineer and I know a lot about computers and stuff, which is a lot more interesting than what you'd think, but not as interesting as being here, and I'm having a cracking time, thank you very much.'

He ran out of breath and tumbled off the table into the waiting arms of several supporters who carried him, and his glass, bodily over to the beer barrel for more well-deserved refreshment. Dillon was next. He decided honesty was the best policy.

'My name's Dillon Wright. I'm a journalist. Most of the time it's not very interesting, except when you insult people, and they set fire to your house. I'm writing a series of articles about religious groups and I haven't said anything nice about any of them yet, so I'll understand if you want me to leave. I've been having such a wonderful time here. I wouldn't want to spoil it. Cheers!'

There was a big round of applause. Several people patted him on the back as he clambered down from the table. Sheryl came over, pressed the palm of her hand on his forehead, and muttered a brief blessing.

'If you are going to write about us, you'd better stay for a while and find out what we're really like. There's plenty of room here for believers and sceptics alike. Stay true to yourself, Dillon, and you will find your own way to salvation. We will be here to help you when you need it most.'

Dillon was quite choked with gratitude and emotion, not to mention the inhibition-reducing effects of the beer. He managed a mumbled word of thanks before Rachel took pity on him and steered him away from the madding crowd and back towards the house.

Megan beat them to the door. She smiled and held it open wide for Boz, who was providing a shoulder for the staggering Sparks to lean on. She waved them towards her sparsely furnished room. Boz dumped his drunken companion on the bed and returned to enjoy the rest of the evening's entertainment.

'Well, that's him sorted out,' Rachel remarked. 'I suppose if you are going to stay for a while, you'd better have somewhere to sleep. We've got a couple of rooms going spare since the Stafford sisters went back to Cincinnati. Why don't you take this one?'

She threw open the door onto a small room with a sloping ceiling. It was peachy. Very peachy in fact, except for the bits that were apricot or possibly nectarine. Every piece of furniture seemed to have some sort of frill on it.

Dillon felt as if he was trapped inside a box of sugared almonds. 'It's very nice,' he lied.

'Of course, it might need some redecorating eventually, but it's got everything you'd need. Here's a wardrobe and a chest of drawers,' Rachel opened them up to show that they still worked despite the ornamentation; 'and here's the bed.' She sat down on the side and patted the covers.

Dillon joined her and carefully put his arm around her. He noticed that she didn't seem to object when he pulled her gently towards him.

'I'm glad you're staying, Dillon. You'll like it here, I'm sure.' Rachel looked him in the eye from a nose length away, then, with a barely perceptible motion, brought her lips up to his. Dillon tried to concentrate on the kiss, but he seemed to be having some difficulty breathing. Also, his nose was starting to run, and his arms were in entirely the wrong place for efficient embracing.

Rachel didn't seem to mind. She popped the buttons on his shirt, one by one, and examined his spreading figure critically. Dillon, meantime, was having some difficulty with the hooks on her dress. The beer and the nerves were making him fumble-fingered, but eventually, he succeeded in the task.

It looked as if Rachel was on the same exercise regime as him. He ran his hands over the flow and swell of her body. Her bra seemed to be holding back quite a lot of pink flesh and he approached its removal with caution. It took both hands and some helpful tips from its owner before he managed to get the thing off.

Soon, he was well beyond thinking and worrying. The whole bed-creaking business may not have lasted very long, but it was extremely enjoyable. Rachel, who had been making noises like the Flying Scotsman at full steam, appeared to have pulled into the station, and Dillon slowly relaxed as she slumped back into his arms.

Charlotte had once told him that he didn't understand her needs. Since she wasn't prepared to describe what those needs might be, he'd started to think he just wasn't up to the job. It wasn't difficult to destroy someone's self-esteem, but it was a lot trickier to restore it. Somehow, in the space of a day, Rachel had managed to make him feel good about himself again.

'Thank you, Dillon,' Rachel whispered, pressing her finger to his lips to stop him from blurting out anything stupid.

'You're fun to be with; do you know that? I feel more comfortable with you than I have with anyone I've met in a long time. You're not afraid to say exactly what you mean, even if it's not what people want to hear.'

Dillon closed his eyes and breathed deeply, as Rachel gently ran her fingers through his dishevelled hair.

'I feel very happy right now,' Rachel continued, 'Do you think you could be happy here with us?'

There was no answer, except for the snoring of the sexually satisfied male. Rachel looked disappointed for a while and then smiled at the peaceful expression on Dillon's face. Quietly, without disturbing his repose, she slipped out of bed, pulled on a few items of clothing, and tiptoed back outside to rejoin the never-ending party.

21 The Road To Hell

A few days later, much to his disgust, Dillon was destined to be back on the road. It was almost as if there was a conspiracy preventing him from staying in one place for any length of time. The first indication of trouble came when he got a call from Arnold Gladman at The Sunday Echo.

'Good work!' said Gladman encouragingly. 'We loved your piece on the Pogoing Pagans. Wherever did you find them?'

Dillon mumbled something about his contacts in the cult world. The truth of the matter was that he had found them in his head, along with the Underwater Monks and the Hermit of Newport Pagnell. He didn't think Gladman was ready for this revelation yet. Not until his pay cheque was safely in the bank, anyway.

'Excellent! But we want you to change tack. We need you in Goonhilly. That's in Cornwall, you know. There's a lot of national interest at the moment and you're the ideal man to cover the spiritual angle.'

'The whole nation is interested in Cornwall?' Dillon said, disbelievingly. 'Since when?'

'The Prophesy, my boy! The Second Coming. The End of the World. Only happens once in a blue moon. Surely, you know. Every crank in the Northern Hemisphere will be there!'

'Oh yeah, TEOTWAWKI, right? I'd forgotten. I'll get right on it. When is it exactly?'

'It's the summer solstice. Surely you knew that? The festival starts next Thursday and all the real doomsday-sayers will be in Goonhilly long before then. The clock's ticking, my boy. We'll be expecting daily reports. Don't let us down!'

Bugger! Dillon thought. The last thing he wanted to do was drive three hundred miles to sit around waiting for the world to end with a bunch of loonies. He had some better ideas of how he could profitably pass the time, and most of them involved spending quality time in bed with Rachel. Perhaps he could just read the newspaper reports and invent some more fictitious cults to keep The Sunday Echo happy.

That idea was soon quashed. Later that day, Sheryl Keane gathered the Wild Things together for a pep talk. 'Sisters and brothers. As you all know, an event of great significance is nearly upon us. I have never set much store by prophecies of doom, as you know, but there is a great gathering in Goonhilly coming. Some are planning a wake for the world and others a celebration. Either way, it's gonna be a helluva party, my friends!'

A big cheer went up from the assembled Wild Things.

'We too must be there: to challenge this false prophecy, to reject this talk of war and damnation, to help drive back the forces of superstition and intolerance. Instead of the end of times, we will show these people the time of their lives! Prepare yourselves. We leave in three days.'

'Bugger and shite!' muttered Dillon to himself. He seemed to be the only one who didn't share Sheryl's enthusiasm for the trip.

'Brilliant!' exclaimed Sparks. 'There's that festival I was telling you about. Lizard Live! Megan reckons we can get in for free. All the top acts will be there. I hear a few rock dinosaurs are playing, so you'll be all right. And there'll be some decent indie bands, for proper music lovers.'

Dillon ignored the dig at his musical tastes and skulked off to find Rachel. She soon put paid to any lingering hopes he might have had of avoiding the whole business.

'Well, I'm going,' she announced impatiently. 'So, if you stay behind it's no sex for two weeks.'

'That's a good point well presented. When do we leave?'

Boz was already working on the group's ancient coach. He'd put on a pair of overalls, especially for the task. Dillon dropped by to inspect his handiwork.

'Needs a bit of a service, but it'll soon be as good as new,' declared Boz, optimistically.

The bodywork had been painted an unpleasant shade of slime green, apparently by someone with a brush and a tin of vinyl emulsion and it had 'Cult Coach' painted on the side, graffito-style. Most of the chassis was held together by rust and filler, three of the tyres were completely bald, and when Dillon pressed on the brake pedal, his foot went straight down to the floor.

'Could you just start her up for me,' Boz asked, from somewhere under the bonnet.

There was a horrible graunching noise and the starter turned a couple of times before dying completely. Dillon tried again and this time the engine caught, briefly, sending plumes of black smoke billowing across the station yard. After a few revolutions, it coughed and spluttered to a halt and no amount of fiddling with the controls would persuade it to start again.

'I think I'll take the Land Rover down to Cornwall if you don't mind. Nothing personal, you understand.'

'But you'd miss out on all the fun of the journey!' Boz protested, 'The chanting! The drinking! The camaraderie!'

'You mean the "Entire Cult Wiped Out in Motorway Death Smash" type of camaraderie. No thanks. I know my Land Rover's not perfect but it's a Rolls-Royce compared to this heap of junk.'

Boz returned to his labours with a hurt look on his face. It was a good thing that he was a patient man because it took him most of the following two days to get the coach anywhere near a serviceable state. Dillon was dispatched to Sheffield with a long list of essential parts, most of which turned out to be obsolete. He then spent a tiresome day crawling around the city's scrapyards looking for replacements.

Ever helpful, Sparks spent the next day downloading manuals and maintenance videos for Boz, while Megan fetched endless pots of tea and explained the principles of the internal combustion engine to him in mime. Despite all this, the work was eventually completed. A crowd of spectators, such as you might see around any good disaster, had built up over the day and there was a somewhat ironic cheer when the coach finally burst into life.

Several of the onlookers accepted Boz's invitation to join him on a test drive into nearby Castleton. They didn't seem quite so keen on the expedition when they got back. A couple of them hadn't returned with the coach and were rumoured to have started hitch-hiking to Cornwall.

Dillon was soon inundated with requests for lifts to the festival. This included two offers of an explicitly sexual nature, which he turned down with great reluctance, having already promised to take Rachel, Megan, and Sparks. In theory, the Land Rover seated six, but only if the entire journey was downhill. It was at times like these that he wished he'd splashed out for one of those nice modern people movers.

The journey south was not without incident. The Land Rover overheated in a traffic jam on the M6 approaching Birmingham. Sparks' attempt to interface his iPhone with the archaic cassette player resulted in him getting another minor electric shock. Finally, when Dillon tried to play his Led Zepplin compilation tape for the fourth time, Sparks threatened to ram it down his throat. They continued the journey in brooding silence.

Traffic was steadily building the further south they got. At every bottleneck and major intersection, everything ground to a fuming halt. All in all, tempers were a little frayed by the time they reached the agreed rendezvous at Truro. Not as frayed, however, as the nerves on the Cult Coach when it finally pulled into the car park some six hours later.

Dillon had thoughtfully left directions to a nearby pub on the windscreen and it was a pale and weary crowd that piled into the bar, desperate for some alcoholic refreshment.

'Jesus H Christ! I need a beer!' declared Sheryl, speaking for the whole group with her usual perspicacity.

Drax, being the tallest and most intimidating, was dispatched to the bar. Soon, a chain of glasses passed from hand to hand towards the travel-weary passengers.

'What happened?' Rachel wanted to know.

'What didn't happen!' said Boz cheerfully, 'We broke down eight times, or was it nine? We've had a police escort since Gloucester. Then the head gasket went at Exeter. The Devon traffic police got one of their trucks to tow us over the border, but this was as far as they were prepared to go.'

'They said something about not wanting a bunch of hippies starting a commune on their end of the M5,' Drax explained. 'Also, Joy did her party trick with the two helmets and the truncheon. That kind of got their attention.'

'So how do we get to the festival now?' asked Boz. He tried to make out he was addressing the pub in general, but the remark was directed straight at Dillon.

'You could walk,' Dillon suggested. 'If you set off now, you might get there in time for the headline act.' Nobody looked very keen on walking. 'Or you could catch the shuttle bus from the park-and-ride. There's one every hour. I checked.'

By now, Dillon was getting heartily sick of watching everyone else drinking (and complaining). He felt it was high time he got the driving over with and could settle down with a refreshing glass of something that wasn't ninety-five per cent sugar. After an hour on the road, he was soon wishing they'd stayed in the pub. With still a full day to go before the event itself started, the traffic on the A39 was horrendous. Dillon began to think they would have been better off walking to the festival after all.

Eventually, when they got within a few miles of the site, the police directed the Land Rover off into a muddy field where they parked up and gathered their belongings together for the long march. An endless column of people carrying bags and boxes, or pushing overladen trolleys filed down the narrow country road, like refugees from some nameless disaster.

There seemed nothing for it, but to join the shuffling masses. The road was a dark and verdant tunnel, with high banks on both sides and a broad canopy of trees obscuring the fading evening light. Dillon did his best to keep them all together but it was a difficult task in the press of people. Several times, he was nudged into the hedge, which he soon discovered was a solid, grass-covered wall with numerous sharp edges to snare the unwary. For a while, he lost sight of the others, and after regrouping, they elected to walk hand in hand like a set of sixties protest singers.

In the humid confines of the lane, innumerable flies and midges swarmed around the sweating crowd. Dillon found himself pressed up against a fat man with a personal hygiene problem, and two women chain-smoking a particularly pungent blend of wacky baccy. To cap it all, it began to rain. Not the gentle cooling rain for which England is so renowned, but a pouring, pounding, tropical monsoon rain, which broke through the cover of the trees in minutes and soaked them to the skin. Party spirit was now sadly lacking amongst the festivalgoers. It was going to be a long weekend.

A few people who knew the lie of the land were climbing out of the lane and cutting across the fields. The unhappy foursome joined them. It was good to be out of the rat run, but they were still some distance from the entrance, with several cow pastures and the high wire fence of the Satellite Earth Station in their way. A large crowd was milling around the main gates.

Dillon peered through the rain at the wooded valley and the watercolour hills beyond, but it was difficult to make out what was happening. Several hundred people were waiting to get into the site and it soon became clear that this was no happy festival crowd: it was a mob. Some were shouting incoherent threats at the staff at the gate and there was a fair deal of pushing and shoving.

At the gate itself, a few lads with no hair and an aggressive appearance were squaring up to the stewards who were trying to search them for concealed weapons and unlicensed recording equipment. A sign on the chain mesh fence advised visitors not to bring in any items that could otherwise be bought at inflated prices from the concession stands inside. There was something strange about the stewards' outfits. Underneath their fluorescent vests, they were wearing long flowing camouflage capes. Dillon started to feel sorry for the lads at the front of the mob.

The crowd was growing rapidly. Those at the back began pushing their way forward to see what was happening. This rippled like the incoming tide until the front row was forced right up against the gates. Two stalwart stewards by the ticket office were beginning to lose it badly, both personally and professionally.

Dillon caught a glimpse of the formidable Sister Charity as she scrummed down with two more of her comrades and charged the crowd whilst Sister Sharon shouted encouragement through a loudhailer. Behind them, a group of unpaid volunteers, wearing orange tabards that identified them as 'Festival Makers', were beating a hasty retreat before anyone could ask them to help.

Dillon guided his friends towards a gap in the crowd. 'All it's going to take is for one idiot to throw something, and we're in for a full-scale riot.' He began counting out loud, as they pushed past countless sweaty and drunken festivalgoers.

On 'twelve', a single bottle arced through the air, spraying its pungent yellow contents on the balding and sunburnt scalps of a group of overweight bikers. It landed with a splat on the mud in front of them. There was a moment's stunned silence then the mob surged forward.

'Keep your head down, your arms braced, and your elbows out,' shouted Dillon over the sudden hubbub. The Lincoln Free Press and Advertiser had forced him to watch a safety video before they would let him help with the football reports. It never came in useful at Lincoln City's bijou Sincil Bank ground, but he was glad of it now. 'Look out for obstacles, and if you fall, try and roll back onto your feet straight away. The last one to the beer tent is a sissy!'

He was immediately deafened by a bloodthirsty, Braveheart battle cry from Megan, who grabbed Sparks by the arm and charged down the hill sweeping all before her. Once Dillon had regained his composure and his hearing, he followed hard on their heels. Running down a rain-soaked hillside in sandals was a perilous procedure, but he skated to the bottom unscathed.

22 I Predict a Riot

It was a relatively bloodless coup. A couple of punches were thrown as the first invaders crossed into the site but faced with a choice of standing aside or being trampled to death, most of the Sisters climbed up the safety of the ticket office roof. Dillon could see that Sister Charity was not happy about this capitulation, but eventually, she clambered up to rejoin her marooned comrades.

When the main bulk of the crowd reached the perimeter, the sheer weight of numbers proved too much for the tiny opening and the fence itself began to bend under the strain. Steel posts buckled and snapped, the mesh was torn down, and Dillon and Rachel were borne across the boundary line on a reckless wave of humanity.

All around the site, punters were taking the opportunity created by the chaos to effect a free entrance to the festival. One man, who looked as if he belonged on a 'Wanted' poster, pulled out a pair of massive bolt croppers from underneath his raincoat and proceeded to demolish another section of the fence. The remnants of the festival makers, and the few police present, soon gave up their attempts to repel the barbarian hordes. It was like trying to push back the sea.

Once inside, Dillon grabbed Rachel, and they surveyed the surroundings. The site was dominated by two structures. The main stage looked impressive with its high gantries and banks of TV screens, but it was completely overshadowed by the massive stone circle beyond which had been built out of roughcast concrete with financial assistance from the Arts Council and placed at the highest point of the arena.

The designer had decided that since most people expected Stonehenge to be bigger than it really was, his stone circle should be more in tune with their expectations. Some attempt had been made to give the structure an authentic look by spreading moss and lichen over the concrete, but it still looked more prefab than prehistory.

Sparks and Megan were waiting patiently by a solar-powered cinema. The four of them picked their way across the sodden ground towards the embryonic tent village, nestling beneath the plantation of uniform pines ahead. Judging by their current rate of progress, the campsite was a long walk from the stage, the stone circle, the beer tent, and most importantly, the nearest toilet.

Megan tapped Sparks on the shoulder and persuaded him employing pouting and fluttering of eyelashes to carry her across the worst of the mud. She leapt onto his back; all eight stones of her wringing wet, and Sparks' spindly legs began to buckle. He tried to step forward to balance the load, but his feet had sunk a good three inches into the mire. There was nothing he could do but topple slowly backwards. Fortunately, he had Megan there to break his fall, this time. There was an almighty splash as they landed in a foul-smelling pool of murky water.

Megan screamed, grabbed a handful of mud, and rubbed it into Sparks' face. Then she began to laugh, as did her mount, once he'd removed the grass from his mouth. She splashed and rolled around in the puddle like a hippo in its favourite hollow. Others came to join them, one young Olympic hopeful doing a perfect swallow dive into a full six inches of water. Soon, a mud wrestlers' pool party was in full swing. Rachel tried to persuade Dillon in with a quick headlock, but he handed her off successfully.

'These are my best trousers,' he protested, pointing to his rain-soaked and threadbare jeans. 'Besides, I can't swim.'

It made little difference in the end. After half an hour of trying to construct their tent, Dillon was as muddy as the rest of them. The campsite had been recently used as a cow pasture and the tent instructions were completely unfathomable.

'Where the hell did you get this contraption from,' Dillon asked, petulantly, after a fourth futile attempt.

'It was a job lot from the army surplus store.' Rachel explained. 'It's the same type they used during the invasion of Afghanistan.'

'Which one? Carry On Up the Khyber?'

He read the instructions once again, but Pole C resolutely refused to enter Slot F, however hard he pushed it. Finally, he decided to leave out the offending parts and everything went a lot smoother. Admittedly, the tent now had twice as many corners as in the illustration, but it didn't seem in imminent danger of collapse. Meanwhile, Megan had pitched the other tent with no apparent difficulty.

'How did you manage that?' Dillon wanted to know, as he crawled out of his lopsided structure.

She held up the instructions, ripped them cleanly in two, and tapped her forehead to indicate the use of logic and reasoning.

'I held some of the poles,' added Sparks, in case anyone thought he'd been slacking.

'I read my book,' said Rachel, who had been slacking, but didn't care what anyone thought.

There was still no sign of the other Wild Things, so they trudged through the mud to the beer tent for some well-earned refreshment. It was Dillon's round. He surveyed the available options with dismay.

'Four pints of pig's piss, please.'

'Which one's that?' asked a youth in a candy-striped corporate uniform, looking up and down the bar.

'It's the one you've laughingly labelled as Best Bitter.'

The beer was as bland and fizzy as he expected, but they drank it anyway. It had been too stressful a day to let even bad beer go to waste. Dillon glanced over at the entrance. Someone very familiar had arrived. Someone who had to duck to pass through the tent flap. Somehow, he wasn't surprised to see him.

'Hello, Ralph.'

'Well met, Dillon. How are you enjoying life with the Wild Things? Is young Rachel Murgatroyd looking after you properly?'

'How did you know…?' Dillon stopped himself. He'd long since resolved to give up trying to understand where Coleman got his information. If it was by conventional means, he wouldn't tell Dillon, and if it was by divine provenance, Dillon didn't want to know.

'And here is the lady herself. I once taught your father, you know, Rachel. Terrible student. I always felt he was destined for the clergy.'

'Can I get you a beer, Mr Coleman?' she enquired, politely.

'No thank you, my dear. I believe they are serving some mass-produced dishwater. We have a couple of barrels of Tribulation Ale in our mess tent. You would be very welcome to join us later. I only came here to speak with young Dillon.'

'How…? Oh, never mind.' There were too many questions bouncing around in Dillon's head. 'Have you come for the festival? Or Armageddon? Or both?'

'It is the solstice that draws us here, in the main. It is unfortunate, though understandable, that the concert will precede it, rather than celebrate it. It is almost as if our esteemed festival organisers believe that the prophecy will render further merrymaking redundant.'

'So you don't believe the Mad Woman's predictions, then?'

'There are many prophecies. If one makes enough guesses about the future, one of them will certainly be near the mark. Though, not this one, I hope and pray to the Mother of the Aeons. Still, this gathering may have significance for many reasons, which I hope will become apparent,' he added, mysteriously. 'Certainly, the reactions of some misguided people may be worth observing.'

'Some of these cults really reckon it's going to be the end of the world?'

'Of course. The true egocentric will naturally expect to be present at all the most significant moments in history. If he or she is of a mystical bent, then surely, these must be the last days. Since they are alive now, everything of importance must happen now. The consideration that vital events may have occurred before their birth or may be scheduled for shortly after their death does not even cross their minds. Unlike Moses, they expect to reach the Promised Land and to stay there for all eternity.

'I was just speaking to one such man who claimed, in a previous life to have been a Saxon nobleman,' Coleman continued in his normal oratorical fashion. 'It seems they were all lords and ladies, movers and shakers of the world. It is a wonder that food was ever prepared or floors swept in the olden days. Now, of course, he is the leader of a raggle-taggle band of misfits and lunatics, but destiny awaits him because he has been chosen. By whom, I cannot say. The ways of an irrational creator are truly mysterious.'

'Are you counting Sheryl Keane as one of your egocentrics?' asked Rachel, when she could get a word in edgeways.

'Both yes and no. I have a great deal of time for Sheryl. To keep such a Dionysian group from destroying itself, she must be possessed of great strength of will. She leads by example and not by decree. I would say that I do not agree with many of her beliefs, but she has many redeeming features.'

'She's been nice to me,' considered Dillon after some thought. 'And she drinks a lot of beer. She can't be all bad.'

'All the Wild Things drink. Indeed, they put us to shame when we last met. I believe they drink because they are aware of their own mortality. They, in common with all living things, will one day die. They view the end as being somewhat closer than most of us care to imagine. They drink to forget the future since they enjoy the present so much. I do not mean to give the impression that they are afraid of what is to come, for they believe in life after death: a rebirth into a non-corporeal state of perpetual bliss, with no hangovers. Am I not correct?'

'Something like that,' admitted Rachel. 'I think Sheryl explains it better.'

Coleman's expression became stern and he drew Dillon to one side. 'Be on your mettle at all times,' he warned him. 'Look around you. There are those here who would wish you ill. But do not fear, for there is a good chance that you will live to see one more dawn, at least. Enjoy the concert! We will meet again. Probably.'.

23 It's The End Of The World As We Know It

After the previous day's events, there was talk of the whole festival being cancelled. However, when the organisers tried this concept out on a focus group in the bar, it nearly sparked another riot. Neither the police nor the organisers were prepared for the task of clearing tens of thousands of angry, mud-splattered people from the area and it was decided to continue "in the interests of public order".

Dillon was about the only one who seemed upset with this decision. The clouds were clearing but he was wet and cold, and not very impressed with the few bands he'd heard so far. In his opinion, this was not a vintage year for music. The charts were full of auto-tuned reality-show winners, soulless soul singers, and endless dance anthems that gave him a migraine.

Most of the musicians he admired had either retired or choked on their own vomit. Even those that were still playing looked as if they were likely to expire on stage. He no longer knew which songs were topping the charts and bands had started doing cover versions of songs he hadn't even heard the first time around. He decided he was getting old, and was quite happy to stay all day in the miniature marquee the Gnostics had erected in one of the drier areas of the camping field.

Sparks, however, had been touring the site and insisted that they should at least see some of the bands on the main stage. 'It's Rosetta on next,' he said, herding Dillon, Rachel and Megan towards the madding crowd. 'You've got to see them; they're a cult band. I mean literally, a cult. They've got their own religion with followers and everything. Apparently, they beamed down from some spaceship hiding inside that comet.'

'Oh yeah?' said Dillon. They sounded like people he should be interviewing, but he wanted to hear how awful their music was first.

'It's true. I read about it in The Beat magazine. They claim their sound is based on the rhythms they heard in the mothership. Mind you, The Beat also reckons the drummer is from Barnsley.'

'How come all these aliens turn out to be from Yorkshire?'

'Dunno, mate,' Sparks admitted, thoughtfully. 'Though I've often felt I'm not of this world if you know what I mean.'

'Just because you're on a different planet, doesn't make you an alien.'

'Yeah, thanks. Anyway, it's a totally new and happening sound. Not that you would know about that. You've got to get with it, Dillon, mate.'

A roar went up from the crowd as six androgynous skinheads, dressed in Lycra, walked out onto the stage. The lead singer gurned at the roving TV camera, swore into the microphone, then strolled over to a pair of bongos, and started to play. He was joined by a couple of guys on keyboards, a shouter/rapper, and someone hitting old bits of scrap iron with a sledgehammer.

The drummer took some time to get to his position, but finally picked his way past numerous percussion instruments and perched himself precariously on a stool, completely dwarfed by the kit in front of him. As the music reached its first climax, he broke into an ear-splitting rhythm and the whole audience started leaping frantically into the air.

Dillon hadn't heard anything as loud as this since that AC/DC tour with the cannons. The bass rhythm pounded against his chest and the whole field appeared to be shaking. Soon, he was bouncing up and down with the rest of them. They were so tightly packed, that he didn't have much of an option. Apart from the rain and mud, the fear that his ears would start to bleed, and some trouble with his breathing, he was starting to enjoy it.

'It's a catchy little number, isn't it,' Dillon shouted in his friend's ear.

'You what, pardon?'

Up on stage, a little guy with a ferret face, goatee beard, and half a dozen keyboards stacked on top of a grand piano, seemed to be trying to weave a tune into the proceedings. The other keyboard player was concentrating on creating strange and repetitive noises with a supercomputer somewhere off-stage left. The overall effect was quite hypnotic in a brain-pulverising sort of way.

The singer also had an impressively powerful voice, though his diction left something to be desired. By the tortured expression etched on his face, he must have had something vital to communicate to his audience, but what it might be Dillon couldn't tell. There was something about black holes and a supernova, plus a chorus in which he seemed to be singing ad nauseam about his yearning for a bucketful of eels.

There were two more bands on before the headliners. Dillon jigged about a bit to the first one just to show willing. They might have been called 'Dog Breath' or possibly 'Cot Death'. Nobody around them seemed quite sure, but, apparently, they were the latest thing in Folk/Rock/Acid Fusion. It was all quite jolly, but Dillon vaguely remembered something similar from the early nineties. Sometimes it seemed popular music had left him stranded; at other times, it seemed to be dragging about twenty years behind.

By the time the next band came on, Dillon was suffering from the advanced stages of festival fatigue. He resolved not to like them so that he could save his appreciation for the headline band. Still, enthusiasm is infectious, and some dedicated fans of the group, whoever they might be, were flailing about wildly in time to the music. This time it reminded him more of the sixties, only with less screaming. Dillon didn't mind this so much, since he was far too young to remember the era the first time around. It was nice of these people to recreate it for him.

Since the music seemed to be moving backwards in time as the evening progressed, it was appropriate that the last act had started performing before most of the other bands were even born. The audience knew the words to all their songs even though few owned any of their albums. Naturally, Dillon had all of them, except for the dodgy one with the Gamelan xylophone orchestra.

Their singer had reportedly been on hard drugs since he was seven and the lead guitarist was only allowed in the country if he agreed to wear a tracker on his ankle. The drummer and the bass player were involved in a long-running feud and had to be searched for weapons before each gig.

There was quite a long break before the headline act came on. Dillon suspected they were waiting for it to get dark so that everyone could appreciate the wonderful light show. Sparks threatened to retire to the beer tent then stayed in case he missed anything; like some girl's irate father trying to strangle the lecherous lead guitarist, or the drummer exploding, à la Spinal Tap.

When the band finally lurched onto the stage, there was a huge cheer. The singer grabbed hold of the microphone for support, said something incomprehensible about the world being eaten by a giant lizard and then they were off playing the first number. They played all the hits and the crowd-pleasers as well as one or two new tunes. Dillon considered it was a good thing for their reputation that no one was going to buy their latest album. They also played a couple of tracks from the early days, which especially pleased Dillon, since he was able to say in a loud voice something like: 'This one's from their first album with Decca,' in the mistaken belief that people would be impressed.

The band finished up with a heart-warming sing-a-long number about prostitution and substance abuse, which sent the crowd home happy. Dillon, for one, was ecstatic. He skipped back to the tent like a two-year-old at Christmas and kept breaking into tuneless versions of his favourite songs before Sparks finally lost patience and pushed him face-first into the mud.

The happy campers had resolved to get some sleep before the great event took place, but there was a constant wash of noise from across the field, as the revellers played all manner of instruments from piccolos to alpine horns. Dillon lay back in the tent and listened to the white noise buzzing in his ears. It nicely obscured the sound of Rachel's fitful snoring, but he hoped his hearing would restore itself in a day or two. If not, he could always sue Rosetta for damages.

Eventually, they gave up on sleep and staggered out into the melee. Some of the music lovers had packed up their tents and headed for home, but most had stayed and excitement was beginning to mount amongst the cult fraternity.

Three separate groups tried to persuade Dillon that this was his last chance to repent/mutate/put an ivy wreath on his head, depending on their particular agenda. He agreed to hang on to the ivy and think about wearing it later. It came in handy for swatting away the flies as he wandered around the festival ground.

Most attention was focused on the giant stone circle. Several hundred people in a variety of outlandish costumes were dancing hand in hand, forming a human chain around the fake stones. Inside, a group of men in medieval armour could be seen, digging away at the centre of the inner ring.

Coleman was watching them with a compass and map in hand. He looked annoyed and swore under his breath. 'They couldn't even read a straightforward map, let alone organise a festival. I knew I should have checked. I can't believe they could be such fools.'

'Which particular fools are these? There seems to be a few around today,' Dillon suggested.

'You find me sorely distressed. I gave our esteemed festival planners explicit instructions on where to place the circle, and they failed me. Look here, on the map. Could I have made it any plainer?'

'Are these ley lines?' Dillon enquired, pointing to the markings on the chart.

'Of a kind. They are lines joining a series of prominent features.'

'What sort of features? Stone circles? Burial mounds?'

'Royal Mail postboxes,' Coleman admitted. 'But it was necessary to direct the planners to an exact spot.'

'Your crossover point is in the woods. They couldn't hold a ceremony in there without chopping down half a dozen trees.'

'Well, possibly that was their reasoning, but it is simply not good enough. Our friends will find nothing in this field even if they dig all day. I shall be forced to intervene and there will no doubt be a price to pay for that.'

The Knights of the Wasteland seemed to have come to a similar conclusion. They were packing up and trooping disconsolately towards their waiting mounts. As Coleman headed off to intercept them, a posse of druids filed into the circle and began a simple ceremony. Several thousand people were now gathered around the monument to watch and to wait for something to happen.

According to the programme, dawn wasn't due for another couple of hours. Dillon wandered off for an Armageddon Kebab with special chilli sauce from Radwan's Mobile Restaurant. On the way back, he bought an amusing 'Cornwall after the Apocalypse' postcard to send off to Steve in Lincoln.

He made his way through the crowds and perched himself on top of a convenient van. It didn't look like he'd missed much. There was a selection of druids and priests drafted in from the various participating sects. Someone had given them holly bushes and other vegetation. There was also a goat that wandered about, eating anything that stayed still long enough, including holly and druid's robes.

Fortunately, the goat didn't seem to be in imminent danger of taking an active part in the proceedings.

The druids themselves didn't seem to be enjoying the experience. They looked as if they would be much happier with their colleagues at the real Stonehenge. Moreover, they were unused to such a large audience and appeared very self-conscious, striking a dramatic pose every few seconds, even when nothing much was happening.

The crowd was still enthralled with the performance, glancing up every so often to check the sun hadn't sneaked up over the horizon without them noticing. The druids began to gather around the central stone altar. Already, one of them had stumbled into the Knights' excavations, but eventually, they managed to form a circle and begin their invocations. The crowd joined in, uninvited, with a cacophony of chants and prayers.

As the sun rose, there was a collective intake of breath from the assembled crowd. The shadow of the great stone arch tracked steadily across the ground as if it were projected from a giant sundial. When it touched the altar, the Archdruid raised a ceremonial stone knife in both hands and as the first sliver of light touched the stone, he brought the knife crashing down on the smooth surface before him. Stone on stone, the sound reverberated around the valley, and following the druids' lead, the people raised their hands in supplication to the sky.

Gradually, the sun's light gathered strength. A low murmur began to build from the crowd. There was no hysteria, no cries of panic, just the sound of thousands of people holding their collective breath. Hands were held and reassurance sought.

Dillon knew in his heart of hearts that nothing was going to happen. He knew this with a certainty founded on generations of scientific knowledge, the overwhelming weight of evidence, and firm personal convictions. Unfortunately, the higher reasoning functions of his brain had been temporarily shut down by a superstitious Neolithic pagan, who was convinced that the Sun God was angry with him for failing to make the proper sacrifices over the past three thousand years. He reached out and grasped the hand of the person nearest to him and received a comforting squeeze in return.

A shaft of light burst out across the sky. It seemed to reach out towards the assembled multitude like a golden ladder reaching towards Heaven. A new dawn. Somebody began to sing a Nina

Simone song to that effect but was soon silenced by those around him. Before long, an ever-increasing orange glow illuminated the sky. There was some cheering and clapping, but most people seemed too embarrassed by their anxieties to make much of it.

Dillon glanced over to his left. He was holding Sparks' hand. A look of horror crossed both their faces and they let go simultaneously, as though electrocuted. Both surreptitiously wiped their palms on their jeans and stared fixedly at the scene unfolding below.

24 Feeling Good

The stone circle was deserted. The druids had vanished. Dillon thought he saw the hem of a white nightie disappearing into a nearby caravan, but he couldn't be sure. Just outside the ring of stones, several disgruntled members of one soon-to-be-redundant doomsday cult were surrounding their guru and demanding explanations. It looked like a few rash predictions were coming home to roost.

On the far side of the ring, a dozen people were sitting cross-legged in the dirt. They seemed oblivious to the crowds milling around them, despite some frantic attempts to attract their attention. Dillon wandered over to see what was going on.

'It's all over,' a woman in a diaphanous headscarf was shouting into the ear of the nearest cult member. 'Can't you see? It's bright daylight!'

'The Light of the World has been extinguished, never to reappear. We are cast into limbo to await the coming of the immortal gods. Praise be to Onos the Gatherer, who balances our fate in the palm of his hands.'

'Nothing happened, you daft hippie!' the woman yelled in frustration. 'It's only dark because you've got your eyes shut. Look around you, for God's sake.'

'Take pity on us, foul demon,' cried the man, pathetically. 'And cease tormenting us with your evil lies. Is it not enough that your master has swallowed the sun and destroyed the Earth, our home? Must you also torment us with the thought that it is not so? You serve a being who can create such cunning illusions, but we are not so easily deceived. Be gone, demon!'

'Who are you calling a demon?' the woman protested, loudly. 'I go to church every Sunday. I'm a respectable woman, I am, and I shouldn't have to stand here listening to a bunch of lunatics like you babbling on all day.' With that, she grabbed the man by his long mane of hair and yanked his head back. 'There! Feel the sun on your face. It's real, isn't it? Or do you think I brought a sunlamp with me?'

'No! No! The endless fires of Hades!' cried the man, mixing his theology eclectically. 'Save us, Onos, or we are surely doomed! We are being dragged by demons into the mouth of the eternal fire-dragon. We shall not be moved. Surely Onos will take pity on his humble servants and lead them safely into the light of redemption.'

Dillon stood nearby, fascinated by this wholesale rejection of reality. It made Creationism look positively logical by comparison. He watched for a while, wondering how long they could keep this up and whether stupidity on such a grand scale could be contagious.

Back inside the stone circle, the doomsday cult had finished their theological debate and had moved on to direct action. Three men were holding their leader down, while others tied what looked like nylon guy ropes to his arms and legs. They pegged him out like Gulliver, spreadeagled on the ground, and tightened the ropes until he was incapable of movement.

'So the world has ended, has it?' a large red-faced man screamed angrily at his fallen idol. 'Well, I've got news for you, pal: we're still here, and we're not happy about it. Not happy at all. I sold my house because of you. My wife left me. She even took the bloody dog with her. So, now it's your turn to suffer. After a few days strung out here, you're going to wish the sun really had never risen.' He bent down and ripped the guru's multi-coloured shirt from his back in one fabric-shredding motion. 'And you needn't think we'll be back with the Factor 50 and the Perrier water. As far as I'm concerned, you can stay here until you rot.'

The miserable band marched away, leaving a couple of their number to guard against interference from passers-by. Not that anyone seemed keen to rush to the guru's aid. Dillon made a few notes before walking away in search of further excitement. It was all a bit of a damp squib, by apocalyptic standards. Of course, he hadn't wanted the sun to be swallowed by angry deities, or have a host of angels chase after him with flaming swords, but it would have made meeting his next deadline an awful lot easier.

Through the rapidly diminishing crowds of departing festivalgoers, Dillon thought he saw someone he recognised. It was hard to be sure, but from this angle, it looked very much like Charlotte and her new friends.

Marcus Hardwick had his arm around a young girl in a khaki uniform, while Charlotte walked alongside seemingly unconcerned. The girl looked as if she should be still at school, though Dillon was no great judge of such things. She was tall and slender and, from the way Hardwick's hand kept wandering, Dillon decided she probably wasn't just his favourite niece out on a half-term treat.

Behind the three of them was an ill-assorted group of militia infantry in a motley selection of military surplus uniforms. They didn't appear to be armed, but Dillon was taking no chances. He slipped behind a stall selling souvenir umbrellas and watched proceedings through a hole in the canvas. Marcus was squeezing his young friend's waist now, and Charlotte was pretending to take an interest in a display of hand-crafted jewellery.

Dillon contemplated the iniquities of life. How many times had he suffered a severe ear-bending from Charlotte for the heinous crime of staring at some girl's cleavage? Now, here was her new hero, with his hand on the arse of some teenage floozy, and she wasn't even batting an eyelid. There was obviously a lot to be said for this Messiah business. You simply explained that God had told you to go forth and multiply and your beloved just had to accept it.

A little while later, Dillon saw Charlotte on her own. She was walking along the edge of the site with her arms crossed and her shoulders hunched. All around the perimeter, now, were tangled heaps of wire netting and broken pillars, where thousands of uninvited guests had trampled the last line of defence into the ground.

Charlotte picked her way over the wreckage and made her way towards the nearby plantation. Dillon looked around carefully then followed at a discreet distance. Once they were in the woods, he called out her name softly. She spun around with a look of fear and surprise on her face.

'What are you doing here, Dilly?' she demanded.

'I could ask the same thing of you,' said Dillon. 'I thought you hated music festivals.'

'I'm here with Marcus, if you must know. He gave a speech on the Mind, Body and Spirit stage. It was very inspiring. We've had dozens of new people wanting to join us. I'm surprised you haven't heard about it.'

'So how is marvellous Marcus getting on?'

The Perfect Fool

'He's fine if you must know. We're getting on just fine.' Charlotte's expression rather belied her words. 'Marcus is a great man. In fact, he's more than just a man, he's the chosen messenger of God. I can't begin to understand how you could say such terrible things about him.'

'So you read the articles, then? I hoped you would. Didn't you like them?'

'I don't care what you say about me, Dilly; I'm not important. But if you insult Marcus, you're insulting our whole faith and you'd better be prepared to face the consequences. It's blasphemy, Dilly. Doesn't that mean anything to you?'

'I think I've already felt the consequences, Charlotte, thank you very much. I was quite attached to that house, you know. I don't suppose that would mean anything to you either, would it?'

'What on earth are you on about?' Charlotte raised her voice in frustration. 'That's just typical of you, Dilly. I'm talking about relationships and religion, and the word of God, and you're talking about that stupid pigsty of yours. Is it surprising that I couldn't stay with you any longer?'

'Not really,' replied Dillon, quietly. 'I can understand you leaving. I'm just surprised that you fell for a slimy con artist like Marcus Hardwick. I thought you had more taste.'

As if summoned by his name, Hardwick strolled into the glade, smoothing back the remains of his hair with one hand. He was smiling, but it was the smile of a hungry crocodile.

'What do you think you're doing?' he snapped. Hardwick seemed genuinely angry, but to Dillon's amazement, he ignored him completely and instead grabbed Charlotte roughly by the arm. 'I've told you not to wander off without my permission. Don't you ever listen to what I'm saying?'

'I'm sorry Marcus.' She seemed on the verge of tears. 'But you were busy talking to Tara and I just thought...'

'You don't think, Charlotte. I don't know what goes on in your head, but it isn't thinking, is it? I leave you alone for ten minutes and I find you cosying up to some heretic. What am I supposed to think?'

'It's a free country, in case you hadn't noticed,' Dillon pointed out.

Hardwick looked at him closely for the first time. His expression grew even less sunny. 'It's you, isn't it? The nosy ex-boyfriend. Well now, it all becomes clear.'

'It isn't like that, Marcus, believe me,' Charlotte pleaded. 'Honestly, it isn't.'

Hardwick rounded on Dillon. 'You're wasting your time here. She is ours now. You can't take her back. I won't allow it.'

'You can keep her as far as I'm concerned. Though I wasn't aware that anyone owned her. Perhaps they re-introduced slavery while I wasn't looking.' Dillon glanced over at Charlotte with eyebrows raised, but she didn't respond. 'I'm more bothered about the state of my house, actually.'

'You look after your possessions and I'll look after mine,' Hardwick responded nastily. 'And I'll thank you to keep your nose out of my business, in future. If any more lackeys of this accursed government come sniffing around my home, I'll know who's to blame. And believe me, I'll know what to do about it.'

'I heard you'd had a visit from DEFRA. It wasn't anything to do with me, matey. Those who live by bullshit, die by it. That's what I say. Try complaining to your MP.'

Hardwick fumed and boiled at this, steam seeming to rise from dew-damp hair. He made a beckoning gesture with his hand.

Dillon heard a rustling in the trees behind him and span around in time to see several militia grunts with sloping foreheads and surplus body hair approaching at speed. Discretion, or more properly, running like hell, being the better part of valour, he legged it into the woods, pausing only to elbow Hardwick in the face.

Dillon sidestepped the tall pines and handed off various inanimate objects in his path. He plunged deeper and deeper into the plantation, not pausing to look behind for his pursuers. He could hear them well enough, shouting and cursing as they fought their way through the undergrowth. They sounded far too close for comfort.

In a race between the military machine against the couch potato, there was going to be only one winner. Already, Dillon was beginning to feel the strain of his initial dash for freedom. His heart was pounding and his breath was coming in raw gasps. He tried to drop back to a more sustainable pace, but the closing sounds of pursuit soon forced him on again. It was only a matter of time before he was caught.

Dillon tried to think like a hunted animal. What was the cunning thing to do? Where could he go to ground? Unfortunately, the only hunted animals he could think of were the hares and foxes he'd seen being ripped apart by hounds on anti-blood-sports videos. It was not a comforting thought. He resolved to make a big donation if ever he got out of this.

All that was left to him now was the element of surprise. Since he didn't know what he was going to do next, maybe it would be a surprise to the hunters too. As he crested a gentle rise, he ducked low and pushed through some tangled bushes into a clearing beyond. Brambles and briars tore at his clothing, but by now, he was oblivious to the pain and forced his way free from their thorny clutches. There was no obvious cover ahead, so Dillon picked up his feet for a final sprint across the clearing.

Loose heather and bracken had piled in uneven heaps over the forest floor and Dillon leapt from gap to gap like an overweight gazelle. As his foot came down heavily on a mound of withered vegetation, the ground gave way, pitching him into a deep hole filled with bundles of dry brushwood.

There was a chorus of sharp cracks, which could have been bones or dry branches breaking, followed by a squelch as he landed at the soggy bottom. He lay there for what seemed like an eternity, hardly daring to breathe, waiting for the Defenders of the Faith to run him down. He heard the heavy footsteps of men running by and shouts of confusion as they searched in vain for their quarry in the dense undergrowth.

Dillon began to move each of his limbs in turn, wiggling toes and fingers and checking for paralysis. Every muscle in his body protested, but at least nothing seemed broken. Soon, the man-made sounds faded gently into the distance, leaving only the distressed cries of birds protecting their young, and the hush of the wind in the high treetops.

Dillon lay back and smiled to himself. His head was pounding and there was a sizeable lump already forming on the side of his skull. His clothes were in tatters and the rest of his exposed skin was either bruised or bleeding. But despite all these woes, he was alive and he was safe. For now, nothing else mattered.

It didn't seem a good idea to shout for help at this point, but once he was quite sure there was no one around, he began to look for ways out of the hole. It was at least three metres deep and there was no way he could climb up the steep sides. Dillon tried forming the brushwood into a makeshift ladder but the branches were far too brittle and gave way as soon as he put any weight on them.

It reminded him of Winnie-the-Pooh's Heffalump trap, but who would construct such a thing in the middle of a Cornish wood? Perhaps someone of very little brain. He'd certainly met a few of those during his recent encounters. As he searched for alternative ways out, one particular group with an interest in excavation, sprang to mind.

It was beginning to get dark and there seemed to be nothing for it, but to wait for the morning and hope something or somebody turned up. Surely, Rachel or Sparks would come looking for him, but where would they look? Maybe they'd call out the mountain rescue. Did they have a mountain rescue in Cornwall? Perhaps the police, or the fire brigade. Someone would come, he was sure of it. Fairly sure, anyway. Dillon tried to make himself comfortable and settled down for a troubled night's sleep.

25 Blinded by the Light

When help arrived, it confirmed Dillon's suspicions. He felt rather like he was being pulled from a burning building by an arsonist.

'Hiya Kevin! Hello there, Althred, me old mate!' shouted Dillon, cheerily, from the bottom of the Heffalump trap. 'How's tricks? I hope you didn't mind me borrowing your little hide here, but it was just lying empty and I thought, well why not just throw yourself in headfirst!'

'Who is this that inhabits our excavations, Sir Roger?' bold Sir Kevin enquired of his second-in-command.

'Methinks it is the hermit of the woods. Who else would reside in such a holy place?'

'Cooee!' Dillon called out. 'It's your old friend, Dillon Wright. Remember me?'

'The hermit names himself Dillon,' said Sir Kevin. 'Tis a strange name for a holy man,'

'Mayhap he is a knight errant who has fallen from grace. You will recall that the noble Lancelot dwelt in the forest, in such tattered garb as this, when, for a while, his wits fled from him.'

'There's nothing wrong with my wits,' Dillon interrupted. 'Though I'm not so sure about yours.'

'Whatever his nature, I think him not evil.'

'Nor I,' agreed Sir Roger.

'Therefore, we should deliver him from the pit before we continue our quest.'

'Indeed, it is beholden upon us to affect his release, since our holy work has been the instrument of his discomfiture.'

'Would you give over wittering and get me out of this hole,' complained Dillon. 'It's cold in here and I haven't had any breakfast.'

On command from Sir Kevin, Althred fetched a rough, handwoven rope from the cart and lowered one end into the pit. It was instantly grabbed by Dillon, who nearly pulled the aged Althred over the edge in his eagerness to obtain his freedom.

A gesture from Sir Kevin brought some half a dozen sturdy Knights to the hole to lend their weight to the cause and he was hauled unceremoniously to the surface.

'Well, thanks, lads,' offered Dillon, grudgingly. 'I'm very pleased to see you, even if it was all your fault in the first place.'

'How came ye to yonder earthworks?' enquired Sir Kevin, with no hint of remorse in his voice.

'I was being chased by the bloody Defenders of the Faith, that's how.'

'We know of them. They are surely numbered amongst the foot soldiers of evil. Why did you not stand and fight?'

'I was unarmed and it was at least five against one.'

'Such odds would matter little to a true Knight,' said Sir Roger contemptuously. 'Why, brave Sir Geraint, of whom legends speak, faced ten armed men with only a staff of wood in his hands.'

'And what happened to him?' Dillon enquired, although he felt sure he already knew the answer.

'He died bravely.'

'Look, I'm not a Knight. I'm not a hermit. I'm a journalist.' Exasperation crept into his voice. 'Surely, you recognise me by now. We keep meeting and every time we go through this same palaver. Would it help if I wore a name tag?'

Sir Kevin peered at Dillon more closely and turned to his lieutenant.

'It seems to me that I should know this man. What say you, Sir Roger?'

'It is in my mind that such a man once travelled with us on the road to the town of Shrewsbury. It was during our last journey in this land if you would recall.'

'Three weeks ago,' Dillon reminded them.

'The passage of time means little to us,' explained Sir Kevin, putting on his mystical voice. 'Though the Earth may have stood still, we have not. We have travelled far from this place, further than your imagination could take you. We have seen things you could not comprehend and returned to fulfil our sacred quest.'

'Have you found it yet? The Holy Grail, and all that jazz?'

'You know of our quest? How can that be?'

'You told me. I wrote about it in the newspaper. We've got a circulation of about two million. Is that a problem?' asked Dillon, innocently.

'You have said he is not evil,' pointed out Sir Roger.

'That is true. It seems we must trust to his discretion,' replied Sir Kevin.

'You haven't understood a word I've said, have you?'

'Since last we met, our quest has met with some success,' Sir Kevin continued, oblivious to Dillon's rising impatience. 'We have not secured our goal, but the grail has been seen. It was in this very spot!'

'It was late one evening,' Sir Roger recalled, taking up the tale. 'We had been hard about our task all day and I was most fatigued. Yet, I felt some nameless power call me back from well-earned repose to this place of toil and sweat. There, an old hag sat shivering in the chill night air. I offered her my cloak and begged her to join my fellows at their warming fireside. She would have none of it but bade me follow her.

'I could not,' Sir Roger confessed. 'My feet were as lead and I could no more lift them from the ground than a tree could hitch up its roots and run.'

The other listeners, well-versed in the story, nodded in sympathy.

'She turned around then and lo! She was transformed into a beauteous and ethereal damsel. In her hand, she held a simple golden cup covered over with the finest muslin. It could have been none other than the vessel that caught Christ's blood as it flowed from his final mortal wound. The grail glowed with unearthly light, which filled the wood with a golden haze. The maiden then made to remove the cloth, and, as she peeled back the covering, I was instantly struck blind, deaf, and dumb, and fell to the earth in a swoon.'

'In such a state did we find him,' confirmed Sir Kevin.

'I have led an unchristian life,' admitted Sir Roger. 'Before I was made a Knight, I communed with women of easy virtue. I have been a gambler. I have been a drunkard. I have even fornicated in a Holy Temple.'

'Bully for you,' said Dillon.

'And though I have repented my sins, tenfold, I shall never be pure enough in spirit to hold the grail in my hands. Yet, there are those who ride with me who may dare this great deed.'

He stared devotedly at Sir Kevin, like a dog with his beloved master.

'We dug deep in vain hope,' continued Sir Kevin, 'that here lay a tomb or vault in which the sacred relic might be hid. But alas, it was not so. Even if such were the case, I fear, Sir Dillon, that your presence may have destroyed the sanctity of this place.'

'Thanks a million. I'm not that unclean, surely?' replied Dillon, both peeved at the suggestion and gratified by his sudden elevation to knighthood.

'It was foolish of us to return, though many begged for a chance to see that which we have sought these long years. Yet perhaps our journey is not in vain. Methinks we were fated to meet with you once more, Sir Dillon. A higher power guides our movements and we must perforce offer you what assistance we may. Wither would you go?'

'Well, I'm not sure,' Dillon admitted. 'I guess I ought to find my car and let Rachel know I'm OK. She might be worried. I hope so, anyway.'

'Such earthly matters are beyond our ken. We shall deliver you safely to one who can answer more closely to your needs. We depart this instant!'

Sir Kevin clapped his hands and the Knights scrambled for their mighty steeds, which had taken advantage of the opportunity to graze amongst the saplings ringing the clearing. Dillon trotted over to the wagon and climbed up next to the taciturn Althred, who offered him a toothless smile and cracked the whip.

This daylight ride past empty fields and deserted villages made no more sense to Dillon than his first journey with the Knights of the Wasteland. They rode hard throughout the day along rough tracks and narrow lanes. Despite Dillon's repeated suggestions that they drop him off at the nearest town, Sir Kevin drove his troop onwards until dusk began to fall.

They finally emerged from sparse woodland into a large brightly lit area lined with hundreds of cars. Dillon was not unduly surprised to see Ralph Coleman waiting for him. He was, however, astounded to find himself at Taunton Deane Services on the northbound M5 motorway.

26 The Knife

Coleman and a couple of his followers were perched on deckchairs in the middle of a tyre-gouged grass verge. Behind them, Dillon could see a bus full of the Wild Things. Boz was standing nearby holding a spanner and an oily gasket. He was wearing a warm winter coat in the chill evening air. Unfortunately, he had forgotten to complement this with any other garments and was currently busy displaying his wedding tackle to a Women's Institute coach party. As they drove past for the third time, Dillon noticed his beloved Land Rover with Rachel in the driver's seat, waving frantically.

The Knights' incongruous medieval procession picked its way through the maze of cars, ignoring the petty inconveniences of one-way signs and fast-food hoardings. Dillon stepped from the wagon to be greeted by a raucous reception party, with Sparks at its head.

'How's it going, mate?' slurred his old friend, breathing beery fumes into his face. 'Took the scenic route, did you?'

'I was in a bit of a hole,' admitted Dillon. 'I didn't fancy a long chat with the Defenders of the Faith, so I decided to go underground for a while.'

'Those lads were asking after you this morning, so we knew they hadn't grabbed you yet. I told them to piss off.'

Megan, standing at Sparks' shoulder by now, shook her head and mimicked the action of a running chicken. Sparks ignored her and carried on his theme.

'I reckon you ought to give that bloke, Hardwick, what for. Running off with your girlfriend. Not to mention him brainwashing people and being a bit of an arsehole as well. You should go and sort him out once and for all.' He did a little shadow-boxing dance, to illustrate his point.

Megan showed her solidarity with a clenched fist salute and nodded vigorously.

'Who rattled your cage?' Dillon wanted to know, looking over suspiciously at Coleman and Sheryl Keane who had their serious faces on. They stepped away from the group and walked up to him.

'The time has come for action, Dillon,' Coleman informed him. 'The Defenders of the Faith aim to subjugate this fair country and all its people. They will stop at nothing until we are all the vassals of a fundamentalist state. This cannot be. If Marcus Hardwick is allowed to continue unchallenged, his canker will spread into every aspect of our society. He is a tool of the evil Demiurge and a symptom of his insanity.'

'He's definitely a tool,' said Sparks, to no one in particular.

'I believe he could be the Antichrist,' announced Sheryl Keane.

'The way to counter such a threat is to meet it head-on,' Coleman added, finally. 'And by using your head, you may find a way to save many innocent lives.'

Suddenly, Dillon felt trapped. Things were happening over which he had no control. Again. Everyone wanted him to act, but he didn't know what to do or how to do it. The tide of events was sweeping him towards something unpleasant, probably a maelstrom, or at least some particularly sharp rocks. He took a deep breath and faced his motley counsellors.

'Look,' he began, 'the Defenders of the Faith, right, they're a real pain in the arse, OK? Dangerous even. But there can't be more than a hundred of them. I've seen them in action. They'd have trouble taking over Rockall, let alone the whole UK.'

Dillon warmed to his theme. 'Take Hardwick, right? He's not a real firebrand cult leader. He's just a second-rate politician on an ego trip. I think you're blowing this all out of proportion.'

'And Adolf Hitler was just a failed artist with a dumb little moustache,' countered Sheryl. 'Appearances can be deceptive. Right now, the Defenders of the Faith are weak. They are in their infancy and Hardwick is vulnerable. We gotta strike while the iron is cold.'

'I thought the Antichrist was supposed to be a great king; some tyrant that takes over the world.'

'That's a revelation,' Sheryl explained. 'A warning. It doesn't have to be that way if we can stop him in his tracks. If you can stop him.'

'Why me?' asked Dillon, not liking this particular turn in the conversation.

'It is the will of the Messengers of Light,' Coleman told him.

'It's fate, mate,' countered Sparks.

'I don't believe in fate,' Dillon protested, weakly.

'That is because you are the perfect fool. An unknowing pawn in a game of chance played by a mad deity,' said Coleman.

'Wrong place, wrong time,' said Sparks.

Dillon stared daggers at him, then looked to Rachel for support.

She had another angle on the situation. 'What about Charlotte? You can't just leave her in the hands of that maniac, Hardwick.'

'Why not? She seemed quite keen on jumping into his arms last time I was there.'

'Would you abandon me in the same way?' she asked, rather unfairly.

'Of course not. You're different.' Though when she stood there, hands on hips with that determined look on her face, she didn't look that different. Dillon couldn't remember ever winning an argument with Charlotte. He steeled himself to try his luck with Rachel. 'Anyway, she abandoned me, I didn't abandon her.'

'So that means you can wash your hands of her, does it?'

'Yes, it does. It's in the rules. The unwritten ones. They're illogical maybe, but that's not important. I know my rights. She left me, so I get the feelings of rejection, and she gets the guilt. It's no good trying to lay that one on me.'

Rachel looked uncomfortable, hugging herself and refusing to look Dillon in the eye. She was probably embarrassed to be involved with someone who could talk such bollocks, or maybe he had accidentally made a valid point for once.

'I'm not quite sure you've got the handle on this girlfriend-boyfriend thing,' he went on. 'You're supposed to be insanely jealous of all my ex-girlfriends and refuse to let me see them, on pain of more pain. You're not meant to encourage me to chase after them like a knight in shining armour.'

Sir Kevin looked up to see if he was required and then went back to polishing his throat guard.

'If you won't do it for Charlotte, what about the others?' pleaded Rachel. 'There are hundreds of people with the Defenders of the Faith now, including lots of women and children. Don't you remember Jonestown? And Waco?'

'They all joined of their own free will, didn't they? Am I supposed to drag them out, kicking and screaming? I don't know what it is you expect me to do.'

At a sign from Coleman, Sir Kevin finally stepped forward. He motioned to Althred, who fetched a plain wooden chest from out of the wagon. The panelling was battered and worn with the marks of great age. It was unadorned and unassuming, but every one of them turned to look at it as if it had a flashing neon light on it saying: Property of Pandora. Do Not Open.

With great reverence, Sir Kevin released the latch and lifted the lid. There was no lightning flash or dramatic music, simply the creak of hinges. Still, Dillon backed away, uncertain. The inside was packed with straw, which was gently moved aside by Sir Kevin to reveal a flat package wrapped in tattered linen, which he presented to Dillon with great ceremony.

There was a faint smell of sulphur, and the covering had an unpleasant oily texture to it. Gingerly, Dillon began to unwrap it, expecting something satanic. He slowly and reluctantly removed layer after layer until finally in his hand he held an ominous, black stone knife. 'No way! I don't want anything to do with this,' he exclaimed with genuine distress.

The knife was rough-hewn from some glassy, volcanic rock. It was no ornament. It was made for a purpose and had a brooding menace about it. There was some gunk stuck to it, which might well have been desiccated blood. To Dillon, it looked like the very definition of an offensive weapon.

'You want me to use this on Marcus Hardwick, don't you? You want me to go and kill someone in cold blood. Someone I don't even know well enough to hate properly. And all because of this stupid religious kick you're on. Well, I won't do it, so there!'

'If it please thee, allow the varlet to draw his weapon first,' suggested Sir Kevin, helpfully. 'Then thou mayest, with a clear conscience, prick him with this bodkin.'

'Is this before or after he shoots me in the head?'

'No doubt the devil of this plan is in its execution. Faced with dire circumstance, a cautious man might hide in the darkness and strike from behind. Such skulduggery would be true to the nature of this gift.'

Dillon examined the knife carefully. Turning it over in his hand and holding it up to the beam of the car park floodlights, it felt heavy. Yet, despite its appearance, it was warm and smooth to the touch. 'So what is this thing? Merlin's steak knife? I don't remember any mention of it in the legends.'

'It is not a legendary device,' countered Coleman, peering at the dark blade with a mixture of admiration and horror. 'It is as ancient as legends, I'm sure, but it was crafted by real people, using real tools and real stone.'

'Tis named Daron in the old tongue,' added Sir Kevin, 'A word that means Devil's Tooth if the scholars are to be believed, for it existed before the Knights of the Wasteland walked this Earth.'

'Darren!' exclaimed Dillon. You seriously expect me to storm a heavily armoured camp, fight off the guards, and murder a religious psychopath, armed only with a Stone Age letter-opener called Darren?'

'Nonetheless, it is your duty,' Sir Kevin's expression brooked no argument. 'It is no shame to die in battle against impossible odds.'

'It's not even sharp, this thing,' said Dillon running his hand down the blade. 'It would be like stabbing somebody with a butter knife.'

'If this weapon is truly blunt, then why do you bleed?'

Dillon glanced down at his hand and nearly dropped the knife in shock. Rivulets of blood were running down between his fingers and dribbling onto the tarmac. 'Bugger!' How did that happen?' He examined Daron more closely. Where his blood had congealed on the blade, the stone appeared indistinct; translucent, even. It was as if there was a knife within the knife, awakened by the taste of his flesh.

Dillon put such ridiculous thoughts out of his mind and concentrated on the practicalities. 'It's bloody lethal, is your Daron. Doesn't it have a sheath or something?'

Sir Kevin found a strip of leather and ran it across the blade. It was instantly rented in two as if it were tissue paper.

'Oh, I see. I shouldn't keep it in my back pocket, then. Perhaps we'd better put it back in the box.' With great care, he wrapped it back in the linen and returned it to its bed amongst the musty straw. 'I don't suppose you want it back, do you?'

Sir Kevin shook his head.

'Well, in that case, I'll stick it behind the jack in the Land Rover.'

'If you need passage, you only have to ask and we shall bear you wherever you wish to go.'

'Oh no, thanks all the same. If I am going anywhere, which I'm not, then it'll be under my own steam. I don't think I could take another magical mystery tour. You never know what's waiting at the other end.'

He carried the chest over to his car, then realised he was missing something important. Rachel came to his rescue, reaching into her bag and producing a set of keys. He took them gratefully, though, in truth, he could open the Land Rover with a lollipop stick, and he didn't have much use for his house keys anymore. She slipped a protective arm around his waist, to reassure him.

'I'm coming with you.'

Megan elbowed Sparks in the ribs.

'Yeah, sure,' Sparks said. 'We'll come along for the ride. Whatever.'

'But you don't even know where I'm going,' Dillon protested.

'I trust you, Dillon,' Rachel said. 'I'm sure you'll choose the right path.'

And there, Dillon realised, was the rub. He liked Rachel an awful lot. And he fancied her something rotten. He probably even loved her, though he hadn't yet said the 'L' word out loud. However, for all her good points, she was still a member of a cult that was permanently and collectively out to lunch.

It came down to who you trusted. The instincts he usually relied on, told him to turn tail and run. The main problem with this was that Rachel would never speak to him again. She might even take on the task herself. He would feel very guilty at her funeral and, though it might be marginally preferable to attending his own, there had to be another solution.

Strangely enough, the one person he did trust was Ralph Coleman. All right, he was as potty as the rest of them, but it was a special sort of lucid madness that allowed him to see things more clearly than many sane people. What had he said? "You may find a way to save many innocent lives." He didn't say, "Stab the bastard with the scary stone knife." There was more to this than met the eye.

At least his choices were becoming clear. He could run away and abandon all hope of sexual congress for the foreseeable future, he and Daron could attack the Defenders of the Faith and perish heroically in a hail of bullets, or he could figure a better way out of this mess.

27 Don't Come Around Here No More

A sizeable convoy set out on the road north. The Knights of the Wasteland quickly fell away from the main group, despite Althred's attempts to whip his Shire horses into racing Arabs. Still, their battle charge along the hard shoulder of the M5 was stirring stuff. It certainly turned a few heads on the busy motorway, including that of an AA repairman whose investigation of a seized water pump was interrupted by several tons of horse and armour cannoning into the back of his van. Mercifully, there were only superficial injuries to men and beasts. Dillon pitied anyone trying to get the Knights' insurance details.

Coleman, it seemed, was hitch-hiking. He used his considerable charm on a woman of indeterminate years with inch-thick make-up and an alarming nest of bright red hair. His efforts won him a lift in a convertible TVR Griffith, not to mention a once-in-a-lifetime offer of in-car entertainment, which he later claimed to have declined in the interests of road safety.

For a while, Coleman's new friend made a valiant attempt to stay behind the convoy. However, open-top motoring wasn't much fun when you're breathing in the fumes from a shagged-out Leyland Bus with a bodged head gasket. Eventually, she got bored of the whole thing, floored the accelerator, and passed them in an angry red flash.

The Wild Things followed the Land Rover up the motorway to Worcester and onto the road to Kidderminster. They drove past two wayside inns without incident, but the third advertised an entry in the Good Beer Guide and a dozen guest ales, and that, pretty much, was that. Dillon pondered the Wild Things' understanding of British drink-driving laws, but Rachel reassured him.

'Boz is completely teetotal. He's so high on his own personality that any other drug makes him throw up. He can projectile vomit a glass of Bacardi the length of a pool table. It's one of his party tricks.'

Dillon wondered how landlords felt about this and how Boz coped with the shock of parking his bare necessities on the bus's vinyl seats in midsummer. Left to his own devices, Dillon found himself inexorably steering the Land Rover and his friends towards the Wyre

Forest and the Defender of the Faith's HQ. His subconscious seemed to have made a decision, even if his conscious mind was still trying to think of a way to get out of this without losing face.

This time, it was no good driving up to the front door and bluffing their way in. Charlotte was bound to have his profile picture pinned to the noticeboard in every guard tower with 'SHOOT ON SIGHT' stamped across it in big letters. Fortunately, the forest was crisscrossed with a series of tracks and firebreaks. There was no way the Defenders of the Faith could watch every approach, so he drove round to the far side, away from the gates, and turned onto an overgrown and rutted forest road. The Land Rover, true to its rally heritage, struggled on through mud and bracken with only the occasional whine and wheelspin.

Finally, they came to a halt about a mile short of the Defenders of the Faith's base. Dillon parked the Land Rover under a magnificent copper beech and covered the car carefully with some loose branches, in the hope that it might go undetected by the Defenders and any particularly undiscerning joyriders. The four amateur commandos walked the remainder of the way, down leafy lanes and drunken deer tracks, until the outer fence became visible through the regimented rows of Scots pine. At a suitably discreet point, they cut through the trees and surveyed their first obstacle.

Surrounding the whole compound was a thick wire fence at least ten feet high, with further strands of barbed wire on top angled towards the outside world. To Dillon's inexpert eye, it looked as if this fence was designed to keep people in as much as to keep intruders out.

Megan pulled out a pair of wire cutters, purloined from the Land Rover's toolkit, but they had little or no impact on the strong steel mesh. After a few minutes of futile effort, she gave up and mimed a suggestion that they give Daron a try. Dillon, however, was unwilling to take the box out of his rucksack and disturb the knife's repose until necessary.

Eventually, it was left to Rachel to show them the way. She scrambled up the most climbable of the nearby trees and worked her way, hand over hand, along a convenient overhanging branch. Once it sagged sufficiently close to the ground, she dropped inelegantly into enemy territory like a disorientated sloth.

Sparks made to follow her, but Megan pulled him back.

'She's right,' Rachel called through the fence, pulling pine needles from her hair as she did so. 'Someone's got to stay behind in case anything happens.'

They agreed that two of them should return to the Land Rover and intercept Coleman and any of the reinforcements that made it as far as the Wyre Forest. Some of the cultists owned mobile phones, but modern means of communication were unlikely to be of much use for contacting the Knights of the Wasteland. Based on past experience, the forces of fate, or coincidence, would bring the various groups together eventually.

Dillon suggested they wait for Coleman to turn up and tell them their plan before they went any further. The others looked at him as if he were missing a few extra marbles.

'Should have thought of that before your girlfriend hopped over the wire,' pointed out Sparks. 'There's no getting back over this way. It's a fate accomplished or whatever. You better go and find out what God's Militia are up to.'

'Ralph doesn't do planning,' added Rachel, through the mesh. 'It's literally against his religion. He believes in spontaneity. Purity of purpose through action rather than procrastination, that's what he told me.'

'But what about the Land Rover? She's a bit tricky to start if you're not used to her,' suggested Dillon without much conviction.

Megan pulled out an oily rag and a can of WD-40 from her rucksack. Dillon bowed to the inevitable, girded up his jeans, and tentatively approached the tree. He clambered up the trunk with the steady rhythm of a sloth on a bad toe day, until he was dangling by his hands over the drop zone. On the count of three, he fell to earth like a paratrooper who had packed his laundry instead of his parachute and lay there winded, but otherwise unhurt, on the forest floor.

As his vision cleared and his lungs began to work again, Dillon experienced one of those 'What have I done?' moments. This looked like a one-way ticket to trouble. Sparks promised to send out for bolt croppers and an oxy-acetylene cutter as soon as practicable. Dillon took Daron out of his rucksack and tied it to his belt by the hilt, just in case he needed to dispose of it in a hurry. He waved a fond farewell to his friends outside the cage and followed Rachel into the heart of enemy territory.

It soon became clear that things had changed dramatically since his last visit. Firstly, there were outposts dotted throughout the woods. They were easy to spot despite the vegetation draped over the squat breeze-block hideouts. Once, Dillon thought he spied the muzzle of a gun protruding from a shadowy opening, but it could have been a trick of the light. He didn't hang around to find out. There was a certain menace about these featureless structures. Like abandoned wartime pillboxes, they reminded him uncomfortably of a time when the prospect of coming under enemy fire was very real.

Further in, a huge mound of earth barred their way. Trees lay uprooted all around and giant boulders were scattered about the site. Dillon at first suspected the Knights of the Wasteland, with their penchant for unauthorised excavation, but there was more of a methodical madness about this work. A defensive structure, maybe. A miniature version of Offa's Dyke to keep the barbarians from invading Hardwick's little kingdom.

The wall was a good six feet high in places, and every hundred yards or so were the beginnings of a guard tower or lookout post. It might have been very effective at repelling an attack from spear-wielding, Iron Age warriors. It might even have given the boys from DEFRA, with their clipboards and sharpened pencils, a bit of a headache. Dillon had to remind himself that he was living in the twenty-first century. A modern tank would drive straight through it. For all that, he didn't fancy sticking his head over the parapet just yet, in case there were other surprises beyond.

They trotted around the perimeter until they found a small landslide and scrambled up through the gap. Peering cautiously between loose piles of rock and earth, they saw the bright yellow livery of a mechanical digger, but no obvious signs of its operator, or any militia patrols.

Emboldened, they clambered across the construction site and entered the inner ward. Distant sounds of activity could be heard coming from the buildings that were now just visible through the trees. Dillon thought he recognised the farm and the shadowy outline of the main hall beyond.

The forest was eerily quiet. There was no background crackle of gunfire, no marching feet, no clamour of voices. It was as if halfway through a battle, everyone had decided to knock off for a tea break. As the group picked their way through the remaining pine trees, they came across another abandoned outpost with an archaic-looking machine gun bolted to the roof.

'It's Sunday!' exclaimed Rachel, suddenly. 'Maybe they're all in the chapel.'

'It's a good thing the forces of evil take a day off for the Sabbath,' Dillon reflected, sarcastically. 'Are you quite sure these people are worth worrying about? I can't imagine the Antichrist taking a half-day holiday.'

'You mustn't underestimate the Defenders of the Faith. I want to see what they're up to. You might be in for a nasty surprise.'

'Oh well,' Dillon sighed. 'No rest for the righteous.' He gave a resigned shrug and continued the cautious advance. To the rear of the old manor house, the woods had been allowed to grow almost up to the ivy-clad stone walls. To one side, in what must once have been the formal gardens, rhododendrons and other rapacious shrubs had taken control to the exclusion of the native plants.

It was relatively easy for the pair to crawl through this undergrowth without being observed until they were virtually at the edge of an open paved expanse that the Defenders of the Faith used as their parade ground.

Suddenly, Dillon hit the deck, pulling Rachel down with him. 'You were right,' he hissed. 'About the nasty surprise, I mean.'

'I don't understand,' complained Rachel, spitting out a mouthful of leaf mould and its many-legged inhabitants.

Dillon pointed across the clearing. The woman standing by the parade ground in smart military attire, complete with a camouflage cap and shiny calf-length boots, was unmistakably Charlotte.

28 Suspicious Minds

Charlotte turned in their direction, giving Rachel a chance to confirm Dillon's sighting. She appeared very animated, waving her arms around impatiently, and giving the impression that she was directing traffic on Hyde Park Corner. 'No, not that way, you fool!'

The two watchers could hear her admonishing a young recruit who was laden down with boxes of provisions.

'We need more rations for C Block. Every block must be self-sufficient. I've told you often enough. I'd hate to have to send you out for more tea bags when we're under mortar attack.'

Dillon, who had some experience of Charlotte in this sort of mood, wasn't so sure. It seemed like just the sort of thing that she would enjoy doing. Rachel, on the other hand, was watching her with obvious astonishment and not a little admiration.

'I'm not surprised you were scared of her,' she breathed in his ear after Charlotte had given a muscle-bound grunt a particularly scathing piece of her mind.

'I was never scared of her. I just didn't want to hurt her feelings.'

'And another thing.' Charlotte's piercing voice came drifting across the makeshift parade ground like a falsetto sergeant major. 'How many times have I told you about chewing gum when you're on duty? It's slovenly and unhygienic, and I simply won't tolerate it. Spit it out, this instant.'

Dillon cringed in reflected embarrassment. This was certainly a turnaround. There was no sign of the unnaturally subservient Charlotte he'd witnessed at Goonhilly. Here she was in her element.

'If I'd wanted .22 calibre, I would have asked for it, now wouldn't I?'

A group of burly infantrymen, dragging a heavily laden trolley, hung their heads in collective shame.

'I gave all the small-bore weapons to the cadets. What were you going to do with this lot? Throw it at the enemy?'

The militiamen slunk away in disgrace, to be replaced immediately by another group under bombardment from her volleys of displeasure.

Charlotte was doing all the practical things the Faithful hierarchy considered beneath them, like distributing the food and organising the toilet-cleaning rota. She seemed to be having more success with the Defenders of the Faith than she'd had in Lincoln where there were only two people on the rota and one of them claimed to be allergic to household detergents. It seemed to him that Charlotte had strayed unwittingly into a power vacuum and was rapidly filling it with her considerable presence.

'Go on, Dillon. She's on her own now.' Rachel shoved him unceremoniously out of the shrubbery and waved him onwards.

Dillon stood there for a moment, blinking in the light and picking dead vegetation out of his shirt. Checking that the coast was clear, he took a deep breath and marched swiftly across the paving stones to where Charlotte stood, hands on hips, glowering at the world. He had no real idea of what he was going to say to her, but something told him she might be useful to their cause. He realised he was taking a big chance and without Rachel's encouragement, it was unlikely he would have plucked up the courage to approach her. It was almost worth the risk just to see the expression on Charlotte's face. She looked like someone who'd run into a recently interred relative in the supermarket. He was about to offer up something witty like, "Fancy meeting you here", or "Shagged any good megalomaniacs lately?" when something in her eyes made him look round.

Away to Dillon's right, Marcus Hardwick was emerging from the doorway, hymn book in hand. Fortunately, Hardwick's gaze was fixed on Charlotte. Dillon dived for cover and prayed that no one had spotted him. Crouching behind a low wall, he fully expected his ex-girlfriend to raise the alarm, but she seemed to be at a loss to know what to do. Charlotte looked from Dillon's hiding place to Hardwick's advancing form and back again. Finally, she gave Dillon an angry nod, and as he ducked his head below the brickwork, she turned to face her leader.

'Hello, Marcus.' As she greeted him, she seemed to lose her air of authority. Her shoulders slumped and she lowered her eyes deferentially.

'Charlotte! What are you doing out here? Why weren't you at prayer?' Hardwick's tone was that of an exasperated parent scolding an errant child.

'There was so much to do, Marcus. Everything's so disorganised still.'

'Are you criticising me, Charlotte?'

'Of course not!'

'Have you forgotten your duty?'

'No Marcus, I haven't. It's just…'

'Sometimes, I'm just not sure about you, Charlotte. You neglect your prayers, and you ignore the Sabbath. What am I to think? You disobey me; you countermand my orders; you make me look foolish in front of my men. Are you ambitious, Charlotte? Do you think that somehow you could manage better without me?'

'No, never, Marcus. You're the most important thing in my life. Truly you are. Everyone here feels that way. Until you came along, I had no purpose. I'm prepared to do anything for you, but I don't know what you want from me.'

'All I require is that you serve me to the utmost of your abilities, without questioning my decisions, without undermining my authority. Is that too much to ask?'

'No, Marcus,' she assented. 'But is that all you want: just another servant? At first, I thought I could be your wife, or girlfriend, or something. But you explained all that, and I now understand I was expecting too much. I know you have to live by different rules to ordinary men. I thought I could at least fight for you, but you don't approve of women going to war, and anyway, I don't think I'm really cut out for battle. I'm too kind-hearted I suppose.'

There was a derisory snort from behind the wall, but fortunately, Hardwick was too far away to hear it.

Charlotte continued her speech unabashed. 'I'm trying to do something useful. I'm a good organiser, truly I am. I'm trying to prepare our stronghold against the coming forces of evil. Don't you approve, Marcus?'

Hardwick smiled one of his ingratiating little smiles, and patted Charlotte on the back, condescendingly. She tried to smile back, but to Dillon, it looked more like a grimace.

'I'm sure you mean well, Charlotte,' Hardwick assured her in his most smarmy tones. 'It must be difficult for a woman in these troubled times. You must learn to support your menfolk, not try to outdo them. A little humility and faith in your purpose is what's required. Go and get yourself into the chapel and pray for these things and for our deliverance from evil.'

'But...' Charlotte looked around and held up her hands in frustration.

'Don't worry your sweet little head now. I'll send one of the chaps along shortly to sort out your little logistical problems.'

Hardwick led her off meekly to the long east wing of the manor. Almost immediately, a squad of militiamen in a pan-European jumble of uniforms ran onto the scene carrying a dozen ammunition boxes. They dropped their burden and looked around in puzzlement. An argument ensued with lots of pointing and waving, before they finally marched off, empty-handed, back in the direction they had come.

Once she was sure the coast was clear, Rachel scurried across the courtyard, tapped Dillon on the shoulder, and led him back into the woods once more. When they were safely out of earshot of the house, she stopped and gathered her thoughts. 'Well, she didn't give you away. That's a good sign at least.'

'Maybe she was worried about what her new boyfriend might think. Somehow, I don't believe Charlotte sees me as a threat to the Defenders of the Faith,' Dillon admitted.

'How do we get you alone with her again?'

'I think she was trying to tell me to come back later, but it doesn't sound like a good idea to me.'

'If we keep our eyes on the parade ground, we might spot her coming.'

'It's probably a trap.'

Rachel ignored him. She was already thinking ahead. 'First, we need to explore this place. Check out the weak spots. If Charlotte won't help you, we'll need a fallback plan.'

'How about we fall back now and get some food,' Dillon suggested. 'I'm always a lot braver on a full stomach.'

'This way!' Rachel insisted, and melted into the trees like a forest deer, skipping over fallen branches with surprising athleticism. Dillon trundled after her, every second step accompanied by the cracking of twigs or the alarm cries of nesting birds.

It was immediately obvious that the Defenders of the Faith were preparing for war. Every man Dillon and Rachel saw was armed to the teeth. They watched as two adolescent boys marched self-consciously across the quadrangle with very real-looking rifles presented on their shoulders.

Everywhere were stocks of ammunition, grenades, and mortars. How they managed to get such a collection of, presumably illegal, arms beggared belief. At every defensible point, there was a pile of sandbags and at least some kind of weaponry, if only a shotgun or a crossbow. The old man carrying this latter weapon would be in his element if the Knights of the Wasteland ever took it into their heads to storm the place. Otherwise, he looked suspiciously like cannon fodder, a useful victim should the tabloid press need some quick shock-horror photos.

The Defenders of the Faith were well prepared, provided the enemy agreed to play fair. Personally, Dillon could see the advantages of a large bomb being dropped from somewhere in the stratosphere. Provided he was nowhere near the target zone, of course. He kept this thought to himself. Rachel still saw this as a mercy mission, to save these poor innocent souls from Marcus Hardwick's evil influence. Dillon wasn't sure he cared what happened to this miserable lot, so long as he was far, far away.

Right now, Dillon was feeling like he was under the influence of every cult in Britain, except Hardwick's mob. Even if he really was on the side of truth and justice, that wasn't much comfort. So long as he was in their camp, might was well and truly on the side of the Defenders of the Faith.

Of the Brainwasher-in-Chief, there was no sign. Dillon and Rachel managed to get close enough to the house, in places, to peek inside, but all they saw were a group of women preparing a meal, and some children playing British Bulldog in the old library. Dillon's stomach rumbled at the sight and smell of food, and he cursed their lack of foresight. Fancy coming on a commando raid, he thought, with only a stone knife and no packed lunch.

Rachel scurried up to an open window and reached around to remove a tray of jam tarts left cooling by the sill. Dillon couldn't bear to watch. There were a dozen women within, busying themselves in the kitchen only a few feet from her outstretched hand, but such was the commotion and confusion inside that she managed to slip away into the bushes unnoticed.

Dillon followed her, making unconvincing barking noises, to point the paw of blame on one of the hungry strays that staked out the kitchen door.

The jam tarts were delicious. Perhaps some protein would have been better for long-term survival, but sweet sticky food was just the thing to perk up their spirits. Somehow, illicit snacks always tasted nicer, and if they were actually stolen then so much the better.

Suitably refreshed, they continued their recce of the compound. Once or twice, they were nearly spotted by the patrols. Either the men were too preoccupied with their duties, or they just assumed that a couple of nutters crawling around in the woods must perforce be members of the Faithful.

Charlotte didn't reappear until the sun was setting behind the distant hills. When she finally stepped out onto the cold flagstone, she looked extremely nervous. She walked quickly across the exposed area and called out softly into the tangled vegetation beyond. 'Dilly? Are you there? We need to talk.'

At first, Dillon made no reply. Suddenly, this didn't seem like such a clever idea. Rachel sensed his hesitation and glared at him. Eventually, and with some reluctance, he crawled out of the bushes on Charlotte's right and made himself known.

Charlotte walked over to meet him and stood for a while as if wondering where to begin. She pulled a sprig of heather out of his hair and brushed the leaves from his shirt.

'I hope you understand that this is all for the best. I'm doing it for you. It's your only hope for salvation, Dilly, don't you see?' She leant forward, let her cheek brush his, and then gently kissed him.

A bewildered expression crossed his face, turning quickly to anger, as she stepped back, and two militiamen leapt from the shadows. In the time it took to say, 'I told you so', they had wrestled him to the ground and bound him tight.

For good measure, one of the thugs banged his head into the paved stone ground and Dillon slumped into unconsciousness. Then, all was silent, save for the sound of a heavy burden scraping across the cold stone slabs. Two women, on opposite sides of the square, each hidden by their own tract of gloom, stifled their tears and prepared for action.

29 Dazed and Confused

It was a tough night for all concerned. Nessun Dorma you might say.

A bandaged and semi-conscious Dillon lay curled up in a foetal ball on the floor of a dark, dank cellar under the stable block. He was vaguely aware of the clop of horses' hooves above, and Charlotte pacing the floor nearby. She was muttering and wringing her hands in her best Lady Macbeth style, clearly lost in her own private purgatory.

Once the goons had left, she had tried to do her best by Dillon. She washed the blood from his matted hair and dressed the wound. He was chained by one hand to an old water pipe, but she managed to manhandle him into the recovery position and stuff a comfy pillow under his head. Then, as a nice touch, she left him a glass of carbonated mineral water and two aspirin.

Dillon tried to talk to her, but he was having difficulty making coherent sentences. In any case, she clearly had no good answers. She kept glancing towards the cellar door, where a young, gun-toting guard was slouched. Eventually, she slunk away into the night with an apologetic hand gesture. It seemed that she had no wish to stick around and explain to her Faithful comrades exactly why she was comforting the enemy.

Dillon appreciated her thoughtfulness, but he could have used something a little stronger to drink, not to mention a large bucket. Instead, he tried to deposit the regurgitated jam tart melange as close to the door as his chain would allow, in the hope that someone would tread in it.

He grabbed the pillow and retreated to the pipework feeling a little better, although it didn't have the same cathartic effect of a good hangover honk. His head was still pounding, his vision was blurred, and his stomach was still engaged in rhythmic gymnastics. He looked forward to making somebody pay for this, just as soon as he found a way to break these chains, smash down the door, and get his hands on some heavy-duty weaponry.

Stranded outside the barracks, Rachel's first thought was to get help. She reached for her phone, but it was gone. She made a quick search of the quadrangle and, although no one seemed to be looking for her, there were too many people nearby for her to stay put for long. Eventually, Rachel began retreating to the perimeter to find Megan and Sparks.

It was easy enough to retrace her steps back through the undergrowth, but now the dyke and most of the outposts were manned. Even though the fortifications were not designed to counter intruders from within, it was still a difficult task to pass through unobserved.

Once out of the defensive ring, she was prey to militia patrols and she arrived at their point of entry in a state of constant panic. Nor was that the end of her troubles. The fence showed signs of damage but had been repaired and reinforced. Of Sparks and Megan, there was no sign. With no trees on this side and no way of climbing back over the fence, there was nothing for it, but to find a safe place to hole up for the night and hope that a new day would improve her desperate situation.

The only safe place available turned out to be a dried-up stream overgrown with bracken and brambles. It was an ideal spot in many ways, except that it wasn't completely dry and it smelt like a badger's bidet. Rachel tried to make herself comfortable, but it simply wasn't possible. Even in the height of summer, Britain's night-time temperatures were rarely high enough for a lightly clad woman in a damp ditch to keep warm. On this particular night, Rachel had too much on her mind for sleep to be more than a remote prospect.

Shortly after dawn, she rubbed her numb limbs into action, and stealthily approached the fence. She tried her best owl impersonation on the deserted forest. It sounded more like a dodgy didgeridoo, but eventually, it achieved the desired response. There was a rustling in the trees, and two unlikely forest dwellers climbed down from their eyrie.

'I can't believe I wanted to live in a tree house when I was a kid,' Sparks remarked, as he stretched his creaking joints. 'If I never see another tree in my whole life, it'll be too bloody soon.'

Megan ran up to the fence and shook the wire in agitation.

'They took Dillon. It was my fault,' Rachel confessed. 'They hurt him. He looked pretty bad, and heaven knows what they might do to him when they find the knife. I don't know what to do, Meg. Did you find Sheryl or Ralph? We need help here, quick.'

Megan pushed an arm through the mesh to comfort her friend who was on the verge of tears. She turned to Sparks for support. He shook his head.

'Yeah, we found them all right,' he said. 'They're on their way here, but I'm not sure what they can do. Sorry, but it's no good fannying about now. It's past being a job for our barmy army. We need to call the police.'

Despite the importance of their mission and all of Sheryl's warnings, Rachel reluctantly agreed with Sparks. Right now, they needed all the help they could get. Megan smiled reassuringly and waved her away. They clasped hands briefly. Rachel took a deep breath and turned around with a renewed sense of purpose. She was still exhausted, cold, and hungry, but she knew what had to be done, and strode purposefully away through the woodland.

Beyond the dried-up stream, there was a clearing guarded by a thoughtlessly conspicuous militia outpost. As Rachel stepped out of the trees, two young militiamen with identical tennis-ball haircuts jumped up with surprise. They waved their guns at her and shouted out a variety of conflicting orders, which she chose to ignore. Smiling disconcertingly, Rachel approached, arms outstretched in a gesture of supplication and gave herself up.

The militiamen couldn't decide what to do with her, but they knew enough to make sure it wasn't their problem for long. They bound Rachel's hands behind her back and drew lots for who would have the honour of bringing in the prisoner. With much prodding and swearing, Rachel was unceremoniously steered through the forest.

Meanwhile, on the safer side of the fence, Sparks was phoning for help, but in his current agitated state of mind, he was making even less sense than normal.

'Er, well, police, I think.' There was a brief silence. 'Yeah, my name is Mark Munro. What? No, I'm in a forest, but I'm not right sure where. Outside that God's Militia place. That bastard Marcus Hardwick has taken my mate hostage. Yeah, that's right, kidnapped. I was hoping you'd come down here and give him what for. Yeah, great. Look out for a knackered Land Rover, parked near a substation.'

He ended the call and breathed a sigh of relief. 'I hate using the phone, don't you?' He reconsidered this remark. 'Well, you're not missing anything.'

Megan held out her hands and looked at him in a questioning fashion.

'They said to head towards the main road and they'll be along right away. I wasn't sure if they'd believe me, but they didn't even ask if I was a hoaxer or anything. You can always rely on the police, that's what me mam used to say, until that patrol car ran over our dog.'

Megan let Sparks babble away to himself as she steered him back to the car. They bumped and scraped their way back to the road once more and drove towards the lane leading down to the Defenders of the Faith's base. Parking by an old, deserted gatehouse, they perched on the bonnet to keep a lookout for help arriving. They didn't have long to wait.

When they saw the first police car approaching at speed, Sparks assumed it was alone, but it was immediately followed by another, and another until it began to look like the Blues Brothers were in town. Sparks was impressed. Perhaps his telephone manner was more effective than he thought. Two NCA officers wearing flak jackets, and armed to the teeth, stepped out of the lead car and began questioning Megan. She referred them on to Sparks, who was beginning to look a little shell-shocked.

'Oh yeah, they're definitely armed. They've got bazookas and tanks and tons of other stuff, I shouldn't wonder,' he suggested, in response to the urgent questions flying at him from all sides. 'There are hundreds of 'em and they're all psychos. There's women and children in there, though, and two of our friends, so you can't just go shooting the place up.'

'We have a hostage situation,' Dillon's old acquaintance, DS Fiskerton, barked into his radio. 'Get the Chief Super' here. I want army backup and air cover, and I want it now!'

By the eager look on the faces of the NCA squad, they had been waiting for this for quite some time.

'Ever since this lot gave the ministry boys a hard time, there's been trouble brewing,' DS Fiskerton explained. 'I don't like religious cranks and I specially don't like them on my manor. Well, this time they've gone too far. You've done us a real favour, son. With any luck, we can flush them out and finish them off this time.'

Sparks wasn't sure he liked the sound of this. He was determined to stick around and help with the negotiations. He was sure it was what Dillon would have wanted.

Officers began to spread out and take up positions around the perimeter, but the bulk of the force headed slowly for the main entrance. More cars and vans were arriving all the time. It was an impressive cavalcade that approached the new gatehouse fortifications.

It certainly impressed the half-dozen or so guards who were loitering around the entrance. Most panicked and ran for the barricades, but one hothead turned and opened fire on one of the oncoming patrol cars, shooting randomly from the hip with his shotgun, just like in the movies. The windscreen shattered and the car swerved dramatically into a decrepit beech tree, covering the scene with a shower of copper and crimson leaves.

Police marksmen spilt out of vehicles on all sides and returned fire. The guard was hit at least three times in as many seconds and collapsed to the ground. Answering shots came flaring out of the rough wooden gatehouse to his left, randomly peppering the forest and the police.

Immediately there was mayhem. Sparks and Megan dived for cover, as everyone with a weapon to hand opened fire on the gatehouse. Two of the guards made a run for it, weaving and ducking as they headed deeper into the compound. A stray bullet struck one of them and he spun around cursing before staggering onto the sanctuary of the woods.

Sparks noticed that the man bore a passing resemblance to Charlotte, though these chinless wonders looked pretty much alike to him. Gradually, he became aware of an authoritative voice shouting above the din. It was a while before everyone heard the command to cease fire. A few parting shots rang out across the clearing, and then, finally, there was silence.

A small group of black-clad marksmen made their way towards the barricades, covering each other as they went. They shouted demands to those inside the buildings as they crouched close to the wall. At first, there was no reply, and then one man emerged, hands on head, looking dazed and shocked, but otherwise unhurt. He exchanged a few words with a couple of the police officers who secured his hands behind his back and led him away. The rest entered the gatehouse cautiously but soon re-emerged to signal the all-clear.

An ambulance was ushered through the jam of vehicles, soon to be followed by two more. Paramedics rushed across the clearing. Three casualties were carried from the building. At least one of them looked in a bad way.

Already, a couple of armoured police riot vehicles had arrived on the scene, and efforts were being made to breach the outer defences. Within the compound, figures in camouflage dress could be seen lurking amongst the trees, but they made no immediate effort to repel the invaders.

'Hardwick is not going to like this much,' Sparks suggested, with characteristic understatement. 'What if he decides to take it out on Dillon?'

Megan slipped her arm around Sparks, but he was preoccupied with the spiked steel fence surrounding the substation. He pulled Megan towards the padlocked gate and began rattling the lock. After a few vigorous shakes, one of the rusting hinges gave way and the whole gate swung inwards, taking Sparks and Megan with it. They came to rest next to the 'Danger of Death' sign, with Sparks' head resting dangerously close to a transformer.

'Phew! That was close.' He wiped his brow and was about to lean back on some high-voltage cabling when Megan grabbed hold of his arm and pulled him clear. Instead of climbing back to safety, Sparks turned his attention to the remains of the gate.

'Dillon reckoned they had their own power plant inside. Well, that's all very well and good, but I bet they're still connected to the national grid. And you know what that means?'

It seemed that Megan didn't.

'Unless they've got some fancy protection relays, then any problems out here are going to cause some major problems for their old turbine generator.'

Sparks managed to free a length of steel angle from the gate and waved it next to the outgoing cables. Megan was hopping about, desperately trying to stop him.

'I wonder what would happen if I lobbed this into the…'

There was an almighty flash, which catapulted Megan and Sparks clean over the wreckage of the gate. It must have been a very loud bang. When Sparks asked Megan if she was OK, he couldn't hear his own voice over the deafening ringing in his ears.

Megan appeared to be uninjured, but the words she was mouthing at him made Sparks wish she had suffered a minor concussion at least. He was considering hiding back in the substation when something struck him.

'Hey look! I did it. It's a blackout. All the security lights have gone out and that CCTV camera is dead. Dillon's going to be so grateful.

30 Dancing in the Dark

When the lights went out in his makeshift prison cell, Dillon wondered what it meant. Nothing good, he could be sure of that. There was a small barred and shuttered window high up in the wall, which did not let in much light or even a glimpse of what was going on outside. The glass had broken in one corner inviting a cold draught into the already chilly surroundings.

He heard the not-so-distant sound of gunfire, followed by a great deal of confused shouting and running about. The place was in uproar. When, a short while later, the cellar door opened and two militia thugs came in, he feared the worst. One of them aimed a kick in his direction, but otherwise, they seemed too preoccupied with their new charge.

Rachel was looking rather more bedraggled than when they parted. Bits of bracken and heather were stuck in her hair, and her clothes were stained with mud, but she seemed otherwise unharmed.

'Aren't you pleased to see me?' she said.

He was, but being glad to see her also filled him with an overwhelming sense of guilt.

'Sure, I was just hoping you'd bring the cavalry with you.'

'Don't worry,' reassured Rachel, 'they're on their way. I think I heard a bugle call just then.'

'Shut up!' shouted one of the guards, a short squat man with no discernible neck and more hair in his ears than on his head. He raised a hand as if to strike Rachel. She gave him such a look of contempt that he stepped back hurriedly and reached for his weapon, oblivious to the fact that he was now standing in a pool of congealed vomit. He pulled out a pair of handcuffs and proceeded to manacle Rachel to an iron grate. She offered no immediate resistance and emboldened, the guard began an overly intimate search for concealed weapons.

'Anything to declare, darling?' he sneered, running his hands over her thighs. Rachel smiled sweetly and then spat in his eye.

Dillon tensed, ready to leap ineffectually to her aid. His hand found the ancient stone knife, still inexplicably hanging from his belt. He eased it from its improvised scabbard, and held it behind his back, ready for a quick throw. Of course, he'd never actually thrown a knife before, but how difficult could it be? After all, he was the reigning runner-up in The Queen in the Wall Novelty Darts Trophy. He eyed up his target and decided to aim for the guard's bulging stomach. He had a feeling Daron's rough edges would make a nasty mess wherever it landed.

The guard grabbed a handful of Rachel's hair and pulled her head back until she grimaced with pain. 'I can wipe that smile off your face any time, darling. Any time. Maybe I'll ask Marcus if I can keep you as a pet. How would you like that?'

The second guard, who could have been his twin brother, appeared around the cellar door. 'Oi, Nonser! Leave it out. There's a war on. You wanna explain how you missed the fight 'cos you were feeling some bird's arse?'

'Bloody hell! It's worse than being back in the army.' He backed out, leering nastily. 'Don't go away now, darling. I'll be back soon.'

The door slammed with a solid thud, followed shortly by the sound of heavy bolts shooting into place.

In the darkness, Dillon slumped against the rough stone wall. It was all too much. He was well known as a man of inaction. A slob, even. Nobody in their right mind would rely on him to sort out this mess. There was nothing he could do but sit back and hope that something or someone would turn up. He took Daron, wrapped it back in the cloth, and wedged it carefully behind the pipework.

'Are you OK?' Rachel's voice was full of concern.

'Not bad, considering. You?'

'Relieved. I thought you were badly hurt; dead, even. I didn't know what to do.'

'You could start by kicking that bastard in the bollocks next time he shows up.'

'Then what?' Rachel wanted to know.

'I hit him over the head, you grab the keys, and we run for it.'

'It's a nice plan. Do you think it will work?'

'No.'

'So, what do we do instead?'

Dillon shuffled uncomfortably. 'Maybe we should wait for the police to come and arrest them all. Then we could go round and kick a whole bunch of bollocks, two at a time.'

'What about Charlotte?'

'I'll leave that one up to you. I expect you understand the female anatomy better. Anywhere that really hurts will do. I've been chained to the wall by a bunch of psychopaths. My head feels like I've spent a week drinking scrumpy snakebite and it's all her fault.'

'You know that's not true, Dillon. Perhaps she didn't have any other choice. She's as much a victim as you are. There's no point being angry with her. Life's too short.'

'I know. Life is short and then you die. All the cultists I've met are obsessed with death. Though maybe your lot cope with it a bit better than most. That doesn't mean you have any more of a grip on the truth than the rest of them.'

'Maybe not but being angry or miserable won't change anything. I can't pretend I know when we are going to die or what happens afterwards. But I believe there's a place prepared for all of us. Even angry atheists.'

Dillon had more practical things to worry about. They were being held captive and there was the sound of gunfire nearby. That was a scenario that hardly ever ended well for the hostages. He didn't want to die, even if there was a nice afterlife arranged for him somewhere. There had to be a way of getting out of here alive, but he couldn't see it. He shook his head sadly and leant back against the cold stone wall.

31 Save Me

It was a long while before anyone came to interrupt Dillon and Rachel's philosophical debate. Every so often, there would be a burst of gunfire and then silence would reign. In between, was the sound of marching feet and shouted orders as soldiers were deployed to their defensive positions.

The two prisoners decided that they had been forgotten in the heat of battle. They were in no hurry to see anyone, especially not Marcus Hardwick and his friends. Eventually, a woman arrived, bringing food on a tray. The distinctive aroma of Italian cuisine preceded her into the cellar. Dillon's stomach began gurgling loudly and persistently. She was the most miserable-looking woman that he had seen in a long while. Rachel tried her best to engage her in conversation, but witty remarks about dying on an empty stomach didn't raise a smile. Still, they were pleased to see her; or rather, they were pleased to see the food. It seemed like an age since their last meal and Dillon had returned that one with interest.

The Defenders of the Faith were careful enough not to supply them with any sharp implements. It proved exceedingly difficult to eat Spaghetti Bolognese with a plastic spoon, and one hand chained to the wall. Rachel was using the fingers of her free hand, with little success. After a few experiments, Dillon settled on the technique of kneeling with his nose almost touching the plate and hoovering up the spaghetti a strand at a time. This was slightly more successful, but the sounds he was making were truly revolting.

This was the pathetic scene that greeted Marcus Hardwick, as he marched imperiously into the cellar, followed at a respectful distance by Charlotte and a couple of minders. Hardwick was armed to his armpits with an unpleasant array of handguns and sharp objects. Charlotte had added a dash of camouflage make-up to her khaki outfit. Dillon was pleased to note that no one had thought of giving them matching his-and-hers firearms.

Hardwick swept the room with a disdainful glance, wearing one of his most superior sneers. Normally, Dillon would have tried to wipe the smirk off his face, but he was feeling about as low as he could get. If Hardwick had told him to sit up and beg at that point, he might have considered it.

Hardwick strode across the room, planted his foot firmly in the pile of puke and went skating across the room in a wild flurry of arms and legs before tumbling to the ground. He lay there for a while, kicking his legs in the air like an upturned tortoise. This lifted Dillon's mood no end.

Hardwick's minders rushed forward to help, but he brushed them away, struggled to his feet, and stood there, hands on hips, glowering at the world. Small pieces of diced vegetable clung to his freshly laundered uniform, and his shiny peaked cap lay crushed in the detritus of Dillon's last meal. Dillon tried not to laugh, he really did, but the look on Hardwick's face was too much. A snort of laughter erupted from somewhere deep inside. It made him gasp for breath and his chest shook until it hurt.

He wiped the tears from his eyes, just in time to see Hardwick aiming a savage kick at his already battered head. Dillon ducked and there was a loud clank as Hardwick's foot struck the pipework. The great leader hopped around the room cursing and taking the Lord's name in vain.

Dillon cowered in the corner. He wasn't sure if he'd get away with a good beating or if they would take him out and shoot him this time. Charlotte placed herself squarely between Hardwick's boot and Dillon's foetal form. It was hardly divine intervention, but Dillon was prepared to recommend her for beatification, just for trying.

'He's not worth it, Marcus, you've said it yourself. People like him are worthless scum, nothing more.'

Dillon nodded vigorously and did his best to look like worthless scum. It wasn't hard.

'His presence defiles our sanctuary. Why don't you send him back where he came from? Surely, God will punish him wherever he hides himself.'

Hardwick appeared not to have heard. He prodded Dillon with the soiled toe of his boot. 'Shall I have you executed, heretic? We are all prepared to die. Are you?'

Dillon said nothing.

'A place is reserved in Heaven for those who perish combating evil. The Day of Judgement is nigh. On that day, I shall stand by the right hand of the Lord as he reads from the great book the names of those to be saved and those who are damned for all eternity. I do not doubt that you will be cast down into the fiery pits of Hell. Are you not afraid?'

'I'm scared shitless,' admitted Dillon, from the depths of his huddle. 'But I really wouldn't kill me if I were you. If you shoot a hostage, you'll have the SAS parachuting in before you can say Bravo Two Zero.'

Charlotte glanced across at him as if something he said had worried her. Dillon couldn't believe it was his threats; they were pretty idle ones, after all. For all he knew, the entire SAS regiment could be out on a pub crawl in Hereford. Hardwick grabbed him by the throat and pulled him to his feet, nearly dislocating his shoulder as he reached the end of his short leash.

'I am not afraid of the SAS. I am not afraid of the police or the army or any earthly force.' His eyes were blazing and there was spittle on his lips as he barked the words in Dillon's face. 'I am God's Chosen One, don't you understand? The Chosen One. Nothing can harm me. If I were to charge those guns, the bullets would pass me by. I am protected by the Shield of God. My troops may fear death, but I do not!'

'I meant your troops, of course,' Dillon blustered. 'Obviously, nothing worries you, being immortal and all that, but what about your followers? Charlotte and Jeremy and all the rest of them out there.'

'Their fears are not important. They are in the hands of God. This is Judgement Day, don't you understand? Whether they live or die now is of no significance.'

Hardwick was starting to look like a proper fanatic. He presumably saw visions of himself clothed in heavenly glory and not some reporter's regurgitated breakfast.

Charlotte was edging out of the door. She didn't look like a woman who considered her life to be insignificant. As Hardwick continued ranting, Dillon wondered what she would do. It was not a comfortable feeling to be relying on his delusional ex-girlfriend for assistance in his hour of need. Still, it could have been worse. He could have been relying on Sparks to be their saviour.

Eventually, Hardwick ran out of messianic vitriol, and marched back out through the cellar door, accompanied by his henchmen. Some minutes later, Dillon heard the crunching of nearby footsteps in the courtyard above, and then the shutters to the cellar window were thrown open. He wasn't sure if this was meant as some obscure act of kindness, or just that he would get a better view of Armageddon when it arrived. Whatever the motive, Dillon was thankful for some more light. Rachel wasn't looking her best, but hers was the face he wanted to see, even if it was bruised, and smeared with pasta sauce.

'I'm sorry you've ended up in this mess. I should never have listened to Ralph Coleman. I should have chucked that stupid knife in the dog poo bin and driven you back to Derbyshire.'

'Look, Dillon, we're not here entirely by chance, you know.'

'Is isn't going to be more of Coleman's pre-destination bollocks?'

'Ralph is very well regarded by a lot of people. There are several organisations dedicated to watching out for dangerous cults and monitoring their activities. Sometimes they come to him for advice.'

'Where is this going, exactly?'

'There were some relatives of people who joined the Defenders of the Faith who got together and took their concerns to the police. This was a couple of years ago and no one was interested at that time. Marcus Hardwick hadn't broken any laws as far as they could, so the authorities decided to leave well alone.'

'I expect his rich gun-running friends might have had something to do with that.'

'Anyway, the relatives were really worried. They didn't like what they were hearing about the Defenders of the Faith, especially the way they threatened anyone who wanted to leave. They spoke to an organisation called Cultfinders who suggested contacting Ralph for less conventional help. He saw the danger straight away. You've only got to listen to Marcus Hardwick for a little while to understand. It's all about death or glory, and there's no glory to be had here, is there, Dillon?'

'I can't argue with that. But what's it got to do with me?'

'Ralph was looking for some way of getting inside information on the Defenders of the Faith. He asked around the Cultfinders network for anyone who had connections to the Faithful. You were the perfect choice, he said.'

'More like the perfect fool.'

'You make a good fool,' Rachel said with a smile. 'In the olden days, the fool was the only one who could tell the king the truth without fear of punishment. It sounds like your perfect job: you get to say whatever you like and no one can retaliate. We could get you a hat with bells on so people would know you were coming.'

'But I still don't understand how Ralph made the connection between me and the Hateful. He can't have been talking to Charlotte, surely.'

'No, not Charlotte. Do you remember who pointed you towards the Gnostics in the first place?'

'Arnold Gladman? Dolores Carter?'

'Arnold passes on information to Cultfinders, but he thinks he's talking to MI6. He's something of a fantasist, I'm afraid. I don't know Dolores, but I expect she is just a particularly well-informed librarian.'

A penny was beginning to drop into the one-armed bandit that formed the problem-solving part of Dillon's brain.

'Dolores mentioned something about a website. One that kept records of cults and religious groups.'

'That's right. Originally Cultfinders was just a loose affiliation of concerned people. It was all a bit haphazard in those days and the information never seemed to get to the people who needed it. They advertised for someone to sort out their databases and make the information more accessible.'

'Sparks! They gave the job to Sparks, didn't they? This is his top-secret contract. The lying bastard could have told me.'

'No, he couldn't. He promised not to. If anyone, it should have been me who told you, but Ralph convinced me that you would be safer if you were kept in ignorance. I'm sorry.'

'I'm still going to kill him.'

'You should be proud of Sparks. His work was invaluable in helping trace missing people and track down particularly dangerous individuals. He had to keep it secret, as there are plenty of people out there who would like access to that data.'

'I did my bit,' said Dillon, still feeling bitter and betrayed. 'I went to beard God's Militia in their den. I wrote the article. Wasn't that enough?'

'I thought that once the police got involved that would be the end of it,' said Rachel. 'But Ralph was still worried about what would happen to the people inside if the police came marching in. He thought you might be able to help achieve a peaceful solution.'

'Peaceful? If he wanted to send me in as a peace envoy why did he give me a scary knife called Daron?'

'I don't know,' Rachel admitted. 'That goes too deep for me. That knife makes my hair stand on end. I don't know where the Knights found it. To be honest, no one seems to know where the Knights come from or who they got involved. Perhaps Ralph does, but he's not saying.'

'Ralph is a Gnostic. He's supposed to know everything. Maybe the Knights found Daron while they were digging up the motorway. I vote we bury it again as soon as possible.'

'So, do you forgive me?'

'Yes, I forgive you,' said Dillon, after a brief pause. 'But no more secrets please, they're too dangerous for my health.'

'No more secrets, I promise.

32 Losing a Battle, Winning a War

Outside the police cordon, Sparks, the doyen of cult-finding and beer-drinking, was helping the police with their enquiries. Chief Superintendent Robert Mansfield, the senior officer in charge of siege coordination, was starting to wish he would stop.

What Mansfield needed to know was the strength of the militia's defences and their leader's likely plan of action. To be told that they had "a shitload" of guns and that Marcus Hardwick was a "tosser" and a "complete nutcase" was not what he wanted to hear. After a few minutes of Sparks' insights into the cult psyche, Mansfield gave him a Crime Stoppers badge and sent him away.

Sparks continued being helpful to several police officers and a large Alsatian named Fangorn. Eventually, Megan took him to meet the posse of newsmen who had recently materialised at a safe distance from the hostilities. Sparks spent the next few hours as happy as Larry; the centre of all attention, giving exclusive eyewitness accounts to all and sundry.

Even without Sparks' input, the negotiations were not going well. The police officers involved were well-trained in criminal psychology. They read the latest negotiating techniques in Hostage Situation Monthly. They learnt how to understand criminals, predict their actions and even think like them. However, even in these apocalyptic times, no one had come up with a good way to deal with religious fanatics. How do you negotiate with someone who thinks you're working for Satan? What do you offer someone who is looking forward to their heroic martyrdom?

Communication had been established with the Defenders of the Faith via their one and only phone, a landline located in Marcus Hardwick's office. Hardwick put across their position in no uncertain terms. He expressed the depths of his dissatisfaction with the police for surrounding his home and shooting his disciples, not to mention them being in league with the devil and so forth. As for the hostages, he indicated that the most likely outcome involved them being sent out in small pieces, as befitted the spawn of Satan. Mansfield considered pushing Sparks in on the end of a long stick to see what effect this might have, but decided, on balance, that it would not enhance his media profile.

There didn't seem much room for manoeuvre. The Defenders of the Faith weren't prepared to surrender, or hand over their hostages, and the Chief Superintendent certainly wasn't prepared to kneel before Marcus Hardwick and declare him Christ Reborn.

Just when he thought the situation couldn't possibly get any worse, the army arrived. It appeared to be something of a token appearance: two armoured personnel carriers and a wagonload of Territorials from Telford. He didn't remember requesting their presence and he wasn't pleased to see them.

In his book, the army meant only one thing and that was trouble. Mansfield wondered if he'd been a little overenthusiastic in his intelligence reports. There were lots of references to guns and religious fanatics, and his superiors were known to be inordinately nervous about such things. He cast about for some excuse to get rid of them before the situation got completely out of hand.

Meanwhile, the military machine came to a rumbling halt in front of the main entrance and purposefully forward of the police lines. Crop-headed squaddies and their part-time colleagues spilt from their vehicles and took up defensive positions, studiously ignoring their civilian counterparts. Their captain swaggered over to the incident room, a cheerless and unheated cabin, where Mansfield greeted him with a cold formality.

'Sorry to have wasted your time, Captain Squires. Don't think we'll be needing you after all. Everything's under control as of now.'

'My information says not, sorry to say,' Squires responded, sounding not in the least bit sorry for Mansfield and his men. 'Heavily armed subversives. Hostage situation. May require special forces intervention.'

Depressingly enough, it sounded as if the man was reading from Mansfield's own report. He considered it most unsporting of the captain to force-feed him his own words on an empty stomach. Maybe, taken out of context, it did sound like a cry for help, but he wasn't going to stand aside and allow some jumped-up Sandhurst graduate to tell him what to do. Mansfield had been waiting for a good siege to come along for years.

'No cause for alarm,' he assured the captain. 'Our trained negotiators are on the scene. A peaceful outcome is imminent. Purely a police matter.'

'For now,' Squires snapped back. He marched smartly over to his men and began barking instructions.

Mansfield breathed a sigh of relief and went back to his cuppa, while the captain concentrated on making sure that none of his men had sneaked off for a quiet smoke behind the lorry.

For the hostages themselves, the intervening time crawled by with all the speed and excitement of a motorway contraflow system. All of their potentially satanic electronics had been removed, including Dillon's digital watch, and they could only guess at the passage of the hours. They quickly exhausted the possibilities of I-Spy, despite adapting the rules to include objects that might only be visible to nocturnal animals.

Currently, Dillon was ahead 53 goals to 47 in a game of cell football. He was just celebrating a spectacular goal, the ball of paper having swerved past beyond the reach of Rachel's unfettered hand when the cellar door opened and Hardwick entered once again. Somehow, thought Dillon, he never seemed to catch them at their best.

Hardwick snapped his fingers and two of his more muscular followers leapt forward to free Rachel from her chains. She was pulled unceremoniously to her feet and dragged towards the door.

'Hey! What do you think you're doing?' Dillon demanded anxiously. 'Where are you taking her?'

'I am releasing her into the community,' Hardwick sneered. 'I have decided that one viper in the nest is quite enough. That should make you happy or are you so craven that you would rather leave in her stead.' He puffed out his chest and smiled condescendingly at his prisoner.

For all his swagger, Hardwick's boyish moon face looked more careworn than Dillon remembered it. Obviously, plotting the military strategy for Armageddon was proving something of a burden, even for the immortal leader.

'I don't believe you,' said Dillon staggering unsteadily to his feet. He was hoping and praying that Hardwick was telling the truth but he trusted the man about as far as he could throw him, which was currently no distance at all.

'What you believe is of no consequence. She is going, and you, my friend, are staying right here until I determine your fate.'

'I'm not going anywhere unless you release us both,' Rachel protested. Her struggles were becoming frantic, but they made little impression on the heavyweight thugs holding her.

Dillon watched her with a combination of anxiety and pride. 'Don't be soft,' he murmured gently.

'I got you into this mess, Dillon, and I'm going to get you out of it somehow, I promise.'

'That's nonsense. And there's not much you can do in here,' Dillon reminded her. 'If you want to help, get to safety, at least it gives me one less thing to worry about. And while you're out there, please try to stop any of those gung-ho NCA types blowing this place up with me in it.'

This little speech didn't calm Rachel completely, but she stopped trying to kick her captor as he manhandled her out of the cellar. He could still hear her protesting loudly and forcibly as the press gang led her away along the passageway. Hardwick bade him farewell and slammed the door. Dillon was alone once again.

33 Messiah Ward

In a strange way, Dillon was quite pleased to be left to his own devices. At least now, if he did anything monumentally stupid, he'd only get himself killed. When your life has so far been one long example of "doing something stupid", this was an important consideration.

Dillon reached behind the pipework, pickpocket style, for Daron's linen wrapping. Uncovering the ancient knife, he laid it carefully on the ground and stared at the rough blade, unsure what to do with it.

Something slightly more modern or high-tech would have been appreciated. The type of device that Q would have given to 007 for a particularly dangerous mission. A biro disguised as a cutting laser beam, or a belt buckle gun, perhaps. Not some Neanderthal Swiss army knife.

Dillon grasped Daron and picked at the handcuffs with the pointy end. Nothing happened, so he jammed it viciously into the lock. The knife slipped, and he narrowly avoided losing a finger. The blade dug into handcuffs' hinges and stuck there, Excalibur-like, stone in steel.

He stared at it quizzically. It was clearly impossible to cut through solid metal with a bit of old flint. He gripped the handle again and began sawing away at the hinges. They parted with minimal effort. It was like cutting a daisy chain with a carving knife. Dillon disentangled himself from the pipework and was free to explore his surroundings for the first time.

Of course, he was still locked in an underground cell, so there wasn't much exploring to be done. Nevertheless, he had broken his bonds and was enjoying a taste of freedom, however limited it might be. He glanced at the door and wondered what would happen if Hardwick and his henchmen came waltzing in. Perhaps he should try to stick the handcuffs back together and pretend that nothing had happened. He examined their remains more closely.

'Cheap steel,' Dillon told himself. 'Maybe not even metal, toy handcuffs or some such. There's always a logical explanation.' He couldn't comprehend why the Defenders of the Faith would use toy handcuffs, but surely an old stone knife couldn't be that sharp.

He didn't feel inclined to test his theory on the remaining steel cuff around his wrist. Healthy scepticism was one thing, but accidentally amputating your second favourite hand was quite another. Instead, he peered through the tiny, barred opening in the cell door. There was no one in sight. After a moment's hesitation, he made his first sensible decision of the day and tried the handle. The door was stiff but mysteriously unlocked, and it opened noisily into an arched brick-lined passageway.

Still, without any clear plan of action, Dillon ran upwards towards an ornate iron archway at the far end. Ahead, the tunnel continued to slope upwards into darkness. To the left, was a panelled wooden door sporting a faded green Emergency Exit sign.

Dillon shouldered the door open and found himself in a tiny room containing four surprised militia squaddies, sitting around a packing crate, playing cards. They stared blankly at Dillon's a dishevelled figure as if trying to figure out if he was an ally or a force of evil.

Dillon stared back, thinking furiously. What would 007 do? Probably much the same that Dillon did: say the first thing that came into his head. 'I need to speak to Charlotte Chaplin. Take me to her immediately!'

The squaddies sprang to attention at the peremptory tone in Dillon's voice. Their leader, who would have looked more at home in a pizza delivery uniform, even saluted.

'Follow me, sir! Are you OK? Things as bad as they say, out there?'

'Worse, soldier. Much worse,' said Dillon, in his best war movie drawl.

He was marched down seemingly endless corridors, all painted in hospital-style spinach green, and dimly lit by flickering fluorescent tubes. Eventually, they arrived at a crudely painted sign featuring a red cross and the words SICK BAY handwritten in shaky capitals.

Dillon waved his escort away and cautiously entered the room. He spotted Charlotte almost immediately amongst the bustle of blue-coated nurses flitting busily from bed to bed. She looked bedraggled and careworn, but still held herself upright in the best military fashion.

He walked through the ward towards her, glancing at each bed in turn. There seemed to be a lot of casualties considering the limited amount of combat encountered so far. Either the SAS really had infiltrated the compound, or the Defenders of the Faith's zeal had got out of hand once the hostilities started. From the way some of the men were glaring at each other, Dillon suspected that friendly fire might well have been involved.

Charlotte was standing by the bed of a young man. Despite the bandages, he was immediately recognisable as her beloved brother, Jeremy. Ordinarily, Dillon would have been pleased to see the odious little prick laid up, but his condition looked grave. He was breathing in rattling gasps, his skin had a deathly grey pallor, and the heavy strapping across his abdomen was soaked in blood.

Charlotte glanced back. The expression on her face was bleak, and she barely registered Dillon's presence. Up close, Dillon noticed that she seemed even less of her old self. There were dark rings around her eyes from lack of sleep and she bore the signs of an inner tension in her manner and her face.

'The police shot him. He was trying to surrender, but they shot him. Why would they do that?'

'Is there anything I can do?'

'He lost a lot of blood. He needs a transfusion, a doctor, a hospital, something...'

'Why don't you take him to the gates? I could help you. If you hand him over to the police, they'll look after him, I'm sure. They must have an ambulance on standby. He could be on his way to A&E in a matter of minutes.'

'I can't. Really, I can't. Marcus won't let anyone leave. He says that if we accept help from the enemy, we will become like them. They offered medicine and food. I heard them calling on the radio. We're desperately short of supplies. But he says it's a trap. We need to put our trust in God, Marcus says.'

'So you're going to let your brother die? Because of what Marcus Hardwick says?'

Charlotte didn't seem to be listening, but Dillon was used to that.

'How did you get out of your cell, Dillon? Did someone let you out?'

'I prayed and the chains fell from my hands,' he lied. 'It was a miracle.'

'You shouldn't joke about such things.'

'No, honestly, it's true. Look!' Dillon held out his arms and showed her the severed handcuffs.

Charlotte stared at the broken hinges, and then at Dillon with a look of bewildered desperation. 'Perhaps you could help. You could speak to them, persuade them to let us be. If only they would leave us alone, everything could go back to the way it was.' She was almost pleading with him.

'Why me, Charlotte?' Dillon wondered. 'It may have escaped your notice, but I can't just wander out and chat to the nearest copper. Why don't you get lover-boy, Marcus, to talk to them? A little diplomacy would go a long way.'

'You don't understand. He has been chosen by God to lead us. Those who attack him must be evil. He can't possibly surrender to them. If this carries on much longer, something terrible is going to happen. Something terrible, Dillon.'

'What's he going to do, Charlotte? Tell me.'

'The forces of evil cannot be allowed to triumph. They must be prevented from defiling our sanctuary. Whatever the cost.' She lowered her head and looked meaningfully at her brother's prone figure.

A cry rang out from the far end of the room, a stomach-churning expression of suffering, while the man in the next bed tugged at Dillon's arm and asked for something to take away the pain.

Dillon felt sick. 'You're right, I don't understand. What forces of evil?' He was raising his voice now; despite the suspicious looks this was generating. 'Look out there, for God's sake. There's not a bunch of Satanists surrounding you, Charlotte, they're just ordinary British soldiers and policemen. You told me your dad served with the Royal Artillery for twenty-odd years. How can they be your enemy? It doesn't make any sense at all.'

'I've been praying for guidance,' Charlotte countered in a quiet, emotional voice. 'Marcus has told us that Armageddon is approaching. I believe him. He wouldn't lie to us. But he never said anything about fighting our own troops. I'd lay down my life for him, we all would, but this…it just doesn't seem right.'

Acting on a hunch, Dillon put his hand on her shoulder and took a deep breath. He felt as if he were poised above a great chasm. A wrong move one way or the other would send them all plunging into its metaphorical depths. 'Everyone around here respects you, Charlotte. I've noticed that.'

She looked puzzled at this sudden change of subject. 'I always try to do my best. I help out wherever I can. There was a lot that needed doing. So much to organise.'

'Well, you're good at organising things. I'll bet you've had to help organise the recruits, haven't you?'

'Oh yes! Some of these officers don't have a clue about work rotas and scheduling. I had to sort it all out, send out the work parties…'

'So, when you told people what to do, they just went out and did it.'

'Of course; the Faithful have proper military discipline. They respond to authority.'

'That's right. Authority. Some people have it and some don't. If I tell people to do things, they just ignore me, but if you tell them, they jump into action. You must have inherited that from your father.'

'Mother always said we were very alike.'

'But if you have authority, you also have a big responsibility, don't you? You can't just stand by, even when it's hard to know what to do. Like now, for instance.' Dillon paused to consider his next words very carefully. 'I reckon that if you told the people here to put down their guns and follow you out of here, they would. They respect you and I don't think they want to fight the army or the police, any more than you do.'

'I couldn't do something like that. Marcus would never agree. It would be like heresy. We must never surrender to evil.'

'But surely, it's evil to let people die, especially when you know how to stop it happening? Sometimes, you have to turn away from evil, not fight it head on. Sometimes, fighting a thing just makes it stronger. Hardwick might be God's chosen one for all I know, but you still have to make your own decisions. You're stronger than you know, Charlotte. It's up to you now. You have to decide what's right and what's wrong.'

'I don't know anymore, Dilly. I just don't know.

34 Hounds of Love

Having imparted his only pearl of wisdom, Dillon planned to get out as quickly as possible. He no longer feared Charlotte betraying him again. She looked like a woman who had far too many other things on her mind. He slipped through a door that led out to an old medicinal herb garden and made his way to a cluster of ramshackle outbuildings.

Another staccato burst of gunfire came from somewhere beyond the potting shed. Dillon was in the middle of a war zone without a flak jacket or a white suit. Time to go. There was just the small problem of getting past the guards, over the fence, and away, without being shot by both sides. All the armed men that Dillon could see had their guns pointing towards the perimeter. This meant he could sneak up behind the men defending the house without being spotted, but what then?

He took Daron out of his belt and looked warily at it. He supposed he could slit somebody's throat if they weren't looking at him. But even if he could stomach the bloodshed, that still left him wandering across open ground in full sight of another dozen or so marksmen.

The thing that worried Dillon more was the reaction of the besieging forces if he ever got to the fence. Would they really shout, 'Armed police; drop your weapon,' like they did in the films, or would they shoot first and apologise later? He thought he might have a chance with the police, but suppose it was the SAS or Counter Terrorism? He hadn't gone through all this trouble and strife just to be terminated by his own side.

No. What he needed was a plan with more cunning and less bravado. A disguise? Or camouflage, maybe? There were lots of shrubs and saplings around. When Birnam Wood to Dunsinane shall come. It had worked for MacDuff, so why not him?

Dillon slunk silently across the neatly mown lawn and dived into the shrubbery beyond. It contained a particularly spiky gorse bush, smelling vaguely of cheap suntan lotion. He pushed his way valiantly though and found himself in a small copse, overgrown with brambles and nettles.

After rooting around in the undergrowth for a while, he came up with a good selection of willow branches in various states of decay, an armful of ragwort, and a strong coil of clematis. Using Daron to good effect, he cut the creeping clematis to length and bundled the branches together into the semblance of a deformed tree; one that had spent most of its life hanging tenuously onto a windy cliff top, perhaps.

Every so often, he conjured up a few more Scottish Play analogies and snorted quietly to himself. Charlotte would make a good conniving witch or psychotic hand-wringing noblewoman.

Finally satisfied, Dillon pushed his way into the middle of his Trojan Tree and practised moving inconspicuously. This proved difficult, partly because trees don't normally walk around, except in fantasy novels, and that wasn't the effect he was looking for at all. He also discovered that, despite never having suffered from any sort of allergy, he now had an irresistible urge to sneeze every time a catkin came anywhere near his nose.

Dillon started to shuffle towards the edge of the copse. There was a tangled hedgerow meandering its way down the hill away from the house. Thinking it ought to provide a suitable backdrop for a mobile bush, he headed that way.

First, Dillon had to navigate the low wall enclosing the copse. This proved harder than he expected since the tightly bound branches allowed him little room to bend his knees. He managed to hop onto the top of the wall and teetered there for a moment before catching his foot on a cunningly concealed length of barbed wire and crashing like a felled oak into the neighbouring field.

He lay there for a full five minutes, waiting for the hue and cry to carry him back to captivity. Nothing happened. Apparently, the sight of a large, animated bush was a common occurrence in these parts.

He tried to pick himself up, but all he achieved was to make himself more conspicuous. He tried rolling towards the cover of the hedgerow. This was slightly more successful, if not very controllable. Dillon started down the gentle slope hoping to meet the hedgerow further down the hill, but unfortunately, his course never quite seemed to converge with the hedge line.

As the hill got steeper, Dillon began to pick up speed. Soon, he was dizzy and had very little idea where he was going. He had no alternative but to let gravity take its course. He wondered what was at the bottom and how much it was going to hurt.

There was a rather soggy splash and a stifled yelp as Dillon and his bush landed in a small muddy stream. Cold murky water trickled down his back and collected in the baggier regions of his underpants. He tried to look on the bright side. At least no one had seen him, and now he was a good two hundred yards from the inner cordon. On the downside, instead of being cold and miserable, he was now cold, wet and miserable.

There remained the question of how he was going to get out of his current predicament before he died of hypothermia. He started to push against the stream bed with the back of his heels and found the force of the water, weak though it was, tended to push him upright. Slowly and surely, he used this technique to move further downstream. Eventually, his head came to rest against a smooth rock, and, with much wriggling and writhing, Dillon struggled to his feet.

He looked for a way to get out onto dry land but there was no way he could climb the slippery banks, hamstrung as he was. Fortunately, the stream was overhung with reeds and willow saplings, providing perfect cover for a wading bushman.

Dillon carried on until the stream ran into the calm water of a fishing pond. There was a rudimentary dam at the far end, which looked as if it had been built by inebriated beavers. More of the Hateful's handiwork, he assumed. He shuffled around the shoreline until he came to a point where the hooves of generations of cattle had worn a path down to the lake's edge. He tiptoed up the path and made for the nearest clump of trees.

Just as he reached the wood, he froze. Coming round the lake was a group of militiamen with guns, and a mangy-looking golden retriever. On any other occasion, it could have been a jolly hunting party on its way out for a pleasant evening's pheasant bothering, except for the fact that assault rifles were generally considered unsporting amongst the hunting and shooting fraternity.

An unpleasant thought crossed Dillon's mind. Maybe they were hunting him. He felt like the lame wildebeest in an African wildlife documentary. It never seemed fair to him that the predator was always the star of the show.

The retriever nosed the ground and led his handler along the lakeside in Dillon's direction. As it reached the cattle track, it barked and bounded up the path towards the wood. The militiaman could hold on no longer and let the big dog run free. Dillon's heart began to pound. He braced himself, ready for the shaggy brute to attack.

To Dillon's relief, as the dog approached the makeshift bush, it slowed to a trot. Instead of biting through the disguise, it sniffed at the branches and yowled inquiringly. Dillon dared not move a muscle. Finally, having rounded the fake bush twice, the dog paused, cocked its leg, and emptied its surprisingly capacious bladder all over Dillon's leg.

You know your life is at a low ebb when a large dog pees all over you and you feel grateful, Dillon thought.

The Defenders of the Faith's hunting party watched the retriever's antics from the shore of the lake, calling to it and shouting abuse all the while. It seemed to be called Scrumpy or possibly Scummy and was more mongrel than pedigree working dog. Dillon viewed the incontinent hound with guarded affection as it lolloped off towards its human pack.

Once Scummy's barking, and the voices of his bickering owners, had faded into the distance, Dillon took stock of his situation. It looked pretty desperate. The bush disguise had got him this far, but it was becoming a liability. With a few quick strokes from Daron, he cut himself free and released his knotted muscles from their bondage.

The relief was exquisite, but soon he felt sharp pains shooting down his legs as blood flowed to the parts it had been previously unable to reach. Dillon hopped around for a while, beating his suffering limbs into submission, until finally the pins and needles subsided.

So far, so bad. He was well outside the Defenders of the Faith's inner cordon but inside the outer cordon. Since both cordons faced outwards, that meant the inner cordon was pointing their guns right at him. If he could somehow sneak past the outer cordon, he would then have two sets of militia guns pointing at him, not to mention the inner cordon of the police who would be facing the outer cordon of the Defenders of the Faith. Thus, leaving Dillon as the designated fowl in a heavily armed chicken run.

Still, the alternatives didn't seem much better. He was hardly going to trot back to the garrison and give himself up. Hardwick would be getting more paranoid as the siege went on and was likely to shoot him on sight.

The only solution was to keep an implausibly low profile, stay undercover, and wait for the storm to pass. Dillon was currently surrounded by some reasonably dense woodland. If he could stay deep in the undergrowth, he should be able to evade capture for some considerable time.

Of course, there was the question of food and shelter. It had been quite a mild day, but now night was falling and the temperature was starting to drop. Dillon's only previous experience of sleeping in the great British outdoors had been in a semi-comatose state, courtesy of the Knights of the Wasteland. He resolved to give generously to a homeless charity if he ever got out of here.

He had also neglected to bring a picnic with him when he made his bid for freedom. Water would be no problem, provided nothing had drowned in the lake recently. The lack of food, however, was already starting to prey on his mind.

Dillon rummaged around in his pockets and came up with the crushed remains of a packet of mints, which he scooped into his mouth. The other pocket held nothing but a small length of rope. It might be useful for strangling small furry animals, but only if he could catch them first. He saw himself more of a gatherer than a hunter, anyway. There were a few late summer fruits around, and some disgusting-looking fungi by the path, which may or may not have been edible. He wasn't that desperate, yet.

The sound of running feet broke into his hunger-fuelled ruminations, and he dived back into the cover of the wood just in time. A stretcher party, accompanied by a young sweat-stained medic, was jogging back in the direction of the house. From Dillon's viewpoint, their burden looked more like a corpse than a patient, but the medic was steadfastly gripping the man's hand and shouting futile words of encouragement.

Dillon crouched down and burrowed deeper and darker into the forest. At first, he was following a faint path, but this quickly diverged. He took the one more travelled, but it made no difference. Within a few paces, he was completely lost. Of course, since he didn't now seem to be going anywhere in particular, this hardly mattered. All around him, he could hear the reassuring sounds of the woods: evening birdsong, the wind in the willows, and that sort of thing. Every so often, the birdsong would be interrupted by the crack of gunfire or the shouts of angry and frightened men, shortly followed by avian alarm calls.

The thick undergrowth that was keeping Dillon undetected was disorientating. Several times, he nearly stumbled onto an enemy outpost in the mistaken belief that they were behind him. Night was falling, but sleep was far from Dillon's thoughts. The sound of voices carried clearly in the quiet of the wood. They often sounded close, but he had no way of knowing if they were heading in his direction or not.

He stumbled upon a track that led out into rough heathland. Here the going was easier, but Dillon felt very exposed. At every bend, he expected to see a phalanx of militiamen heading towards him. He was hoping to spot some landmark, maybe even the perimeter fence stretching out in front of him.

Eventually, his nerve failed him and he ducked back into the safety of the forest. By the dappled light of the moon, he stumbled along the edge of the treeline, fighting with throat-level branches and ankle-high brambles. After a few hundred yards of this slog, he came up against an immovable obstacle: a high brick wall covered with ivy and rambling vines.

Some of the creepers looked strong enough to support his weight. Thinking this might be a way out of the compound, or at least a good place to shelter for the night, Dillon hauled himself up to the top of the wall and peered over.

There in front of him was the unmistakable outline of the Defenders of the Faith's headquarters, just as he had left it several hours earlier. He mouthed a silent stream of invective and banged his fist in frustration on the uncaring brickwork.

35 Blood on the Rooftops

Dillon perched on top of the wall and considered his options. He couldn't face going back out into the grounds to be shot at by both sides or be used as a doggy toilet. Reluctantly, he decided to take his chances in the buildings around the Hateful's headquarters, where the hiding places were warmer and there was the prospect of snatching some hot food.

Unfortunately, there were militiamen posted all around the old manor house and no realistic prospect of sneaking in through the servants' entrance. After casing the joint for a while, Dillon realised that they were on guard duty because no one would trust them to do anything more challenging. They were making little effort to look beyond their noses and were following such a regular route that Dillon could set his watch by them. After timing the patrols for the third time, he lowered himself down into the garden and scurried across the dew-damp lawn to a windowless corner of the house.

From his experience of playing hide-and-seek as a kid, Dillon knew that searchers usually concentrated their efforts at ground level and seldom looked up. Climbing the outside of the manor house looked tricky, but not impossible. A rusty fire escape ladder led up to a first-floor balcony. From there he was able to shin up a cast iron drainpipe to the guttering which ran along the outside of the parapet. He just had time to secrete himself behind the mock-Tudor castellations, before the guards passed obliviously below. Once they were out of sight, he levered himself onto the roof with the help of a convenient gargoyle and settled behind a large chimney, jammed between the brickwork and the steeply pitched slates.

It wasn't going to be a particularly pleasant place to await the dawn, but it seemed preferable to the confines of his cell, or more sleepless hours wandering lost in the woods. From his eyrie, he spied a possible escape route: through the abandoned kitchen garden and via an avenue of ancient lime trees towards an abandoned gatehouse. It was less well patrolled than his failed circuit of the grounds and he seriously considered climbing back down and giving it a go.

Something stopped him. Not just his previous failure, the prospect of being fired upon by all sides, or the fact he was cold, wet, and weary, but rather a strong feeling that the unfolding of events required him to stay right here. Not only to wait, but also, at some ill-defined moment, to act. What he was supposed to do, Dillon wasn't quite sure. He had no intention of completing his original Mission from God. He was still of a mind to get revenge on Marcus Hardwick, even if he wasn't prepared to stick a stone knife in his back.

Every so often, Dillon could hear distant cries of alarm and the sounds of small groups of the Faithful beating their way through the undergrowth around the house. If they were searching for him, they were going about it in a particularly inept way.

Beyond the distant fence, in the darkness of the forest, uniformed figures weaved their way through the regimented lines of trees, more arriving every minute. He saw a black-clad man in a balaclava skulking around the defences and wondered if the SAS really had arrived but, on reflection decided it was probably a member of the press corps with a head cold.

A chopper swept the area with searchlights and monitoring equipment, staying carefully out of rifle range. Dillon waved. No doubt his thermal signature was being drowned out by the heat seeping through the uninsulated roof. No one thought to look out of the helicopter window. That would have been far too low-tech.

As the thrum of the helicopter blades faded into the distance, Dillon heard voices from the room below. He was sure that the loudest of them belonged to Marcus Hardwick, but he could only pick out odd phrases. Hardwick was shouting about glory and death, but mostly death. There was the odd cheer, but the general lack of enthusiasm suggested that not everyone in the room thought their soul was ready for an audience with its maker.

With a great deal of puffing and blowing, Dillon unfolded his body into the rough approximation of a standing position. From his new vantage point, he could see dozens of cracked and missing tiles and, in his opinion, most of the chimney stacks were in serious need of re-pointing.

There were a lot of chimneys, more than seemed necessary even for a house of this size. Decorative and pointless spires protruded from the many corners of the building, giving Dillon the choice of convenient and uncomfortable hiding places. Sticking his head cautiously above the parapet, he inspected the unfolding scene below.

Slowly but surely, in the pale morning light, the Defenders of the Faith were falling back from the outer defences. They did this surreptitiously, crawling commando-style through the undergrowth before scurrying past the manor house in great haste.

Dillon wondered what was going on. Were the Hateful preparing to napalm the perimeter? He followed the progress of a pair of young recruits as they slunk along the wall beneath him. They were blissfully unaware of his presence and seemed more immediately concerned with escaping observation from within the house.

He watched as they made their way through the arched entrance to the old stable yard and joined a growing crowd of their comrades on the parade ground. Without risking life and limb, it was hard to get a good view of the proceedings from the rooftop.

By hanging on to some ornate stonework and leaning out beyond the farthest spire, Dillon could make out about fifty men, women, and children milling around the quadrangle. All of them were looking towards a slightly built figure in khaki battledress who was busy organising them into neat, orderly lines. With her military bearing and golden hair spilling out from beneath her smart junior officer's cap, it was unmistakably Charlotte.

Yet more people came flooding into the parade ground. They seemed hesitant, unsure whether they should really be there. Charlotte's presence appeared to reassure them.

Once everyone was assembled and all were arranged to her satisfaction, she gave a signal to a young corporal. He disappeared back into the house and quickly returned leading a party of stretcher-bearers, and a host of medics assisting the walking wounded.

These medics all appeared to be women wearing black hooded cloaks. Dillon didn't recall seeing any nuns amongst the rank of the Faithful, but when one of them turned to speak to Charlotte, he recognised the stern fur-trimmed face of Reverend Mother Sophia Hildegard. Dillon had no idea how they had got into the compound unless Charlotte had let them in. He had to admire their courage. He didn't think Hardwick would hesitate to execute a few heretical nuns if they got in the way.

Charlotte went over to the first stretcher and laid a comforting hand on her injured soldier's brow, presumably her brother's. She took a deep breath, walked stiffly to the head of the parade, and turned to face her people. Presented on masse, they were a mixed bunch, not the grey-faced collection of Puritan thugs that Dillon had envisaged. Some of the men had a military bearing and haircuts to match, but far more were overweight or undersized, and some looked frighteningly young to be facing Armageddon. For the first time, Dillon began to feel some sympathy for them.

From her gestures and the intent look on the faces of those in the assembled ranks, Charlotte seemed to making a speech. Whatever she might have said, it was short and to the point. Those who were able snapped to attention, threw back their shoulders and held their heads as high as they could without fracturing a vertebra.

Having said her piece, Charlotte gave the order to advance and marched steadily along the gravel driveway with the raggle-taggle bunch of misfits following her, three abreast. It was an impressive sight. Even the civilians and the wounded attempted to leave their stronghold with the most dignity they could muster.

From his rooftop perch, he was relieved to see that none of the marchers were armed, and Charlotte seemed to have a furled white flag about her person. Hopefully, that would protect them from any trigger-happy marksmen on the outside.

He was less sure about the situation within. There was no way of knowing how many of Hardwick'ss cronies remained within the building. The departing ranks were making enough noise with their marching to rattle the windows beneath him. It was only a matter of time before someone noticed what was going on.

Sure enough, just as the columns passed the ornate wrought-iron gates, a top-floor window flew open and a peak-capped head poked out. The man gave a started cry and bobbed back inside. Seconds later, Hardwick appeared at the window to see his departing disciples for himself. Judging by the colour of his neck, he was having an apoplectic fit.

'Charlotte!' Hardwick screamed. 'Get back here at once! What in God's name do you think you're doing?'

Whatever Charlotte had told her troops, it must have been good. Not a single one broke rank and only a few backmarkers looked around. Perhaps it had been the manic quality of Hardwick's voice which had risen to a shrill shriek. Dillon imagined he could see blood spitting from the man's mouth. Perhaps if he'd tried to reason with them, his militiamen might have turned back.

Hardwick didn't even try. Presented only with the retreating backs of those on which he had pinned all his schemes, he completely and utterly lost it. 'Traitors! Scum! How can you do this? Betray me, and you betray God. I am your Chosen One. You disobey me at your peril. Turn back this instant, I command it. Turn back or you are cursed for all eternity.'

He pulled out a handgun and began waving it at his departing followers.

'Damn you all to Hell! Whether we live or die is not important. It is God's will that we fight the forces of evil, no matter what the odds.'

Hardwick screeched away at the top of his voice and pointed the gun at those below with what looked like murderous intent. Several other windows opened and the officers pointed an assortment of lethal-looking weaponry at their own men.

Some of the deserters glanced back over their shoulders and froze. Charlotte saw what was happening and looked around desperately for some cover.

Seeing that things were about to get nasty, Dillon decided it was high time he made his move. James Bond would have swung from the roof, grabbed the gun, and filled the room with bodies before Hardwick could say 'Sodom and Gomorrah'. Dillon was just trying to stay out of the firing line.'

He soon discovered how difficult it was to run on a steeply slate roof, especially one as dilapidated as this one. Inevitably, his foot slipped causing him to land heavily on a section of roof timbers favoured by woodworm and deathwatch beetles for their annual picnic. There was an ominous crack and two dozen slates disappeared through the roof, shortly followed by Dillon himself, flailing his arms wildly. For a second, he thought the attic floor might save him, but the rotten joists gave way, sending the whole ceiling crashing down, gold-painted light fittings and all.

Dillon landed with a bone-crunching thump directly onto the central conference table in all its solid mahogany glory. There was a stunned silence as ashen, plaster-coated officers took in the scene of devastation. Some of them made a vain attempt to brush bits of broken ceiling from their freshly pressed tunics. Some just sat there, stunned.

Outside, the Faithless deserters took the opportunity presented by Dillon's impromptu entrance to make a break for it, carrying the sick and injured with them as best they could. A few shots were fired from the windows, but the marksmen's eyes were filled with dust, and the bullets went harmlessly into the trees.

Dillon stood up gingerly on the polished tabletop, showering the officers with another layer of debris. He wiped the plaster from his face and felt round to check that all his limbs were intact.

Hardwick was standing at the head of the table pointing his large and impressive handgun directly at Dillon. His hand was shaking violently but, from this distance, it didn't look as if Hardwick could miss.

Dillon reached for his belt and pulled out Daron the knife. There wasn't much else he could do. The ancient blade looked small and ineffectual to Dillon, but it had a profound effect on the men surrounding him. Several of them were carrying weapons that could have blown him to kingdom come from a hundred metres, but each, in turn, backed away from the table and stared at Daron in horror. Dillon waved the knife around for effect and was gratified to see a few turn and run for the door.

Outside, he could hear vehicles approaching. The sound of running feet could be heard on the gravel path. On the floors below, windows were shattering into a million pieces. It was only a matter of time before help arrived. Dillon did not have time on his side.

Hardwick gripped the gun firmly with both hands and raised it until Dillon was staring straight down the barrel. He forced himself to look into Hardwick's eyes. There was nothing to see. Just a blank, all-encompassing madness, burning and consuming all rational thought.

Hardwick's index finger tensed on the trigger, and then with one dreadful, fluid motion, he swung back the barrel until it kissed his lips, thrust the muzzle into his mouth, and pulled the trigger.

Dillon recoiled in horror, expecting a shower of blood to come raining down. Nothing happened. The gun gave a series of muffled clicks but refused to fire. Distraught, Hardwick threw it to the floor and fell to his knees howling at the world.

Gazing down at the pathetic sight, Dillon experienced mixed emotions. Revenge was supposed to be sweet, but to be honest, he just felt sick. A thunderous explosion sent his ears howling with white noise and what seemed like every armed police officer in England came charging through the door.

The time for action was over. Dillon breathed a sigh of relief and stood down.

36 Celebration Day

In the immediate aftermath of the siege, Dillon was inundated with requests for interviews and personal appearances. He even became a minor celebrity for a while. It was all very gratifying (not to mention profitable), but eventually, answering the same questions over and over again began to wear him down. Tired of all the attention, he began passing the requests on to Sparks who was very keen to talk about his experiences to the media. They, however, were even keener to find a way to get him to shut up.

Rachel refused point-blank to discuss the whole thing and effectively cut herself off from the outside world. Megan, on the other hand, was happy to give any number of interviews to the tabloid newspapers who found her, in many ways, the ideal subject.

It didn't take long for public interest to wane, and Dillon and Sparks returned to Derbyshire considerably richer, but probably no wiser, for the experience. They were welcomed with open arms by the cult and soon settled back into a normal routine (normal by Wild Things' standards, that is).

Dillon, for one, could not remember being as happy, at least since he started wearing long trousers. The Wild Things were like one great extended family. He'd forgotten how much he missed that feeling of belonging. Despite their obvious eccentricities, he felt completely at home with them. They cared for him, laughed with him, drank with him, and he had grown to love them all dearly.

Rachel, however, proved to be more of a problem. 'I let you walk into a trap. And then I ran away and abandoned you to your fate. You could have been killed in there, and it would have been all my fault.'

'Coulda, woulda shoulda,' said Dillon. 'It's not your fault those Defenders of the Faith knobheads decided to kidnap me. All's well that ends well.'

But Rachel clung on to her guilt trip, and they skated around each other for quite a while, until Sheryl had a maternal word with Rachel and metaphysically banged heads together.

The only cloud on the horizon as far as Dillon was concerned was Sheryl's insistence that there were yet more mysterious tasks for the cult to perform before this eventful year was over. After a long period of communion with the late KC Ducatel and a large bottle of whisky, she advised her followers to prepare to journey north soon and to purchase warm clothing. Even Boz was seen perusing the hiking shops in Hathersage for loose-fitting Arctic gear.

Dillon tried to persuade Sheryl that they'd done enough questing for the time being and it was someone else's turn to charge around the country on mystical missions. She waved away his protestations with a smile. She was equally uncommunicative when other members of the cult asked her exactly which frozen wasteland they were heading for.

The uncertainty gave life in Hope a rather frantic edge to it for a while. The mood in the Wild Things' camp was broodingly expectant, almost to the point of hysteria.

The American traditions dear to the hearts of Sheryl and many of her flock made Thanksgiving the most important festival of the year and an excuse for much partying and celebration. Exactly what they were giving thanks for varied depending on Sheryl's latest enthusiasm. This year, they were mainly celebrating their deliverance from evil, and possibly the birthday of Akhenaten, the Heretic Pharaoh. The party started unofficially around the end of October and showed no sign of abating as the festival approached.

Finally, the day arrived and it was time for the Thanksgiving feast itself. Daron the knife, as well as being ideal for whittling wood, proved invaluable when it came to carving the turkey. Dillon had to shrug off the sudden desire to plunge the knife into the still-beating heart of a sacrificial bird and settled for slicing off a nice piece of breast for everyone instead.

All in all, it reminded Dillon of those halcyon Christmases of his childhood. The only problem was that, due to the non-stop partying, he couldn't honestly remember a great deal about it, except for the warm glow in his heart, which nicely counteracted the crippling indigestion. He did wonder for a while if he was developing a drink problem, but on the whole, it only seemed to be a problem when he stopped.

He vaguely recalled Coleman and his chums coming around to deliver a barrel of beer and a message for Sheryl. The Gnostics of Albion's leader was full of the usual bonhomie and dire warnings about the evil Demiurge. Dillon nodded a lot, as he was wont to do when Coleman got into his stride.

'You deserve this celebration,' Coleman declared, nearly crushing him with a Russian bear hug.

'It was nothing,' asserted Dillon, who was trying hard to forget about the whole Defenders of the Faith thing with the help of Coleman's excellent ale.

'Nonsense; you helped save the lives of more than a hundred lost souls. There's not many can say that.'

'So I went to all that trouble to rescue a bunch of tossers from their own stupidity. Hardly seems worth it,' said Dillon dismissively.

'I agree that they are not the most pleasant of individuals and that they did indeed contribute to their own misfortune. They deserved to suffer, perhaps, but I ask you: did they deserve to die?'

'No, I suppose not,' Dillon acknowledged. 'But if I could have killed that bastard, Hardwick, I would have done, you know.'

'Then all would have been lost. Do you not realise that your greatest achievement was to prevent Hardwick from becoming a martyr? Dead, he would have been a potent symbol for like-minded demagogues. In his present pathetic state, he inspires nothing but pity.'

'Then it's a good thing I wasn't armed; that's all I can say.'

'Did you not have Daron in your hand,' Coleman reminded him.

'Well, yes, but I'm not much of a knife thrower.'

'I have a feeling that such a dark device would not have missed Hardwick's heart.'

It was stifling hot in the converted station's waiting hall, what with the roaring log fire and the press of people around him, but still Dillon shivered. 'You're probably right. I still wanted to kill him though.'

'But you did not,' Coleman asserted. 'You had the chance, but you stayed your hand.'

'No idea why.'

'I think you do,' Coleman contradicted him. 'We mere mortals cannot make life, and therefore it behoves us not to unmake it. There is enough sorrow in the world already. You brought a proud man low and thus made him powerless. It is enough.'

Of the Knights of the Wasteland, there was no sign. It seemed that whatever they had stumbled across in Cornwall, it was sufficient to keep them out of trouble for the meantime. When pressed on the subject, Coleman would only tell him to wait and see. He had the air of the great magician about him; waiting for the right moment to pull the celestial rabbit out of the hat.

There was more good news for Dillon on the way. Ever since the siege in the Wyre Forest, he had been fearful that Charlotte, now freed from her Faithful bonds, would come and try to claim him back. He had rehearsed all his arguments time and time again, but he knew Charlotte to be a truly forceful character and he couldn't rule out the possibility of him being dragged off by the sheer weight of her persistence.

It seemed he had misjudged her. So distraught was she by her treatment at the hands of Hardwick and the male-dominated society of the Defenders of the Faith, that she had forsworn men altogether. The Magdalene Sisterhood, having seen her interviewed on national television had offered her support and sanctuary at their sanctuary in Belchfield Magna.

After giving this some thought, Charlotte had graciously accepted and was currently reorganising the cult into the efficient, streamlined religious machine that the Sisters hadn't previously been aware that they needed. Some sections of the Sisterhood were so impressed that they were ready to declare her the long-awaited female messiah. Sister Patience, however, was known to have declared her a 'bossy cow'.

As for Charlotte's former colleagues in the Defenders of the Faith, many of them were now facing trial on various charges ranging from attempted murder to firearms offences, and for keeping unlicensed livestock. Hardwick was currently under guard in a maximum-security mental hospital, after another attempt to take his own life, and after several attempts to help him were made by disgruntled former comrades. He was, by all accounts, a shadow of his former egotistical self.

Shortly after Charlotte's conversion to the cause, the Sisterhood hit the headlines in impressive fashion. A former Defenders of the Faith officer had been released from prison on compassionate grounds. The fact that the Home Secretary played golf with his father was thought to have played some part in this unexpected offer of clemency. However, after tasting freedom for little over a week, he was kidnapped by female persons unknown; then tarred, feathered, and bound naked to the foot of Nelson's Column (an allegedly phallic tribute to male aggression) as a warning to other enemies of womankind.

The perpetrators of this outrage were never caught, but the timing itself was sufficient evidence for Dillon to suspect the hand of Charlotte Chaplin in there somewhere.

37 Afterglow

Somewhere out on a wild and wuthering moor in West Yorkshire, a group of men were building an Iron Age hill fort from items purchased from the local DIY store. None of them possessed so much as an NVQ in fortification construction, nor did they have planning permission or third-party liability insurance. What they did have was a library book entitled How Ancient Britain Was Built and the boundless enthusiasm of truly world-class eccentrics.

This group, calling themselves The Yule Men, though lacking in building skills, were led by a couple who had organised some of the UK's major folk festivals. They planned to use the fort as the centrepiece of a colossal fire festival, complete with music and dance, rhythm and ritual. The whole event would climax with the symbolic torching of their newly constructed fort.

The local council were strongly opposed to all of the above. However, when their building inspectors took a close look at the fortifications, they declared them unsafe to the point of insanity. No demolition contractor would be foolhardy enough even to make a risk assessment of the work involved. Since it was the Yule Men's avowed intention to burn it down themselves, the council thought it best to let them get on with it.

Dillon and Sparks were largely oblivious to the furore associated with the festival. The Wild Things considered watching the news to be far too dispiriting. Besides, Dillon was far too relieved to have escaped the clutches of the Defenders of the Faith to be worried about what was going on in the conventional world outside.

When Sheryl Keane called the Wild Things together on a bitterly cold December morning, most of her followers had no inkling of what was in store. They all stood shivering out on the platform in the chill north wind, it being the only way she could address them on masse. A few flecks of snow settled on her hair, as she stepped onto an upturned water trough to make her pronouncement.

'Dearly beloved,' she began, 'I didn't gather you all here today just to freeze your asses off on this fine English winter day. I come bearing news. I know y'all been wondering what we have planned for our next big party. Well, I gotta tell you, we ain't gonna have one.'

Her audience cried out with feigned disappointment, waiting for the twist they all knew was coming.

'Instead, we, the wild and wonderful Cult of Eternal Joy, are heading for the frozen wastelands of Yorkshire. We are going to be a part of the biggest winter solstice party of all time: the Great Baildon Fire Festival!'

There was an outbreak of cheering, which Sheryl cut short. 'Let me tell you, we have been asked to play a vital role in these festivities. And what is more, good people, they gonna have a dozen bars on site and we get free access to them all. May the gods bless you all and comfort you. Now let's get the hell inside!'

Dillon wasn't sure what to make of all this. To him, the fire festival sounded like a pyromaniac's garden party with some religious mumbo-jumbo thrown in for good measure. Still, with the Wild Things in attendance, it was likely to turn into a huge multi-denominational piss-up, whatever the organisers might have intended.

Sparks, who was no lover of the great outdoors, recalled visiting Baildon Moor as a child.

'It's the kind of place where Brontë buffs go to die of exposure. Like Ilkley Moor, only bigger, and you don't have to sing about Mary Jane and the bloke with no hat.'

'It sounds like a bit too much like the Allendale Fire Festival,' said Dillon. 'You remember the Guisers?'

'You mean those drunks dancing around with flaming tar barrels on their heads. How could I forget?' complained Sparks, bitterly. 'Anyway, it must have been minus several at least. How I let you talk me into that, I've no idea.'

'I read about it in a travel magazine when I was waiting to see the dentist. It sounded like a good crack at the time.'

'I'd rather spend New Year's Eve having my teeth drilled.'

'I know what you mean. I used to like bonfire night, but after having my home burnt down, I'm not sure I'm ready to celebrate the joy of fire again.'

Sparks, having started the said fire, had similar misgivings.

Dillon phoned up Dolores Carter at her desk in Lincoln Central Library and persuaded her to email everything she could find on Baildon and the fire festival, as a matter of urgency. He and Sparks hurried down to their nearest online communication hub: the Copper Kettle Café, in Hope. Over a cup of tea and a toasted teacake, they scrolled through the pages of information.

Most of it was historical pagan stuff. Baildon Moor was once a prime site for Beltane celebrations and sacrifices. What exactly they sacrificed is not recorded, but there were reports of Lancastrians going missing around solstice time.

In addition to all this fascinating, but useless, information, there was also a limited amount of data about the upcoming festival. Its organisers had a chequered financial history and a poor health and safety record. Acting on a hunch, Dillon phoned Ralph to see if he knew what was going on.

'Where shall I begin? Have you heard of Coleman's Finest Ales? They're very good, you know.'

Dillon admitted to having sampled a pint at some beer festival or other.

'The brewery was set up by my late grandfather. I inherited the business some twelve years ago. I transferred ownership to the Gnostics of Albion and, since they are a registered religious organisation, it has become the only brewery in the country with charitable status.'

Dillon had to admire the cheek of it, but he didn't see the connection with the fire festival on Baildon Moor.

'When the Yule Men put the bar concessions out to tender, we, of course, applied. Since our product boasts certain tax advantages, we were able to undercut our competitors and win the contract. This is going to be a major undertaking. We need to recruit additional staff for this endeavour: people who will encourage the customers to have a good time and consume more of our marvellous product, people who have boundless enthusiasm and can hold their drink. So naturally, I contacted Sheryl Keane and requested her help.'

'Thank you, Ralph,' Dillon declared. 'It's all becoming much clearer. It still sounds seriously dodgy, though. Is there anything else I should know before we get to Baildon?'

'There are many things, Dillon, but I am not ready to offer enlightenment just yet. It would spoil the surprise, my friend!'

The road to West Yorkshire was full of surprises. Not least was the number of beaten-up cars and campervans heading north. Dillon and his friends started out with the Land Rover, an old Peugeot van, and the smoke-belching bus. By the time they reached the M62 intersection, they had collected a convoy of about thirty vehicles and their like-minded occupants. This was before they met the Gnostics of Albion and their fleet of antique wagons delivering Coleman's Finest Ales to the festival.

The next surprise was the lack of any hold-ups on the route. With roadworks suspended for the Christmas holidays and most of the traffic incapable of breaking the speed limit, it was one of the most hassle-free trips Dillon could remember.

Finally, they reached signs for the Elland Road football ground and the convoy passed a troop of horses bearing a dozen men in full medieval armour along the hard shoulder. The Knights of the Wasteland were on their way to Baildon under full police escort with flashing lights and a mounted patrol. At first, Dillon assumed they were under arrest for violations of the Highway Code. However, the mounted police in particular appeared to be treating them with a great deal of respect.

'I must have forgotten to mention it, my friend,' said Coleman when they arrived at the festival site. 'The Knights of the Wasteland have been commissioned to demonstrate the art of horsemanship to the celebrants of Yorkshire. Merrie England, jousting tourneys and all that. It should be an excellent finale.'

'There seem to be quite a few things you haven't mentioned,' grumbled Dillon. 'Anything else you'd like to add before we go in?'

'I would recommend taking advantage of the ample provisions we brought with us. Perhaps a picnic and something wholesome to grill on the great Baal fire.'

'And why, exactly?'

'Because it is my belief that the food stalls, though wonderfully exotic, are run by the Omo Peace Collective. I imagine you have heard of them.'

'Would that be the group commonly known as the Poison Chicken Cult?'

'The very same,' Coleman agreed.

'How on earth did they end up with the food concession?'

'They put in the lowest bid. After all, if one intends to commit ritual suicide before the end of the tax year, there's no point in incorporating excessive profit margins. Their food is excellent, by the way, but I would ask one of their chefs to taste it first.'

'Anything else?' Dillon demanded.

'Well, I shouldn't concern yourself unduly, but the firework display is under the control of the group responsible for the very impressive display of pyrotechnics on the South Wales coast last year.'

'Oh my God. The Abergavenny Arsonists! Are you sure this is a good idea?'

'Put it this way, Dillon. If you were caught up in a riot, where would be the safest place to hide?'

'In the middle of the rioters,' Dillon said, without hesitation. He had a journalist's natural survival instincts. At least, he thought he had until the events of this last year.

'Well then, I guarantee you will be in the most secure place imaginable to celebrate the winter solstice.' Coleman reassured Dillon, patting him paternally on the back.

'Is that the lot?'

'Almost. There is one more thing that will become immediately obvious as you approach this Brobdingnagian fort.' Coleman refused to elucidate further.

Finally, the happy band arrived at a disused quarry, which was doubling up as a car park, or possibly a scrapyard, judging by the state of most of the vehicles. There were very few spaces left, but one corner of the quarry was reserved for staff and VIPs. They waved the appropriate bits of paper at the disinterested stewards and abandoned their vehicles next to some rusting excavation machinery.

It took a while for the un-athletic cultists to ascend the steep path to the moor, but eventually, they crested the ridge and staggered over a litter-strewn wasteland, towards the phoney hill fort dominating the skyline ahead.

It was certainly an impressive sight. Apart from its sheer size, the most impressive thing about it was that it was still standing. It looked like the sort of thing that Heath Robinson might have constructed had he been around in the Iron Age. There were leaning towers perched on leaning walls adorned with leaning spires. The whole thing was propped up by flying buttresses made from pallets and packing cases. The only things stopping it from collapsing like a pack of cards were a giant web of cargo netting and some bloody great nails.

Coleman led them towards one of the more solid-looking entrances to the festival. Exactly what he had meant became abundantly clear when they reached the gate.

Waiting to greet the crowds was a line of Festival Makers in ecclesiastic camouflage. The first woman, instantly recognisable by her sheer size was the Magdalene Sisterhood's first line of defence, Sister Charity. Her colleague, Sister Sharon, stepped forward to greet the festivalgoers.

'Welcome to the Baildon Fire Festival! We hope you will enjoy your visit. If you require any assistance, please don't hesitate to ask one of our friendly Fire Guides. Happy Solstice!'

She handed them each a map, a programme of events, and some instructions on what to do if your clothes unexpectedly caught fire. Sister Charity didn't appear to be enjoying their visit, or anyone else's for that matter. She motioned to one of the stewards.

'Search this lot,' she barked. 'And make sure their passes ain't forged.'

Coleman patted the steward on the head and walked straight through. The man made a valiant attempt to search the rest of the motley group of cultists but got short shrift from the Wild Things. He did manage to stop Dillon and remove Daron from his belt but took one look at the stone knife and hastily returned it.

Just inside the gates was another posse of the Sisterhood, selling programmes. Each one came with a free inspirational pamphlet entitled The Dawning of the Age of Woman. The woman organising this hive of commercial activity was Charlotte. She was haranguing the disinterested visitors with a megaphone which garbled whatever message she was trying to convey.

'Archipelago is a tombola ping-pong to the wombat archangel. Guinea-fowl indigo bon-bon now!'

She stopped when she saw Dillon approaching. They stood facing each other, avoiding the other's gaze and shuffling uncomfortably. There was not much to say, beyond a few bland pleasantries.

'How's it going?' Dillon asked her.

'Oh, you know, keeping busy. Quite good on the whole. And you?'

'Not so bad. Getting everyone licked into shape, I see.'

'Yes, that sort of thing.'

'Look, I never really thanked you for sorting out things with the Defenders of the Faith.'

'It had to be done.' She seemed about to add something more, but the moment passed.

They exchanged their farewells and Dillon trotted away to catch up with his friends. Charlotte stared after him for a while and then turned back to her sisterly duties, and her new life.

38 Supernaturally

Once safely past the security cordon, the whole party made a beeline for the backstage bar. There were still a couple of hours before the main attractions were due to open, and plenty of time for a pint or two before duty called. Strangely enough, no one had thought to trust Dillon or Sparks with complex tasks, like pouring drinks and adding up. Coleman told them to circulate and help with any bottlenecks.

After necking three pints of Dead Nag, Dillon's head was beginning to circulate of its own accord. He looked around the bar, to see if there was anyone to badger for his next article. Apart from Sparks, who looked set for the night, the rest of his friends had left to take up their posts.

On the far side of the room, a small, bearded man was engaged in a fierce conversation with two chisel-faced minders in identical grey overcoats. Convinced that it was Salman Rushdie, Dillon scurried across to compare notes. By the time he had pushed his way through the crowd, the men had vanished. He was disappointed. As a writer persecuted by religious extremists, he was sure they had a lot in common.

He collared Sparks and dragged him outside to check out the stalls. His drinking partner was none too pleased to be plucked from the warmth of the free bar to go wandering around a craft market in the depths of winter.

'It's all a load of crap,' Sparks insisted, determined not to enjoy himself until somebody put another pint in front of him. He picked up a particularly livid tie-dye T-shirt and waved it under his friend's nose. 'My dad had a shirt like this in the seventies. I've seen the photos. He looked a right fool in it. You ought to get one, Dillon, mate.'

Dillon, who had been genuinely looking forward to the event, was also beginning to tire. He wandered over to the marquee hosting the charities that stood to benefit from the festival's projected profits and signed a petition in support of a place he'd never heard of, at the urging of a particularly attractive environmental activist.

At the far end of the marquee, Dillon found himself staring at a display on overpopulation. As he stood reading its distressing predictions, uncountable hordes of festivalgoers pushed past him. The air was suddenly a lot thicker and the tent much smaller than when he came in. He was starting to find it difficult to breathe.

Sparks, seeing his opportunity, grabbed Dillon by the arm and rushed him past the first aid post, into a tent signed The Baal Beer Bolthole. To one side, Coleman was giving an illustrated lecture entitled Holistic Brewing (with free samples). Behind the rows of hand-pulled ales, Rachel, Megan, and a dozen others were manning a bar, which heaved with eager customers. Megan handed over a couple of pints of Apocalypse Ale.

'Ta, love,' said Sparks. 'And one for my friend, please.'

She gave him a quick gesture indicating that two was all he was getting. Dillon gratefully sipped his drink and glanced at his watch, tipping some of it on the muddy ground in the process.

'Only five hours to go before we all go up in flames,' said Dillon. 'Might as well have another drink. It's not often you get offered free beer.'

'Too true,' said Sparks, cradling his pint in an unsteady hand. 'It's been a good old year, all told.'

'Yeah, pretty good,' agreed Dillon. 'Apart from being taken hostage, of course.'

'Right. I forgot about that.'

'And our house burning to the ground.'

'Look, there was something I meant to tell you about that…'

'And Charlotte leaving me.'

'Well, every thundercloud has a silver lining,' Sparks suggested. 'You found Rachel instead.'

'And Megan found you. Poor girl.'

'We made friends with a man who owns a brewery.'

'Right!' Dillon was pleased to be looking on the bright side again. 'So, pretty good all in all, I guess.'

'Do you believe in all this Armageddon crap? There's been a lot of weird stuff going on recently. All these nutters reckoning the world's going to end. Could they be right?'

'Shouldn't think so. Not yet anyway. I mean it's bound to end sometime, like in a hundred million years or so. Just not yet.'

'Good.' Sparks seemed convinced by his friend's argument. 'I'll drink to that.'

'How about we go and check out the concert?' Dillon suggested, concerned that they might be missing out on the only interesting part of the whole event.

'Can we take the beer with us?'

'I don't see why not.'

'Fine. I'm with you then.'

Sparks tottered up to the bar. He returned with two fresh pints plus Rachel and Megan. The four of them made their way through the labyrinth of canvas and wood to the fort's asymmetrical courtyard and jostled their way to a suitable viewpoint.

Dillon began to wonder if they should have paced themselves. The concert wasn't due to finish until two in the morning and there were still the fireworks and the towering inferno to come. He felt rather woozy, and the whole proceedings started to appear a little distant and unreal.

On stage, a procession of has-beens and never-will-bes from the world of rock and roll trundled their way through their greatest hits. Many of the stars were much the worse for drink or drugs, or possibly both. So was most of the audience, who covered up their mistakes with a drunken chorus of epic volume, which drowned out much of the music. Dillon didn't recognise many of the songs, but he sang along all the same. He was starting to have a good time and was happy to share his mood with those around him.

The last band, an angry Anglo-Australian collective, marched on stage and grasped their instruments with more of a sense of purpose than the preceding acts. They launched straight into a rocking little number about alcohol abuse and armed robbery, carrying the audience with them on a roller-coaster ride through the murkier depths of human behaviour.

As the last power chord merged with the roar of the crowd, the lights dimmed, and a fusillade of mortars pierced the darkness with a shower of silver and golden sparks. Rockets and Roman Candles burst into Technicolor flames, threatening to ignite the more exposed sections of the fortifications with every incendiary arc.

Bearing in mind all the warnings about the organisers' pyromaniac tendencies, Dillon pulled his comrades away from the fort. Already, some of the support struts were starting to smoulder and it was becoming appreciably warmer. The fireworks built up to a final explosive climax of sound and colour that deafened everyone within a three-mile radius. Then there was silence.

A mellow chiming sound slowly built to a crescendo which insinuated its way into the crowd's consciousness, past the ringing tinnitus and the buzz of puzzled conversation.

Heads turned as an elderly man trotted gracefully into the fort on horseback, holding a brass bell before him. The bell was of no great size, but the sound it made rang out clearly above the hubbub, each tone seeming to grow stronger, with every passing minute.

Dillon recognised the man instantly: it was Althred the cart driver, and he was accompanied by Sir Kevin and eleven other Knights of the Wasteland. They formed an honour guard, pushing back the crowd on either side. They drew their swords, each holding them at the hilt like a crucifix.

Behind them came six monks dressed in long black robes, bearing between them a man lying on a rickety and unhygienic stretcher. They lowered him to the ground and then, with some difficulty, helped him into an ancient oak throne, which appeared from the swirling smoke.

Dillon and his friends were pressed close to the action by the mass of people, and when Althred beckoned him forward, Dillon looked around to see who was behind him, but already, many hands were gently pushing him towards the space cleared by the Knights.

As he approached, he recognised the man he had seen in the castle at Shrewsbury many months ago. The man wore his golden chain with an air of great authority, and he was still clutching at his seemingly wounded stomach.

Dillon's knees buckled and he found himself kneeling in front of the ancient throne. 'What ails you, sir?' he asked, the words coming of their own accord without any input required from his befuddled brain.

The old man took his hands away from his stomach. Dillon could see dark blood seeping through the rough woven shirt. He glanced around, looking for the first aid tent or St John's Ambulance. He felt a burning sensation on the small of his back and for a moment wondered if a stray firework had lodged in his back pocket.

He reached around and removed Daron the knife from the waistband of his jeans where he had stuffed it to avoid difficult questions. Why he had decided to bring the knife with him had been a mystery. Maybe this was why. The hilt was hot to the touch, and when he stripped away the oilskin covering, wisps of black smoke rose from the blade. He held the knife out to the old man, who grasped Dillon's open hand and brought the tip forward until it touched his wound.

Dillon, who had been known to faint while watching surgical procedures on the TV, stared at the man's stomach. The blood was congealing and the wound was closing. The man was sat bolt upright. Colour had returned to his cheeks, and he was staring into the far distance.

The knife blade seemed to have melted away like a chocolate poker. Dillon was left holding the charred handle. As his presence didn't seem to be required further, he let it drop to the ground. He staggered to his feet and backed slowly away from the scene, to be reunited with his waiting friends.

The old man pushed himself up from the oak throne and stood for a few seconds with his arms out in a gesture of welcome, and then keeled over, falling face down in the mud. The black-robed bearers stepped forward once more, lifted his inert body onto the stretcher, and carried it out through the crowd.

'Did I do something wrong?' asked Dillon. 'Should I have waited for St John's Ambulance after all? This mystical first aid is a lot more complicated than it looks.'

But no one was paying any attention to him. People craned forward to see the next part of this unexpected pageant. When they caught a glimpse of what was coming, they gasped in shock, and a rippling silence spread through the whole crowd.

Four women, dressed all in white, approached the Knights. There was something insubstantial about their appearance, their bodies translucent and indistinct. They seemed not to walk across the ground, but to float, as if they had no need of the earth beneath their feet.

The first of these ethereal maidens carried a spear, more solid than herself. Drops of crimson fell from the blood-soaked tip onto the earth, where it left no mark. The second bore a bright silver dish, partly wrapped in pure white muslin. The third held aloft a heavy golden candlestick, the flames from which refused to flicker in the gentle breeze. Lastly, came a woman, cradling in her hands, with great reverence, a plain gold cup. A soft glow penetrated through its covering, illuminating the look of total serenity on her bloodless face.

Sir Kevin detached himself from the lines of motionless Knights and followed the ghostly procession. Raising the hilt of his sword high into the air, he cried out, 'Stay, I pray you, my Lady Blanchefleur. In the name of God, stay.'

To the astonishment of the watching crowd, the cortège paused and the maiden turned to face him. Sir Kevin lowered his sword and fell to his knees. The majority of the spectators followed suit. Bowing gently, she offered the cup up to the knight's eager lips and drew back the cloth.

An intense light flared from the grail, slowly filling the space with its brilliance, until it was too bright for the gathering of mere mortals to bear.

When the assembled multitude opened their eyes once more, there was nothing to see. The Knights and the Grail procession had vanished. It was as if they had never existed.

39 Fool on the Hill

There was a stunned silence. Dillon wasn't sure quite what to think. Was it just a perfectly choreographed pageant? A high-tech illusion? What did it all mean? Was there more to come?

The crowd stood in reverential silence as if waiting for the rapture, but the trumpets never sounded and no angels appeared on the stage. After a while, they began to relax, and the hubbub of conversation grew steadily, as people congratulated themselves on surviving another doomsday prophesy. Somewhere, a lone voice began to sing Jerusalem and the bulk of the crowd joined in, humming where they didn't know the words.

'And did those feet in ancient time, walk upon England's mountains green?'

Probably not, thought Dillon, who was fairly sure that one of the Grail Maidens had been wearing white stilettos under her cloak. However, walking across Baildon Moor in high heels probably counted as a miracle in its own right. Who could say what the regulation attire might be required for supernatural guardians? Anyway, it was a rousing song and, after what he had just seen, he was prepared to consider anything possible.

'...I will not cease from mental fight, nor will my sword sleep in my hand....'

Finally, the floodlights came back on and people started heading for the exits. They all knew what was coming next and they wanted to be a good safe distance away. Sparks suggested Bradford, or possibly Sheffield.

A sizeable bonfire had been lit on a small mound about a hundred metres from the hill fort. Dillon assumed that this was the symbolic Baal fire. Hordes of people plucked burning brands from the flames, and danced around, clutching, chanting, and singing a cacophony of different songs.

The more energetic festivalgoers were leaping over the lower flames as their pagan ancestors once did. There was the occasional yelp of pain as a fire jumper mistimed their run-up and had to be dowsed with water.

With a fearsome battle cry, a bare-chested man in a leather kilt charged up the hill, clutching a burning branch in one hand. He was followed by dozens more frenzied fire starters. Dillon recalled reading that it was good luck to bring a fiery brand home to the hearth. This lot looked as if they would be lucky to be going home uncharred.

The kilt-wearer threw his brand into the bales of hay piled up against the outer walls of the fort. Even on this damp winter's night, they burst instantly into flames and began to consume the ramshackle structure. More and more bales caught alight as the also-rans arrived. Soon, flames were leaping high above the moors.

Even from where Dillon was standing, a good fifty metres away, the heat was intense. The whole heather-topped hillside began to steam and smoulder. Fortunately, the vegetation was too sodden to burn properly, but the crowd was continuing to edge away from the conflagration just in case.

Finally, the walls began to topple inwards. Golden sparks flew high into the night air as the towers crashed down onto an ever-increasing pile of flaming debris. The crowd watched the shrinking inferno for a long, long time until it was nothing more than glowing embers. Gradually they turned away to buy roasted chestnuts from opportunistic vendors or start their weary journey home.

No more mystical events unfolded, other than the magical relocation of the beer tent to the bottom of the hill, helped on by a host of willing volunteers. As dawn approached, Dillon and Sparks found themselves standing next to Coleman watching the streams of festivalgoers flow downhill to the nearby towns of Baildon and Bingley, where they could safely await the promised night buses and early morning trains.

'That was a miracle, wasn't it?' Dillon suggested to the towering Gnostic leader. 'An honest-to-God miracle. How am I going to explain this one to my editor? He'll never believe it.'

'Quite possibly you are right. Miracles do happen; of that, I am sure. Although, they sometimes require an earthly helping hand.'

Dillon was even more confused than normal.

'If you look closely enough, there are miracles all around,' Coleman explained. 'Take that wellhead for example.' He pointed to the water bubbling out of the rock a short distance away.

By torchlight, it was hard for Dillon to make out the colour, but it looked suspiciously dark and frothy. A small group of revellers were drinking enthusiastically from it and they looked decidedly worse for wear. Dillon dipped his hand into the brackish liquid and sipped cautiously.

'More of Coleman's Finest Ales?' he speculated.

Coleman took a swig and sniffed the liquid in the fashion of a true connoisseur. 'I could not possibly say. It could have been miraculously brewed from the waters of this hallowed moor.'

'Hmm, I see what you mean. But that was the real Holy Grail, wasn't it? Just like in Monty Python.'

'Well, it was a grail, certainly,' agreed Coleman. 'A most holy and mystic vessel.'

Dillon was a little shocked by this revelation. He had just come round to the idea of believing in miracles when here was the dealer in mysteries himself refuting a wonder he had seen with his own eyes.

'You mean it's not the one from the last supper?' Dillon asked plaintively. 'It doesn't hold, you know, the blood of Christ, or whatever?'

'Well, theologically speaking, it does. For those of the Roman Catholic faith, anyway.'

'Would you care to explain that for the ignorantly speaking.'

'It was once, I believe, the communion cup of Saint Hugh of Lincoln,' explained Coleman. 'On the underside of the vessel, was his swan motif. I would hazard that it was given to him by one who returned from the crusades. It most likely predates the Christian era. From the history of its usage, I would suggest that it contained wine; transubstantiated, no doubt, by the saint himself.'

'And then magically preserved?' suggested Sparks.

'Indeed. And occasionally topped up by the holy order into whose hands it was entrusted some nine hundred years ago.'

'So, it was all a trick,' accused Dillon.

'Not exactly, my friend. The Knights of the Wasteland sought a grail and I found them one. In truth, their quest was becoming not only tiresome but also dangerous for all concerned. It was time they returned to good and noble deeds, like feeding the poor and rescuing those in peril. Even in the modern world, there are dragons and monsters which require slaying. And if they do not take that path, there are caves in the Welsh mountains said to hold the sleeping enchanter, Merlin. Potholing in armour is difficult but perhaps not impossible.'

'But what happens if they find out it wasn't the real Grail?' Dillon demanded.

'I think that is unlikely. Unless they are familiar with the techniques of DNA analysis and happen to have some earthly remains of the Christos to hand. A Grail is a Grail after all; it was finely crafted, of the right age and origin, and mystically received, just as it should have been. Such relics are said to be authentic by common acclamation, not by documentation.

'I have it on good authority that the cup which Joseph of Arimathea brought to these shores was purchased in the gold market at Calais on the way and was melted down sometime in the eighth century by penniless monks who had more need of bread than legends.'

'What about King Arthur? Won't they be a bit upset when he doesn't turn up?'

'They have waited many years; I'm sure they can wait a little longer,' Coleman responded, rather harshly. 'Perhaps the current threats of war and environmental catastrophe are not yet sufficient to stir England's saviour from his long slumber. In the meantime, I shall encourage our worthy Knights to good works, so that their master will be pleased with them on his return.'

'So, he's not coming back then,' sighed Dillon disappointedly. 'That's a real pity. I know it's only a legend, but I always hoped it might come true one day.'

'I find it unlikely that even a legendary king could survive a sword through the stomach, especially with medieval medical techniques. Nonetheless, I have been wrong before. Nothing would please me more than to see King Arthur come riding through the streets of London to reclaim the throne of England.'

'Yeah. That really would give the royal family something to worry about.'

Dillon was still confused. Many things remained unexplained and he had a feeling he wasn't going to get any more answers from Coleman. What about the old man on the throne? How did the Grail Maidens disappear like that? Would Coleman give their phone numbers so he could interview them for the paper? He settled for asking the one question that was consuming him.

'Why me?' he asked. 'What's my part in all this?'

'Are you familiar with the legend of the Perfect Fool?' Coleman enquired cautiously.

'Sort of. I got the potted version from Sparks and Dolores. And even Rachel called me a fool. I'm not as stupid as everyone thinks, you know,' complained Dillon, turning away in disgust. He immediately tripped over a rather charred deckchair and fell face-first in the ash and the mud.

Coleman and Sparks rushed up to give Dillon a hand and pulled him to his feet. Someone handed him a rather grubby handkerchief, and he tried to restore some dignity by distributing the mud around his face more evenly.

Coleman continued his explanation as if nothing had happened. 'The Great Fool has many names. In Welsh, he is Peredur; Wagner called him Parsifal, and in the Arthurian tales of Chrétien and Mallory, he is Perceval. According to legend, he finds the Grail Castle but fails to ask a ritual question of the Wounded King. He then wanders in the wilderness gathering knowledge before he can regain the Grail Castle and heal the king.'

'And is that what happened?' asked Dillon, in an awed voice. 'You're talking about the Fisher King, aren't you? I thought the name Pelles sounded familiar. Was it really him? Did I heal his wound? He didn't look too well afterwards.'

'According to legend, once healed, the king is permitted to die and the Wasteland may flourish once again. Of course, that is only a legend. But when enough people believe it, legends have a strange way of imposing themselves on reality. I could tell you that Sir Kevin found the old man sleeping on a cobbled street in Lincoln, but he may still be the Fisher King. I could tell you that the veiled women hail from the Dengie Hundred in deepest Essex, but does that mean they cannot be Grail Maidens? Truth and legend are intertwined. You must decide for yourself.'

Dillon looked at Ralph with a growing sense of mutual understanding and shared experience. There was little else to say. After all that had happened, they were both still alive. They wished each other well, shook hands warmly, and went their separate ways.

Sometime later, Dillon could be found perched on a mound not far from the smouldering fort, engaged in a group hug with the Wild

Things, looking for all the world like a colony of drunken penguins trying to keep warm. To the east, the sun was gradually transforming the sky into a patchwork of crimson and orange as it rose above the moors.

Most festivalgoers had left to avoid hypothermia and the risk of being roped in to clear up the mess. A few dozen stalwarts remained around the ruins. A group of women were taking it in turns to walk across the glowing embers barefoot. Judging by the whoops and hollers coming out of the smoke, they hadn't focused their inner energies sufficiently for the task. Three local lads had tied hazel twigs to a harassed-looking Friesian and were trying to drive it through the ashes. The poor cow didn't appear to appreciate the symbolism of the experience and felled one of her tormentors with a well-placed kick.

As the sun warmed the blackened earth, Dillon broke free of the shivering huddle and stretched his weary limbs. Where the Baal fires had burnt away the dormant heather, small white flowers could be seen poking their heads through the charred roots. Dillon bent down to inspect them; they looked a little like snowdrops except that their petals pointed directly up to the sky, like tiny silver goblets. It was far too early for spring flowers, and he hoped they would be spared from the frost.

Rachel got up to join him, leaving Sparks lying on the mound with his head in Megan's lap, snoring gently. Dillon put one arm around Rachel and with the other, caressed a flagon of miraculously preserved ale. He took a swig, settled back to watch the sky and wondered if he was finally living happily ever after. Certainly, he was happier than he had been while standing outside his smouldering house or being held at gunpoint by religious fanatics.

Happiness, of course, was only ever a fleeting state of affairs. You had to make the best of whatever life threw at you. You had to seize the moment before it slipped from your grasp forever. After all, the best that you could ever hope for was that the best is yet to come.

ACKNOWLEDGMENTS

The Perfect Fool started out as a piece of instant writing, which then turned into a short story called The Wild Things. For such moments of inspiration, my thanks go out to all the writers' groups I have been a part of, especially Havant Writers for their many years of support and encouragement.

The wonderful Dunford Novelists helped me hone the first chapters and encouraged me to finally get this story published.

Thanks to Loree Westron and the Portsmouth Authors Collective for help with marketing and sales.

I'd like to thank my beta readers, the amusing Steve Shepherd (author of the Dawson and Lucy comedy thrillers) and the amazing Lesley Talbot (who will one day finish her fantastic novel).

I have to thank my wife, Chris, the Blackwater girl, for all her support.

Finally, I'd like to thank you, the reader, for making it all worthwhile. Extra thanks if you've left a nice review on Amazon, Goodreads, etc. It makes a huge difference. If you haven't done it yet - go on you know you want to...

ABOUT THE AUTHOR

Nick Morrish is a chartered engineer, turned writer, from Leeds. He began writing to entertain himself while working away on offshore oil platforms, power stations and shipyards. His career has taken him all over the world to many unusual locations and introduced him to some remarkable characters.

Writing as Chris Blackwater, his first novel, Emergency Drill, was shortlisted for the Crime Writer's Association Debut Dagger award. His short stories have appeared in a variety of publications and anthologies.

In recent years Nick has gradually drifted down to the south coast of England where he now spends his spare time kayaking and sailing on the Solent

Printed in Great Britain
by Amazon